Die Trying

A P Bateman

Die Trying

Copyright © 2024 by A P Bateman

All rights reserved.

No part of this book may be reproduced in any form or by any electronic or mechanical means, including information storage and retrieval systems, without written permission from the author, except for the use of brief quotations in a book review.

I lost my mum while writing this book. She was probably my most avid reader and it was rare to see her without one of my books in her hand. She re-read them so many times that she undoubtedly knew the characters better than I did. I remember when I was starting out and she was the first person to read my novel. It was hand written and rough. I hadn't yet learned to type. I asked for feedback and she said it was "Ace". I asked her to be more specific and she said, "Er, absolutely ace..." I got upset because her feedback wasn't constructive, but I wish she was here to tell me that again.

This is for you mum
X

Also by A P Bateman

You can find all the links for A P Bateman's previous work at Amazon Author Page

The Rob Stone Series:

1) The Ares Virus

2) The Town

3) The Island

4) Stone Cold

The Alex King Series:

1) The Contract Man

2) Lies and Retribution

3) Shadows of Good Friday

(a series prequel/standalone)

4) The Five

5) Reaper

6) Stormbound

7) Breakout

8) From the Shadows

9) Rogue

10) The Asset

11) Last Man Standing

12) Hunter Killer

13) The Congo Contract

(a series prequel/standalone)

14) Dead Man Walking

15) Sovereign Power

16) Kingmaker

(a series prequel/standalone)

17) Untouchable

18) The Enemy

19) Die Trying

The DI Grant Series

1) Vice

2) Taken

Standalone Novels:

Never Go Back

The Most Dangerous Game

Short Stories:

The Perfect Murder?

Atonement (an Alex King thriller)

Chapter One

Cadiz, Spain

The sand was warm and fine, shimmering like golden castor sugar in the sunlight. White clouds scudded through the azure blue sky and the sea was sapphire blue. But King saw none of this as he stared into the muzzle of the Colt .45 just a metre from his face.

"She didn't call off the contract, then?" King asked, staring, like so many of his own marks had, down the barrel of the gun.

"No," the man replied somewhat effeminately. "She wouldn't do something like that. It's quite ridiculous of you to think that she would." He paused. "You crossed a line. I hear you visited her husband, threatened her family. She upped the bounty on your head, and more like me will come after you if I fail... which clearly, I will not," he said, moving the weapon so that it lined up with King's face, just in case he hadn't seen it.

King noticed that the man wore the same red bikini bottoms, which now looked like a Speedo, but he had lost the bikini top, and the oversized woman's sunglasses were pushed up on top of his head. He was thin and lithe, and his body was completely hairless. Curiously, King felt somewhat miffed that if he was going to die, then this was not the sort of person who should do it. The man certainly did not look like a tough guy – hell, King had even been attracted to the man's legs when he had been in the guise of a woman sunning herself on the rocks. Of all the soldiers, well-trained agents, and hardened criminals he had cut down over the years, this was not a fitting end. As ridiculous as it sounded in his head, he felt cheated somehow.

"Are you scared?" Franz Oppenheimer asked. He had thought of himself as Frankie while sunbathing on the rock, and *she* had lured many men to their fate. Now it was down to Franz for the kill.

"No," King replied, choosing to stare the man in the eyes rather than look at the gun barrel.

"Are you going to beg for your life?"

"No."

"Good," Franz replied. "Because it wouldn't do you any good." He paused, glancing around longer than King ever would have in the same situation. Then, looking back at him with determination in his dark eyes he said, "Because I'm an assassin, it's what I do…"

King had already slipped his hand underneath the towel beside him as the assassin had briefly taken his eyes off him. There were no second chances in this game. He fired the speargun through the towel and into the man's sternum. The spear travelled through the man's aorta and halfway out through his back and as the line briefly unspooled and coiled at the man's feet, he dropped the rolled-up towel and the .45 Colt hidden within and fell onto his knees. "Me, too..." King said coldly, gathering up the pistol and glancing around the beach. The two men fishing on the edge of the bay were still casting and reeling from the rocks, quite oblivious of what had just transpired in front of them.

"You've killed me..." Franz managed through snatched breaths. "Oh, my god... you've killed me..."

"It's the business you're in, pal," replied King. "Suck it up..." He drew the diving knife from the hard plastic sheath strapped to his ankle. "Now, are you going to talk?"

"No..." Franz started to wobble. "But your world is about to come crashing down around you..." he wheezed.

"Enough bullshit..." King said and slashed the blade across the man's throat and when he fell dying on the sand, King got to his feet and covered him up with his own towel.

Two hundred metres from the shore, the yacht bobbed on the growing swell. He could not see Caroline, but they would be ready to sail as soon as he returned in the tender. The plan had been to sail to the Canary Islands, and he did not see why that should change. The contract on his head would still be open, but the distance would give him the time and space to figure things out. King cut the line and tossed the speargun into the tender along with the pistol and the net of fish he had earlier speared, along with his mask and fins. He pushed the prow of the rubber boat off the sand, and the transom and engine met the building swell and lifted easily as King leapt in and started the engine. He heard the explosion, felt the 'whump' of the concussive shockwave inside him, and even as he turned his head, he knew what he would see. Or what he wouldn't. The yacht was gone, only flotsam in its place. There was no part of the hull intact, and the mast was gone. King felt a wave of nausea inside him, his blood surging and heart skipping as he powered on the tiller and the tiny boat rose above the waves. Ominously, perhaps even fittingly, the sky had greyed, and black clouds loomed on the horizon. The once blue water was now grey and impossibly black on the horizon. The swell was growing and a squall was coming in. The gunshots hammered into the water beside him, and King knew that they were high-velocity rifle rounds because of the metre-high plumes of water they created, splashing his face. He turned around, briefly catching sight of the two fishermen running for their lives across the rocks, then found the gunman a hundred metres to his starboard side, crouched behind a large rock on the other side of the horseshoe bay, muzzle flashes giving away his position. King thought he heard more gunshots but could not place them. He picked up the .45 and emptied the weapon's seven rounds in the general direction, then tossed the weapon over the side. It was enough to make the gunman duck for cover and break his aim, which had been getting ever closer to the tiny rubber boat. King had only one option. There was nothing left of the yacht and no sign of Caroline. He was running on adrenalin and survival instinct alone. He needed distance between the gunman and himself and he could only get that by veering away from the wreckage and heading out of the bay. If he ran at maximum revs and jerked the tiller randomly to veer off course, then he would become a more difficult target and every twenty metres he gained the gunman would have to adjust their aim and watch where the rounds hit before they could be sure of a clean shot. Another hundred metres and he could safely put the headland between them, and he would have a chance at getting to the next beach before the gunman could get there

Die Trying

by road. But that was all well and good. Right now, he could barely care less about his life. He needed to find the woman he loved. King snatched up the mask and dived into the water twenty metres from the floating wreckage. He slipped the mask on as he swam downwards and tilted it and blew through his nose to clear the build-up of pressure. Above him, bullets speared and fizzled into the water making tendrils of bubbles two metres deep, and he observed them all rapidly depleted of all energy, falling harmlessly to the seabed.

The seabed was scattered with wreckage and the mast was pinning the forward part of the hull to the sand. King was all but out of breath when he reached the seabed and peered inside the hulk. Their possessions were scattered everywhere, and he could see that the explosion had blown the boat completely in half. He knew enough about demolition to know that this had not been an accident with the boat's gas, and nor with the small amount of fuel on board for the yacht's outboard engine. There were scorch and impact marks all over the remains of the hull that were conducive to shaped charges. He paid this little attention, desperate to find Caroline, but there was no sign of her. He could see a shimmy of light and water inside the broken hull, and he knew that it represented a pocket of air. He swam desperately, the last of his breath escaping his lips as he pressed his face into the air pocket. It was no larger than a bucket, and he spat and coughed and heaved gratefully for breath, and above the sound of him panting, he heard an eerie wail, and realised somewhat despairingly that it belonged to him and with it the realisation that Caroline was gone.

That's it, lad. Take a breath and fight on... he could hear the gravelly Scottish voice of his old mentor echoing in his ears, as clearly as if the man had been there beside him and not six feet under the ground in an unassuming MI6 graveyard. King blinked, realising that for the first time in years he was alone again. Strangely, he had to pull himself out of the despair as if it were a physical rope anchoring him to the spot. He cleared the mask and took in all the precious air that his lungs could carry, and he dipped back under and made for the flattened wreckage of the stern and the bosun's locker, which was now gaping open with its contents scattered over the seabed. He snatched up the scuba tank and switched on the valve, then slipped himself into it and bled some air into the BCD until he drifted off the seabed and found negative buoyancy. Progress would be difficult without a set of fins, but even as he drew near, he could see the remnants of the tender drifting loosely on the surface as if it were a large rubber blanket. The gunman had found his range and had ripped the tiny rubber boat to shreds. King kicked on and used his arms to make up for the lack of fins. He knew that he had forty minutes of air and he set the bezel marker on his vintage Rolex at thirty-five minutes. He could already see the rocks of the headland to his right, and he kicked on past and took a path to his left, hoping without a compass that he would cross the next bay and reach the opposite headland rather than swim further out to sea. He would surface in ten minutes and get his bearings, and as he kicked and sculled with an aggression and determination he had not summoned in himself for some time, he vowed that he would find the gunman, and the people behind the bomb and he would exact a wrath upon them beyond anyone's imagination. When he was done, they would pray and beg for even a painful death. Because anything would be welcome after the pain King would inflict upon his enemy.

Chapter Two

L ondon
 Three weeks later

"Anything after the phone call?"

"Nothing," Lomu replied. The big Fijian was six-four and eighteen stone of muscle and known affectionately as Big Dave to those he worked with, and a whole lot of trouble for anyone intent on crossing him. "When I rang back the dial tone was dead. King probably tossed the phone as soon as he ended the call."

Neil Ramsay nodded, pondering on the man's report. He looked up as Mae entered, a no-nonsense looking woman in her early sixties with grey hair pulled back in a tight bun. She carried tea and coffee on a tray and pinned a file to her ribs with her elbow. It was just like her to multi-task, and she had been a godsend in the setting up and running of the new department under the umbrella of MI5 yet operating independently until the Security Service could seal their recent security breach. Ramsay knew that it would not be without repercussions, but he had been in intelligence work long enough to know that you simply had to fight the fire when you felt the flames. "Ah, thank you, Mae," he said, barely looking up from his desk.

Big Dave gave her a wink as she handed him his tea. Jack Luger took his coffee and smiled. She seemed more taken with the big Fijian, and Luger felt she acted a little more matronly in his presence. It must have been an age thing. He did not mind, though. His school matron had been more of a mother figure at his boarding school than his own birth mother ever had. When he thought about it – and he had tried not to over the years – he had grown up in a household with a nanny, been sent to boarding school aged seven and then gone away to university. The family naval tradition followed, and he now viewed his family life as snippets from stuffy Christmases and easters where church service played a larger part than presents or easter eggs and even the long summers had been spent in Italy or France with the family nanny in attendance. It irked him somewhat that his younger brother had attended a local prep school as a day pupil and had a far closer relationship with their parents than either he or his older sister would ever have. Only his aunt had provided him with a semblance of family, and she had encouraged him to leave the navy and come and work with her at MI5. And now she was dead, and that thread of emotional support and comfortable familiarity was gone forever. He would take Mae's manner with him as something akin to matronly, whether she meant it or not. It was practically the only care he had ever known.

"The Spanish police did not come up with anything helpful," said Luger once Mae had left the room. "Other than the obvious signs of an explosive charge being used.

Die Trying

Unfortunately, a squall whipped up the ocean and scattered the debris both far and wide ..."

"What's a squall? I thought that was a female red Indian..." Big Dave said seriously.

"We call them native Americans now," Luger corrected them. "Anyway, that's a squaw. And that's a racial slur, too."

Big Dave shrugged. "I'm black," he told him. "I can't *be* racist."

"Oh, you can," Luger replied earnestly.

"He's, I believe the term is, messing with you," Ramsay said tersely. "He did it to me all the time when I worked in the field. I don't miss it one bit."

Big Dave smiled and sipped his tea. "My bad..."

"And that expression makes no bloody sense whatsoever," Ramsay said, looking at the file that Mae had just brought in. "Thank goodness I don't have to hear it so much these days..." He paused and stared at Jack Luger. "Why a squall and not a storm?"

"It literally picked up for less than twenty minutes. Heavy wind and rain, big seas and then just as quickly, it was calm and clear, and the sea settled down. I used to see a lot of them in the Caribbean when I was in the Royal Navy."

"And that ruined any chance of essential recovery," Ramsay mused.

"Caroline's body, most of all..." Big Dave said sullenly, leaving his words to hang in the air. "Let's not forget that."

"I never would," Ramsay replied.

"I know," the Big Fijian shrugged. "Just sayin', that's all."

Jack Luger sipped his coffee. He was new to the team, and he knew when to contribute to something, and when to sit back. He had liked Caroline but would be the first to admit that he did not know her well.

"So, we arrive at King," Ramsay said heavily.

"No sign," said Big Dave. "He was seen by two eyewitnesses leaving the beach in a small craft. That craft was later found in the rocks torn to shreds by bullets."

"And that's it?"

"No," Luger interjected. "At the next beach over, a man was seen swimming to shore. He was observed walking away from the beach towards town. Later, a scuba tank washed in. From the description, it was most likely King. Someone helped themselves to the tank and BCU, so it couldn't be tested for King's DNA."

"Yeah, later a man walked into a clothes shop in just swimming shorts. He helped himself to everything he needed and walked back out again." Big Dave paused. "The CCTV system hadn't worked for months, so again, we couldn't verify. Although who else could it have been?"

"Nothing on the traffic cameras in Cadiz?" Ramsay asked.

"No. But that's what King has been trained to do... disappear," replied Big Dave. "If we could find him, then it would be because he wants to be found," he added knowingly, having tailed King once before. His brief then had been simple: *protect King at all costs, but don't let him know you are there...* They had thought he had been blissfully unaware, but the man had known all along and when he wanted to shake them off, he disappeared like a puff of smoke on the breeze.

"With an open contract on his head, and with assassins getting close enough to kill Caroline, then he's not about to sit out in the open," Luger offered, but the mirrored expressions from both Ramsay and Big Dave told him that the ice was thin around the subject of Caroline Darby, and he had better mind his step. "I mean... there's no body..."

"It's the Atlantic," Ramsay pointed out. "But more than that, it's the Gulf of Cadiz. I shouldn't have to tell a navy man that the tides are strong near the mouth of the Mediterranean. The current rushes up the coast to Portugal." Ramsay reached for a sheet of paper and said, "Here, I asked a marine biology contact of mine to generalise the area for me. Now bear with me; scientific types tend not to use three words when they could use thirty instead. The Gulf of Cadiz is a sub-basin of the north Atlantic. The northern, eastern, and southern limits are well defined by the south-west coast of the Iberian Peninsula, the Strait of Gibraltar, and the Moroccan Atlantic Coast. Because of its location, the Gulf of Cadiz is a very dynamic and complex system being an area where an important vertical mixing promotes the exchange of properties between the Atlantic Ocean and the Mediterranean Sea through the Strait of Gibraltar. This aspect has motivated great interest in the scientific community and different studies have already been carried out about the interconnection of both sub-basins. The Strait of Gibraltar has a longitudinal extension of about sixty kilometres in length and it is fifteen kilometres wide, presenting a minimum transversally averaged depth of two-hundred-and-eighty metres and a maximum of nine-hundred metres in the eastern part. It is also characterised by a system of sills; Camarinal Sill and Espartel Sill which constitute the main exit of Mediterranean outflow water to the Gulf of Cadiz. The mean circulation pattern at the Strait of Gibraltar can be approached as a two-layer exchange, inflowing Atlantic water by an upper layer and outflowing Mediterranean waters by the lower one. This mean circulation creates several types of fluctuations with different time scales. The first type is the low frequency variability (seasonal and interannual), which is mainly driven by the climatic forcing over the Mediterranean basin. A second type is that associated to the sub-inertial variability, with oscillation periods between a few days and a few months, which is mainly controlled by changes in atmospheric pressure over western Mediterranean and local wind. The third type is the fluctuation originated by the effect of tides, which are the main source of variability in the Strait of Gibraltar, being the most energetic process and achieving values higher than 2.5 ms^{-1} Finally, within a fourth type the shorter than tidal periods fluctuations are included. In the context of the Strait of Gibraltar oceanic dynamics, it is noteworthy that persistent and intense easterly winds in the Alboran Sea have a significant impact. These winds not only weaken the Atlantic Jet but also give rise to a Coastal Counter Current along the Alboran Sea's northwest coast, extending towards the eastern entrance of the Strait of Gibraltar. This CCC has the ability to interact effectively with the weakened Atlantic Jet, causing it to shift southward and even aiding its disconnection from the upper branch of the Western Alboran Gyre. The presence and behaviour of this CCCs during episodes of intense easterly winds have been well-documented. These phenomena collectively contribute to the intricate oceanographic processes in the region..." He looked at the two men and said, "In other words..."

"It's a bloody great washing machine off the coast, and there are too many variables to predict body recovery locations..." Big Dave suggested. "There is a place like that in Fiji. Once you're in the water, then you're in it for ten miles and just have to accept the ride."

"This sounds altogether worse," said Ramsay tersely.

"The currents wash up and down, left and right and every direction in between with temperature fluctuations, and god forbid, predators." He paused. "My marine biologist contact went on to note various species of shark prevalent in the area..."

Jack Luger coughed, but there was nothing wrong with his throat. The team had suffered a heavy blow, and if he could get matters back on track, then he would. Talk of shark predation on her body was the last thing they needed. "Do we go back and look for King?"

"No," Ramsay replied. He wheeled himself out from behind his desk and turned his back on them to survey the Thames through the large bay window. "King knows how to survive."

"But we can look for him and protect him while he hunts for the assassins who are searching for him," Luger ventured.

Ramsay shook his head. "I have a more pressing concern for you both," he said heavily. "Anyway, I have Rashid making tentative enquiries as we speak." Luger leaned forwards eagerly, then felt a little foolish as Big Dave remained seated comfortably, somewhat too comfortable given where they were. He had finished his cup of tea and seemed to be searching for something. "Damn it, man, what are you doing?" he asked irritably.

"Your budget isn't running to biscuits these days?"

Ramsay shook his head and pressed a button on the telephone. He asked Mae for some biscuits and stared back at the big Fijian. "Happy now?"

Big Dave shrugged and beamed a big, white smile at Mae as she bustled in with a plate. Her demeanour was clipped and hurried, but it said more that she was busy than eager to please.

"Chocolate, Mr Lomu," she told him putting the plate down on the desk, before gathering up the empty cups. "I suppose you'll all be wanting another brew…"

"No, thank you, Mae," Ramsay said curtly. "They will be leaving soon…" he waited until the woman had closed the door behind her and said, "There's something I want you to look into. It's not really our sort of thing…"

"I have no real idea of what our *thing* is," said Big Dave.

"I'm glad someone said it," Luger said, raising an eyebrow. "Our remit is pretty broad…"

"And broadening by the day," Ramsay said, wheeling his chair around. Paralysed by a traitor's bullet, he had lost the use of his legs just over six months ago and nobody thought he would return to work, let alone head up a new department with MI5. Never a true field agent, as an officer of MI5 he had found his remit slipping and the gifted analyst had been thrown into several missions accompanying the team in the thick of it. The assassination of the key higher echelons within the Security Service had given Neil Ramsay a series of battlefield promotions and seen big changes in the way MI5 approached field operations and their ever-crossing of concentric circles with MI6. "Drugs," he said, wheeling back to the desk. "Or rather, the availability of drugs supplied by Iran and Russia to Europe."

"Is this the Iron Fist?" Big Dave asked, having just put down a cyber-attack by a group of agents representing Iran, Russia, North Korea, Belarus, and China. Five countries, represented as five fingers of a fist. The trail had now gone cold, but with MI6, MI5, the FBI, and the CIA all making hunting the Iron Fist a priority, it would not remain cold for long.

"I'm not sure. But Iran shares the longest border with Afghanistan and the world's supply of heroin comes from

Afghanistan. However, Iran's recent activity supporting the Houthi movement and their intentions to control and disrupt the Suez Canal, our analysts have thrown the suggestion that the increased shipping activity taking alternative routes will make the smuggling of drugs harder to police. Satellite footage is showing a huge increase in traffic over the Iran-Afghan border, meanwhile the European drug trade is being significantly boosted."

"Define European," Luger said pointedly.

"Western Europe," Ramsay replied. "The United Kingdom, France, Spain, Italy, Greece and Germany."

"Particularly?"

"Yes."

"The main contributors to NATO, and certainly the best and largest in terms of military force."

"That's the MOD's take on it as well," said Ramsay.

"What am I missing?" Big Dave asked, picking up his sixth chocolate *Hobnob*, and also the last of the biscuits.

"Our enemies want weak opponents," said Luger. "Ex-military generals and serving members of parliament have all recently voiced our readiness in military action against Russia and her allies." He paused. "The notion of national service is being debated, and the public are being extremely vocal of their outrage on social media. This isn't nineteen-thirty-nine. The youth has changed."

"Exactly," Ramsay smiled, a rare occurrence and especially these days.

"I'm still missing something..." Big Dave asked through a mouthful of biscuit.

Luger said without any hint of condescendence, "If the supply was plentiful and inexpensive enough to create more junkies, to weaken society enough, then Russia wouldn't even have to invade. The fear of them would be enough.

Think about it... Russian men drink, smoke, fight. Many are routinely homophobic, sexist, and racist. They are men's men from fifty years ago... the youth of European society barely know how to identify gender. Factor in nations of drug addicts without the will to fight... well, it's a worry. The perception of who would win would be threat enough."

"My worry indeed," Ramsay concurred. "So, imagine the worry when police in Plymouth picked up a consignment of heroin that for all intents and purposes, arrived for free..."

Chapter Three

Devonport Dockyard, Plymouth

"We rounded up the usual suspects," DI Dermott said. "The links in the chain soon buckled. Many had so much prison time behind them that they're in for a ten stretch just for being in possession for as little as a Henry..."

"A Henry?" asked Big Dave, taking his eyes off the frigate and Royal Navy support vessel towering over them in the berth.

"Henry the Eighth." He paused, then added, "An eighth of an ounce."

"Of what?" Luger queried.

"Of whatever... puff... speed... blow... snow... It was just an expression." The Detective Inspector frowned. "You're not drug guys, are you..."

"No." Big Dave shrugged. "But we're terrorist, assassin and mafia guys..."

"And we're real quick learners," Luger added.

"And we're investigating the latter, with our path crossing the former."

"Alright," the detective inspector conceded. "What do you want to know?"

"Start with the arrest and finish with where you're at now," Big Dave told him.

"Well, this was a routine layover..." He swept his hand towards the freighter. "Customs cleared it and we had no interest in it, but we have our own watchlist and a couple of the players found their way here with some of my team on their tail. They aren't the smartest bunch, but if there are drugs being moved from here to Truro or up to Bristol, then these toerags are generally behind it."

"What tipped you off?" asked Luger as they made for the gangplank.

DI Dermott cleared them through the armed police cordon. This was one of the largest drugs hauls ever seized in the country and security was tight. Outside the cordon, Royal Navy police and a dozen Royal Marines stood at arms. The police inspector had told them of their plans to take the contraband to a secure location before incineration. The plan included an armed escort from the Royal Marines alongside armed police officers and a major road closure. Having seized the heroin there was no way that Devon and Cornwall Police were going to lose it to opportunistic thieves. "Typical druggy scumbags. They do what they do, and they largely get away with it, but every once in a while, a tosser will buy a Range Rover and get it vinyl wrapped in iridescent yellow or buy a Nissan Skyline and fit an exhaust you could hear in the next county." He shrugged. "Just the usual crap that puts them on our radar. Lately it's gold. Tons of the stuff hanging around their neck like a bad impression of Mr T..." He looked at Luger as they reached the deck of the freighter. "You don't know who I mean, do you?"

"No."

"I pity the fool..." Big Dave said, in a pretty good impression of the eighty's television star. He laughed and looked at the police inspector. "He still doesn't get it..."

"You'll have to find it for him on video," DI Dermott chided.

"What's a video?"

"Bastard..." Big Dave punched Luger playfully on the shoulder, moving the young man several feet and sending him into the wheelhouse door.

"Sorry," said Luger. "I forgot how touchy you older guys can get. You probably both need an afternoon nap or something..." He looked at the detective inspector and said, "They were blinged up and driving flash cars. I get it. But what happened here?"

"A man called Tommy Jury usually brings the stuff in for these guys. He's a London criminal who was swimming in a very large pond. He did some county lines stuff and ended up, like so many Londoners, coming down this way. Branching out and pissing off the yokel locals. But instead of all this second home bollocks, this Londoner came down to run things for a major player called Colin Haskell. Skip forwards three years and Haskell was found floating in the sea off Teignmouth and Tommy Jury is running the show. Fishing accident the coroner ruled. But we know different, just couldn't prove it in court. Tommy Jury pays for the consignments and sells it off to the foot soldiers. About ten in all, who in turn have a network of a dozen or more dealers. Those dealers may well have their own foot soldiers, but we hardly ever stick with them. They are the ones who cut deals so we can get further up the chain." DI Dermott paused and opened a packet of cigarettes. He offered one to them and they both declined. He pulled a face as he lit a cigarette and took a grateful drag. "But here's the thing. Tommy Jury did not pay for this consignment."

"Then who did?" asked Big Dave.

"Nobody did," the detective inspector replied. "And it doesn't look like anybody did. Likewise, the ten dickheads with the gold chains and the shitty cars, they didn't pay a thing. But they have all been paid to distribute it. For free."

"Then what's to stop them selling for a price?" Luger asked with a shrug. "I mean, there's no better profit than getting something for free. Even selling for twenty-percent less than usual would likely double their typical profit."

"What's to stop them?" Dermott chuckled. "Fear. Plain and simple. But a fear like nothing you could possibly imagine. Because one man talked and now, he's dead." He paused, looking at the cigarette with disdain before tossing it over the side into the slick water. Evidently the man was struggling to quit. "And the man he was being held on remand with killed himself after he cut the dealer's throat with a shiv…"

Chapter Four

Cadiz, Spain

You never forget your roots. Sometimes you may need a heavy prompt, but people who grew up a certain way know how to get back there. It's just a matter of time or desperation.

King hadn't forgotten how to steal. He hadn't forgotten how to rob, either. From the moment he had walked out of the sea with nothing but a pair of swimming shorts and his watch on his wrist, he had reverted to the person he had once been. However, that person now had twenty years of experience in the intelligence field, with the dirty tricks needed to operate and survive in hostile territory taught to him by the clandestine operations wing of MI6.

He soon had clothes on his back. After perusing a tobacconist and calmly picking out a pay-as-you-go mobile phone and some toiletries, he asked the cashier to show him one of the Swiss Army knives from the locked display case on the counter, he calmly turned and walked out of the shop, turned left, and took the myriad of alleyways into the old town, stuffing the goods into his newly acquired jacket. As he melted into the crowd he felt for the cashier and the business owner, but his need was greater, and he had known that his crime spree would not stop there. He charged the phone at a café, taking time with a pot of tea and some pastries to establish a plan. He still needed a phone card to register the phone, but that would have to wait until he had some money, which came as he left without paying and swiped the payment and tip left on a plate at a recently vacated table on his way out. Outside, a couple were standing to leave and as the man counted out the notes, King's hand slipped inside the woman's tote handbag, and he pocketed her purse as he side stepped around them. He turned off the street and into another alleyway and by the time he had emerged at the other end, he had binned the purse and slipped forty euros and two debit cards into his pocket. In another tobacconist he bought a fifty-euro phone card and a map and paid contactless with one of the woman's cards. He couldn't steal the phonecard because they were handed out upon payment, and he needed the till receipt to register.

Next had come the car. Nothing flashy or memorable. But people didn't tend to give up their car without a fight. A vehicle was generally the second most expensive purchase a person would ever make, so King knew that he would have to be ready, and he would have to play it right to avoid blood on his hands. He spotted the carpark at the rear of a small supermarket. Spanish supermarkets tended to be smaller than in the UK, although there were many to choose from. The carpark was free for patrons and took around thirty vehicles. There were no barriers and only a single CCTV camera on the entrance and exit, which was divided by a single bollard. The cars were a rather humdrum collection of hatchbacks with the odd higher end brand mixed in. He would avoid the brand-new Mercedes coupe and the convertible BMW in any event - far too flashy and memorable - but rather than choose a car, he would choose the owner. Minimum effort, maximum reward.

King waited patiently pretending to scroll on his phone under the cover of the partial roof, which he supposed had been erected for shade rather than for inclement weather. He ignored a young mother and her child, sitting in the shopping trolley. Likewise, an old man struggling with two shopping bags as he limped towards his old Fiat. But when a woman wandered out with a bottle of wine in one hand and her phone in another, he pushed himself away from the wall and took notice. She was mid-twenties and stopped to take a picture for either Snapchat or Instagram as she walked towards a silver Peugeot. She pulled a standard social media pose – puckered lips and pout, head tilted sideways and no warmth in her expression – and continued to walk to the car, checking the phone to see if she had any likes already. King found the whole process quite amusing. He stepped out from the shade, apparently engrossed in his own phone and as she fumbled her key fob from her handbag. When he was a metre from her, he looked up as if to apologise for his distraction and pocketed his phone. She held her phone and key fob in one hand and the bottle of wine in the other, and he simply knocked the bottle from her hand with his elbow and turned to apologise as it smashed on the ground. He grabbed the key fob and her phone, and ignoring her shock, pressed the key fob and watched as the Peugeot's lights flashed as it opened. The woman shouted in Spanish, but

King simply opened the door and tossed her phone into the open wheelie bin amid rubbish and flies swarming around the lid. He had the vehicle started and was pulling out before the woman could protest further, and the last he saw of her, she was reaching into the wheelie bin to retrieve her phone. He had been tempted to take the phone, but he did not want to leave the young woman high and dry, and she would have called the police from inside the supermarket, likely gaining him just thirty seconds.

King drove confidently and rapidly through the streets, then pulled into a narrow residential street and parked. He got out and checked around him, then set about removing the number plate of a similarly aged vehicle with the Swiss Army knife. The process took just three or four minutes, and he dropped the plates into the rear footwell and got back in the car. On the outskirts of Cadiz, he found some waste ground that had become a dumping ground. King parked and removed the vehicle's numberplates then replaced them with the stolen set. He was back on the move withing five minutes, filling up with fuel and a bag of drinks and snacks, using one of the two debit cards he had stolen. The transaction went through, but King had dropped both cards in the bin beside the fuel pump as he returned to the vehicle.

Now, four days after the yacht had been blown apart, and his life along with it, he sat in a cheap hotel room in Santander, having pulled a dozen other crimes and had finally started to grieve for the love of his life.

Chapter Five

Devonport Dockyard, Plymouth

"This must be the biggest case you've been involved with," Luger commented as he stared at the blocks of heroin resin that were all wrapped in greaseproof paper, like neat little cakes at a village bake sale. Wooden pallets had been brought in and the blocks painstakingly stacked in what DI Dermott had told them were five hundred blocks to a pallet.

"I see murders as my biggest cases," he replied curtly, then conceded, "But yes, this is as big as it gets. Upon discovery, we had the ship towed around here where the Royal Navy can keep it safe. His Majesty's Naval Base, Devonport, is the largest naval base in Western Europe. It will be safe here. And it's never going to hit the streets."

"With a proposed resell value of… nil," Big Dave mused.

"And that simply makes no sense," DI Dermott said irksomely. "It's hard enough doing this job, but now there's a whole new slant on it. They want to get people hooked to create a market that might... no... almost certainly wouldn't have been there. College and university kids with a tight budget and tuition fees, youngsters on a night out, works dos for thirty and forty-somethings who never tried drugs, but now feel reckless enough to try... just hooking people in for free." He paused. "It's like giving out huge loans with no repayments for the first couple of years..."

Luger nodded, but he did not divulge Ramsay and the MOD's fears on why Russia would want a nation - or a continent no less - of drug addicts. "So, what was the method of smuggling?" he asked.

DI Dermott scoffed. "It was packed in Egyptian cotton sheets and various spice barrels."

"I can smell turmeric," said Big Dave. "And cumin."

"They were all extremely pungent spices," Dermott replied. "Smoked paprika and chilli powder, something called kaffir lime leaves as well." He paused. "But the method of smuggling was underwhelming."

"You sound disappointed," Luger ventured.

The police officer shrugged. "A bit of an anti-climax, that's all. You get the haul of all-time, but some mugs just wrapped up the heroin and waved off the boat from the dock. And the people at this end have about five brain cells between them."

"They got Al Capone on tax evasion, despite the FBI investigating him for years," Luger proffered. "I guess it's better just to get the drugs off the street than to worry about semantics."

"I suppose," the detective sighed.

"What about this Tommy Jury character?" Luger asked. "The local gangster."

Dermott scoffed. "Can't find him. He's disappeared."

Die Trying

"Lying low with the shipment seized, I suspect." Big Dave walked over to the nearest pile of heroin and picked up a package. "That's way heavier than I thought it would be. What is it, a kilo?"

"Should be five hundred grams. That block has a street value of over a hundred grand."

"Jesus... there's thousands of them..." Big Dave weighed it in his hand and shook his head. "That's a kilo, though. I'm certain of it."

"No, five hundred grams."

"There's no way," the Big Fijian insisted. "I've handled enough kilo packages in my time."

"I didn't think you worked with drugs before," the detective said dismissively.

"He's talking about his steaks," Luger grinned, trying to lighten the mood.

"I'm talking about plastic explosives," Big Dave said curtly. "And that is not half a kilo, brother..." He took out a penknife and started to cut into the package.

"Hey! That's evidence!" Dermott protested.

The big Fijian ignored him and inspected the blade. "Were all the packages hidden in spices?"

"No. I told you. Some was hidden by Egyptian cotton."

"How?"

"On wooden pallets, just like the ones we used to stack the others." He paused. "The cotton sheets were stacked all around and on top."

"Show me the packages that were hidden in the spices." The detective frowned, but he led them past the enormous stacks and handed him a package. Big Dave handled it and said, "Now, that's half a kilo."

"Just like the others..."

"What's wrong, Lomu?" Luger asked, frowning at his colleague.

Big Dave held out the blade for the detective. "Is that heroin resin?"

Dermott inspected it closely and smelled the tip of the blade. "Absolutely."

Big Dave nodded. "Well, we've got a problem," he said. "Because the twenty pallets hidden by Egyptian cotton sheets, about a hundred tons of what you think is heroin, is Semtex plastic explosive..."

Chapter Six

Cadiz, Spain

Diego Pascal sipped his second espresso as he waited for the call to come in. His contact had sent him to Cadiz because that was where the target had been seen last. He had never met his contact, but they had always provided a wealth of information and prompt payment. The Spaniard knew that his contact had to work in the intelligence or security community, but he did not know for whom, except that it would have to have been a Western intelligence agency because many of his previous targets had been Islamic extremists or Russian mafia. So, with that in mind, he had always felt vindicated in a profession full of doubt and self-loathing.

The early summer sun was warm on his face, but the breeze was cooler than his home of Madrid, the wind blowing in strong from the Atlantic whereas the capital was leaving a cool winter behind and warming up for what would soon be another oppressively humid summer. He sipped more of his espresso, then called the waitress over and ordered a third, draining the remnants of the cup as she bustled inside. He would need it for the six-hour drive.

The contract was in limbo. There was little to be gained in remaining in the picturesque city, and with an increased police presence it was foolish to chance being pulled over and questioned. Especially as he carried illegal weapons in his vehicle and no doubt they will have been used in various crimes across the continent. He planned to ditch them in a reservoir that he had scoped out on the way back to Madrid. Swimming was prohibited at the body of water, so when he disposed of the guns there was little chance of them being discovered, unlike off the coast where the waters were frequented by divers and snorkellers throughout the summer months.

The waitress brought his espresso and whisked away the empty cup and Diego Pascal sipped the frothy surface as he checked his messages.

Stand down. The mark's status is still unknown. Wait for further contact.

Well, he knew as much. So now it was official. And if the mark was already dead, then he would not get paid. He had known that with the parameters of the arrangement changed, without his contact agreeing to half the fee upfront, it was clear that other contractors were engaged in the contract. He had made the right decision to leave the city. With multiple contractors involved, mistakes would be made, and the police could get lucky. The thought that both a pistol and a rifle were in his vehicle, just fifty metres away set him on edge. Spain had stringent firearms laws, and just

Die Trying

being in possession of an unregistered weapon could lead to five years in prison, and once he was in the system then connections to unsolved crimes could be made, and for the things he had done, he would never be a free man again. He looked up, frowning as the man sat down opposite him. He was of medium height and weight, fit-looking and well-muscled with a rugged face. Pascal thought him to be Middle Eastern, perhaps Indian, but his eyes were light, almost blue hazel. Quite striking. Perhaps he was a direct descendent of Alexander the Great, like some Afghans or Pakistanis.

"Put the phone down, Señor Pascal," said Rashid. "Nice and easy..." He showed the man the sleeve of his leather jacket and the thick suppressor edging out. "Don't lock the screen, there's a good lad..." He watched the Spaniard put down the smartphone and slide it across the table towards him. The waitress swept in and picked up the phone, replacing it with a lungo. Rashid smiled appreciatively as she walked away and he sipped the coffee gratefully, the weapon still trained on the man in front of him. So far, so good. The woman wasn't a waitress at all. She was called Jo Blyth and she was new to Ramsay's department, having come over from MI5 as an analyst wanting field experience. She had convinced the café owner that she was an insurance agent and she wanted to catch someone making a false claim, and she had paid the café owner fifty euros to take one coffee to a table and her apron was now folded on the counter and she was already fifty metres down the street inside the van and plugging the phone into a laptop to copy Pascal's contact list.

"Who are you?" asked Pascal, trying to keep his composure. "A competitor?"

Rashid shook his head and sipped some of his coffee,

placing it back on the table without his gaze ever once leaving the man's eyes. "Not exactly..."

"Well, you are not police," he said pointedly. "Police don't use suppressors."

Rashid nodded. The weapon up his sleeve wasn't so much a pistol with a silencer attached; it was a dedicated build. Essentially just a small, rifled barrel with a suppressor attached, the single 9mm, hollow-point bullet was already chambered with a bolt released by the user's thumb instead of a traditional trigger. Just ten inches overall with a cap on the end and a spring and firing pin in the rear half made a simple, yet effective concealable weapon that was virtually silent. "I think you know..."

"You work with the mark?"

"Put a name to him."

"Him?" Pascal frowned. Rashid watched the man's eyes flicker but said nothing. Enhanced interview techniques had taught him to allow the other person to fill the gaps. Sure enough, the Spaniard added, "The contract isn't for a man."

"Then who is your mark?"

"I can't tell you that."

Rashid shrugged. "There's an infinitesimal chance that we could have crossed wires..."

"I do not understand..."

"Let me make it simple for you..." Rashid leaned in, but the weapon did not move. "Give me the name and if it's not someone I know, then I'll get up from the table and walk away."

"You said a man..." Pascal ventured. "The contract is not for a man..."

"A name..."

"Caroline Darby," he replied, holding his hands out to

emphasise that it was merely business. "Thirties, blonde, slim. Attractive, I suppose..."

Rashid hoped that his expression did not belay his surprise. The initial contract had been for King. This changed everything. And then he thought that it really changed nothing at all. The man was on borrowed time. "Were you behind blowing up her boat?"

"No," he shook his head. "I don't know who that was."

Rashid leaned back in his chair, and still his arm and the weapon up his sleeve did not move. "So, your contact set up a contract with multiple contractors?"

The man shrugged. "It looks that way..." He paused. "Bad for me because I might not collect on the bounty. Bad for her, because with multiple hitters vying for a bounty, well..." he trailed off leaving the rest of the sentence hang in the air.

"Who is your employer?"

"You can't seriously expect me to answer that?"

Rashid smiled. "Let's stop wasting time, Señor Pascal. So, we go someplace quiet and dark and where you'll be tied to a chair and we get busy on you with pliers, hot irons, electrodes, a hammer even, and you'll eventually talk. And if you don't, well there's waterboarding and digit removal, and a whole host of things I don't want to do, and you most certainly don't want to have done to you." He paused pulling a pained expression. "And then there's testicular torture, eyeballs, skin peeling... Come on, man! You don't want that, and I don't want that. But you *will* talk. Everyone does, eventually." Rashid held the man's stare. He had no intention of doing these things, although he had roughed up enough people in his time. But the imagination was an unlimited entity and he hoped that the man had pictured some of these things and did not want to risk it.

"They'll kill me..."

"So will I after we've put you through all that hell," he replied. "So, let's skip all that crap and just get to the nitty gritty..."

"Qué?"

"The nitty gritty... cut to the chase? Get to the point?" The man nodded and Rashid said, "So, get to the point. Tell me who you are working for."

Diego Pascal shrugged. "I get a message. That's all I know. Many of the marks are enemies of the West, so it may even be you guys..."

"And who do you think I am?"

"You sound British, but you don't look it."

"I think you're behind the times, pal..."

The man shrugged. "Secret service?" Rashid did not reply, and the man said, "But I think it is the Americans. The spellings and language used is sometimes different to what I was taught in school. They spell things differently, you know?"

"I've noticed. But I don't think they know that they do..." Rashid paused. "Is it a man or a woman?"

"I don't know," the man replied, measuredly as he gave it some thought.

Rashid's phone rang quietly and unobtrusively. He fished it out of his pocket, all the while showing the Spaniard that the weapon was on him. Rashid had been expecting the call over a text message because he did not wish to take his eyes off the killer in front of him.

"The phone's good. It didn't lock me out. His contacts are now ours..." Jo Blyth's silky tone reeled off. Rashid liked the young woman a great deal, but he had not been able to so much as put a chink in her armour, and as much as it

pained him to admit it, he had started to think that she was not interested in him.

"Any names?"

"The mark," she replied. *"Caroline Darby. The contract was initiated five days ago."*

Rashid thought about his orders back in London. Ramsay had been quite clear. He had typically wheeled himself around his desk and taken to the bay window with its view over the Thames. The man was battling personal injury and life-changing circumstances, but to a man like Ramsay, giving the order to kill someone was neither easy, nor one he would take lightly. He had told Rashid unequivocally: *Find and eliminate any known assassin suspected to be hunting King.* Well, Caroline was his friend, and he had enough leeway to make necessary decisions.

"Thanks," he said and ended the call.

When his thumb released the bolt, the sound was no louder than a champagne cork popping and the man's chin dropped to his chest, the 9mm bullet hole leaving a small, red stain on the man's shirt directly over his heart. Rashid stood and dropped a ten euro note next to his empty coffee cup. He walked past the café and down the parallel alley, disappearing completely by the time the owner stepped out onto the pavement to light a cigarette. The café owner took a long drag of the cigarette and blew the smoke out through his nose appreciatively, then recoiled as thunder rumbled across the city. The noise was followed by a reverberation and with it the glassware, cutlery and crockery rattled on the tables. He watched incredulously as the man in the chair did not move. The café owner thought him to be asleep, but nobody could have slept through that thunder, and what struck the man was the perfectly clear blue sky. Thunder in a clear sky, he had never known the like. When he walked to his customer, he saw that the man's eyes were open, and a trickle of blood had run down the man's white shirt from a red mark that resembled a rose. The blood had pooled at the man's feet and the man he had been talking to had gone, and with him, the insurance agent posing as a waitress, who had paid him fifty euros to deliver a single espresso then leave. And by the time the café owner realised that something was wrong with the man in the chair, Rashid was seated beside Jo in the van and driving down the coast road.

Chapter Seven

"But it has no smell. Plastic explosive smells of almonds, doesn't it?"

"Not Semtex," Big Dave replied as he started removing blocks of the explosive, digging to get inside the stack. "That's why all the terrorists favour it. Sniffer dogs can't smell it, either." He looked up at the detective and said sharply, "Raise the alarm and start evacuating, and get bomb disposal here... the navy guys will be the best bet... and you'll need a cordon in place."

"How large?" Dermott asked as he took out his phone.

"Not here! No electronic devices!" Big Dave snapped. "Not here. Make the call at least a hundred metres away."

The detective nodded. "And the cordon?"

Big Dave shrugged. "I don't know. Judging from this lot, about two miles..."

"Seriously?"

"This isn't about drugs," Luger said adamantly. "Whoever sent this consignment knew that it would be intercepted, knew that it was such a haul that it would be impounded here." He pulled at Big Dave's shoulder, but the man was immovable. "We need to get the hell out of here..."

DI Dermott was already outside, shouting a warning to the armed police who appeared to be sneaking cigarettes alongside the Royal Marine contingent, and casually evaluating each other's weapons. He sprinted down the gangplank to reach the advised hundred metres to make the calls. The police officers seemed perplexed but at the mention of an IED, the Royal Marines – all likely to have served in Afghanistan – did not need to think long about their paygrade and sprinted back towards the barracks.

Undeterred, the big Fijian continued to unload the kilo blocks of high explosive, then froze. "Shit..."

"What?"

"It's a mobile phone receiver..." he replied. "There's a spaghetti portion of coloured wires as well."

"How much signal?"

"It's hovering between one and two bars..."

Luger yanked the big man by his collar and this time Big Dave stumbled backwards. "I'm calling it!" he shouted, still pulling at the man's jacket. "Bomb disposal can jam the signal and do what they're trained to do!"

They hit the gangplank together as a faint ringtone chimed behind them, then stopped.

"It hasn't got enough signal to detonate!"

Big Dave didn't say as he ran, but the set up would have required a full connection for detonation, likely three or four rings, but that could wait. For now, distance was everything and with the device receiving a call attempt then it was highly unlikely the bomb disposal team would have anything left to point a signal jammer at.

DI Dermott was talking animatedly on his phone as Luger almost crashed into him and shoved him in front of

Die Trying

him as they ran. A few uniformed police officers got the message and ran ahead of them, shouting for anyone in the area to get clear. Luger guided them up a grass slope with a monument on top and as they reached the monument they could see why; the slope was a steep knoll that they stumbled down, giving them some shelter from the blast. Dermott wasn't a runner, and he was probably regretting an adult life of thirty cigarettes a day and a lot of pints after a tough shift. Luger pressed him onwards and they were picking up stragglers all the time. An air-raid siren sounded and added to the feeling of panic and pandemonium, and as Luger glanced to his left people were evacuating office portacabins and running in their direction.

The detonation sounded like a dull thud at first. And then the air seemed to suck them back at first, almost halting their progress as effectively as trying to sprint through chest-high water. Luger glanced behind them to see a mighty mushroom surging vertically, and then the explosion bellowed, and he felt it in his chest and stomach, complete deafness forced upon him at once, followed by a piercing ringing forcing him to cry out in pain. And then he was weightless, driven off his feet by the shockwave and lifted outwards. He did not know how far he had been thrown by the blast, and he was sure that he had blacked out for a few seconds, but he did not recall hitting the ground. He simply came too, his internal organs aching dully, his ears screaming in protest. He called out, but could not fathom what he had said, nor could he hear the other screams around him. He rolled onto his stomach and clawed himself onto all fours. A young woman stared at him; her Royal Navy uniform almost torn completely from her. She had blood at her temple and there was something impossibly still about her, an incomprehensible sadness in her eyes.

Luger knew that she was dead. He looked to his right and saw Big Dave struggling to get up. The man had tried too soon and fell back down. Luger caught his eye, and they shared a look that told the other they were ok, but only just. DI Dermott was shouting something, but the man's voice was muffled. He struggled to stand and as Luger surveyed the scene, he could see others struggling. There were bodies, too. The young woman hadn't been the only fatality.

Gradually, Luger's senses returned to him, although his ears were still ringing, and his throat was unimaginably dry. He helped DI Dermott to his feet and watched as Big Dave tended to casualties. They had all escaped the heat blast and shrapnel of the explosion, but the shockwave had thrown people unexpectedly into the air, and landing had been merely down to chance. Sirens sounded as ambulances, fire crew and military police arrived on the scene. Within minutes the gates opened, and civilian fire fighters, paramedics and police arrived.

"You'd better go and get this lot organised," Luger told Dermott.

The man shrugged. "I have a feeling this has already gone way above my paygrade..." But nevertheless, the detective turned and walked dutifully back towards the grassy knoll.

Big Dave backed away as help came and both men walked back up the knoll, then stood still and surveyed the scene.

"Standard operating procedure calls for assessing the risk of a secondary explosion," Big Dave commented flatly.

Luger nodded. "But you'd need something left for that..."

The frigate was all but gone, just the rear fifth from the stern remained, likely held out of the water by the submerged hulk. The frigate was on its side and a rescue operation was already underway with helicopters winching crew and small inflatable craft going to the aid of casualties in the water. Surprisingly, the supply vessel – an enormous craft of some thirty-seven-thousand tonnes – had buckled midship and both stern and prow were pointing skywards, with a third of the vessel underwater. The port was littered with barrels and boxes, lifejackets and debris, and a sheen of oil gave a glossy blue and red hue to the surface. Smaller craft had either capsized or been swamped by the waves caused from the sinking of the frigate, and a few boats had been thrown out of the water and onto the quayside. More poignant, though, were the bodies floating in the water. As the two men watched, the bodies started to sink one by one, indicating that many had been alive when they hit the water and had either perished from their injuries, or taken on water and drowned. The bodies would only float again after putrefaction and the build-up of methane, hydrogen sulphide, and carbon dioxide, which typically took three or four days in warm, shallow water, but in the cold, deep waters of Plymouth and a tide running through the dockyard, might never resurface at all.

"What do we do?" asked Luger.

"We're no use here," replied Big Dave. "We'd just be in the way. Besides, we came down to look at a drug bust, and that's now at the bottom of the sea."

Luger nodded. "I was based here for a while," he said solemnly. "For a year when I was with naval intelligence."

"I'm sorry..." Big Dave replied.

Luger shrugged. "That's okay."

"No, it really isn't," he persisted. "Plymouth is a bit of a shithole..."

"Idiot..." Luger shook his head, but it had made him

smile. He was used to it, though. Gallows humour they had called it in the navy, and he knew it was the same in all the armed forces, and indeed the intelligence services, too. Anywhere, for that matter, where life and death is prominent. It's what got you through. Luger took out his phone as it chimed. The signal was relatively acceptable on top of the knoll. He read the alert and frowned. "Shit..." he said quietly.

"What is it?"

Luger simply held the phone for him to see.

Sky News alert: *Global terrorist attack. Massive bombs exploded in docks at Plymouth, Barrow-in-Furness, Algeciras Bay (Cadiz, Spain), Toulon (France), Port of Trieste (Italy). Italy, Spain, the UK, and France's largest naval ports attacked, along with Barrow-in-Furness, home to the UK's submarine manufacture and development. NATO on full alert as initial death toll estimated at 3000 and expected to climb. Multiple vessels destroyed.*

Chapter Eight

Cadiz, Spain

"What on earth was that?" Jo Blyth exclaimed.

"An explosion," Rashid replied.

"Are you sure?"

"Yes," he replied somewhat tersely that his judgement should be called into question. "I've heard more than my fair share..."

The young woman said nothing as she continued to drive along the coast road. Overhead, helicopters flew towards the port and the sound of sirens grew. She pulled to the side of the road as police vehicles, fire crew and ambulances caught up with them and raced past.

Rashid's phone chimed and he read the message:

Sky News alert: *Global terrorist attack. Massive bombs exploded in docks at Plymouth, Barrow-in-Furness, Algeciras Bay (Cadiz, Spain), Toulon (France), Port of*

Trieste (Italy). Italy, Spain, the UK, and France's largest naval ports attacked, along with Barrow-in-Furness, home to the UK's submarine manufacture and development. NATO on full alert as initial death toll estimated at 3000 and expected to climb. Multiple vessels destroyed.

"Trouble?" she asked.

"Trouble. Looks like an orchestrated attack on the strongest European naval contingent of NATO. Five ports bombed at once, two in Britain, the rest in Spain, France and Italy."

"Well, I guess Cadiz was one of those ports," she said. "Do we investigate?"

Rashid shook his head. "No," he replied. "Until we're told otherwise, we work our way down the list..."

Chapter Nine

Bayonne, France

People said that crime didn't pay, but King had run series of snatch and grabs since Cadiz and had two thousand euros in his pocket and was now driving his third car with a set of stolen French numberplates. He had used a selection of stolen debit cards to buy mid-range mobile phones and then sell them for cash to thrift shops and pawn brokers. He had paid for his food with the cards, ditching them when they were either declined or he felt he was pushing his luck. Nobody had been physically hurt during his crime spree, but he did know that he had caused inconvenience and stress to individuals but found it easy to discount because he was in a situation of life or death, and he put his own life far above the inconvenience of strangers and the financial hit that the banks and insurance companies would take.

When he compartmentalised this – the fact that it was the faceless corporations that charged their customers extortionate fees that truly suffered - he found it easy to live with.

King stopped at the service station and refilled the Audi estate that he had taken from its owner in a similar manner to the Peugeot. This time a harassed mother who had been admonishing her child excessively, but not too harassed to put down her phone and Instagram feed. She needed to wake up, pay attention to the world around her and appreciate what she had, and King had been pleased to give her that lesson. He had left Saint-Jean-de-Luz and found a suitable numberplate on a similar aged vehicle in a quiet, leafy village five miles off the A63 autoroute.

After buying some water and a simple, yet delicious ham and cheese baguette which he ate on a low wall overlooking the river, he tossed the empty bottle and paper wrapper into a nearby bin and checked his phone. It was a force of habit, and the fact that there were no numbers displayed reminded him how alone he was, and that he would never see Caroline again. But he could not let go of the fact that the police and coastguard had not recovered her body. And that was the worst thing about it. No body meant a scintilla of hope. His mind wandered back to the operations and jobs he had taken on over the years where he had taken a life and left no closure for the friends and relatives. He had thought nothing of it at the time, disposing of a body – his mentor Peter Stewart had taught him well and no body generally meant no crime in many cases – and besides, the people he had been sent to kill had all been enemies of his country. More or less. Sometimes less, and as he grew older, he knew that many had been simply pawns in somebody else's game and unknown agenda. How those grieving families lived on never truly knowing what had happened to their loved one was beyond him, and he had started to see Caroline's death as penance for his sins. He was not a religious man but doubt often presented itself when a person reached their lowest ebb.

Chapter Ten

London

"Well, that was unexpected…"

"Tell me about it," Big Dave replied.

"It's terrible," Ramsay said, pausing the news footage on the tv remote. To his left, a large television taking up a third of the wall had been switched to Sky News. "All military ports across Europe are on high alert, as are land bases in case they try similar attacks using vehicles. Flight exclusion zones have been extended around airfields and military bases as well." He paused. "You both look battered and bruised."

Big Dave shrugged. He supposed that for Ramsay the comment may have come close to concern, but it sounded like an observation at best. Luger thought it best to follow the Fijian's lead and did not reply either.

Ramsay glanced at some papers in front of him and said,

Die Trying

"Nobody, has claimed responsibility, yet. However, in today's socio-political climate we cannot discount Russia or Iran and if this is the case, then we cannot overlook the Iron Fist."

"We lost all leads to the organisation with the death of the General and Ahmadi." Luger paused. "And whatever information MacPherson and Sir Galahad Mereweather might have had died with them..."

"A great deal died with them," Ramsay commented flatly. "Not least personal agenda and interference in Britain's security..."

"If Iron Fist even existed," said Big Dave.

"The top security analysts in the Security Service suspect otherwise," Ramsay countered. "Unless you have any intelligence to the contrary?"

Big Dave shook his head. "I'm not doubting a Russia-Iranian partnership. Iran has supplied Russia with missiles after they depleted their supply in Ukraine. But I never bought China as being threatened enough by the West to join such an allegiance, nor Belarus as being important enough. Russia moved some nukes there, to stop Belarus being invaded by NATO during the early days of its Ukraine campaign, but Belarus is hardly a world player. North Korea is barely credible, despite their leader's sabre rattling from time to time."

"Some sound points," Ramsay conceded. "But at the end of the day it's just opinion and a hunch. We need credible facts only."

"China are too concentrated on their new-found capitalism and consumer production. Outside of Taiwan, are they even looking to expand their borders? Do we, Europe, even stack up as a target?" Big Dave shrugged. "We're an influential partner and top contributor to NATO, so we are well protected, and we have little manufacturing production and vast consumerism. China is filling that segment for us. What's to be gained by them attacking us?"

"He has a point," Luger observed. "China is actively hacking us, but mostly it's aggressive consumer research… passwords and contacts, purchases and conversations."

"Do let me know if either of you would prefer a desk job, won't you?" Ramsay replied offhandedly. For the man everybody looked at as on the autism spectrum, it was an unprecedented display of sarcasm. "But I do wonder how much disinformation Sir Galahad Mereweather planted to use Ahmadi as an asset. I know that the man's family were slain, and British intelligence was blamed for that, and that only went to further bolster Ahmadi's resolve. Though we do have solid evidence that Iran took major traffic of heroin over its border with Afghanistan, and we know that Russia would benefit from a Europe where fighting aged men and women have little resolve because of enabled drug addiction. I still think, that despite the attacks, it's a valid line of investigation. Russia is up to something and has Iran's help. And because they are always backed by China on the world stage, we cannot afford to discount the world's second largest superpower."

Big Dave nodded. "So, what about King?"

Ramsay did not hold the man's gaze, instead glancing at some papers and said, "King and his association with us is compromised until the contract on his head is lifted." He paused, placing the papers in an impossibly neat pile in line with the edge of the desk. "We are taking measures to see that this horrible episode can be closed."

"We?" Big Dave asked.

Ramsay ignored him as he picked up the phone and said, "Mae, tell Jim to meet Lomu and Luger in the car…"

Die Trying

Jack Luger frowned as Ramsay replaced the receiver. "We're going somewhere?"

"Those shits across the river have something that may be of interest to us..." Big Dave had never heard Neil Ramsay use profanity, but he guessed even he could be prone to curse when talking about MI6. Ramsay added, "Take Jim in with you. He has a brilliant memory and eye for detail, despite being as socially sensitive as a hog roast in a kubutz..."

Big Dave raised an eyebrow as he stared at his friend and boss. Swearing, sarcasm and humour in the same day. He would have had a laugh with Caroline about that. The two had a shared kindred spirt, and he often felt a connection to her that he did not feel towards the others, and he suspected that they did not towards her. A sibling bond, perhaps. Certainly not sexual, but he did know that he cared for her a great deal. The thought of her being killed by an assassin filled him with a rage that he struggled to quell. All he did know was that if he ever met the assassin face to face, he would tear their tongue out of their throat with his bare hands.

Chapter Eleven

Sisto-Palkino, Leningrad Oblast, Russia

Piotr Krylov could not believe his luck. Not only had the woman sat and drunk with him, but she had truly been interested in him. The conversation had been easy. She had touched his thigh and bought rounds of vodka with her own money. She was a bored housewife and had headed for a bar far from St. Petersburg where she could relax without fear of being seen. She had made it clear that she intended to find a man to screw and there had been an unspoken agreement between them that they would end their evening having sex. The anticipation was insurmountable. Sex with prostitutes always felt so ungratifying. The surge of excitement was nothing when it was not reciprocated, and after what he had found to be a rushed and uncaring performance, there was never an afterglow or the chance for another performance. The transaction had been done and the woman could not get out of there quick enough. But sex with an unhappy married woman? She would be trying hard to impress and at the same time, eager to make the experience memorable for those dark, sleepless nights when she could fantasise next to an uncaring, cold husband. She would try to reach climax, and he would do his best to help her.

He had floated the idea of a small hotel he knew of near the harbour, but she had not wanted to take the risk. The car would be fine, and fortunately, she owned a large, black Mercedes SUV that she would get even more of a kick out of screwing inside, because her husband had bought it for her. The large, dark vehicle would go unnoticed off the road in the edge of the woods beside the quiet road into Sisto-Palkino.

The night was black, with enough cloud to mask the stars in a moonless sky. Krylov could barely see the trees when the woman switched off the lights. They had kissed passionately in the carpark outside the bar, and he had fondled her inner thighs and teased at her crotch with his fingers through the satin briefs she wore under her leather skirt, disappointed that she was not yet wet, though confident that would soon change. She had teasingly brushed his hand aside, telling him that there was more than enough time for that when they parked, and not to excite himself too much because she wanted to explore as many positions as they could inside the vehicle.

Outside, the silence was absolute. The only sounds were that of the engine ticking cool after the drive. Krylov was so aroused, so excited at what lay ahead with the beauty beside him, that he could hear his own pulse pounding in his ears, his own heartbeat thudding in his chest.

"I want to lay on the hood," she said, her English vocabulary shaped by American movies and popular culture. "I want to feel the warm metal from the engine on my back as you pleasure me orally..."

Krylov felt the surge of excitement in his lower regions, scrabbling for the doorhandle and clambering out of the vehicle. He tore at his jacket and shirt, the early spring air still bitterly cold. No matter. He would soon warm up. His belt was already unbuckled as he walked around the front of the Mercedes to meet her but froze when he saw the muzzle of the pistol in the gloomy illumination of the vehicle's interior light.

"What the fuck is this? A robbery?" he asked incredulously. "Do you know who I am?"

"Yes."

"Well?"

"You're a low-level criminal with an inflated ego and ideas above your station."

Krylov took a step towards her, and she raised the pistol. It was a 7.62x25mm Tokarev and it packed a hell of a punch. He froze, something about the coolness of her that sat uneasily with him. She placed her mobile phone on the warm bonnet, and he could see that it was recording.

"What is this about?" he asked. "I have money. A great deal of it..."

"You have what Lukov has allowed you to skim off the top. He is not a stupid man, he knows that you take more than your share, and he can accept that," she said, the pistol as unwavering as her stare. "But he does not like excessive greed. Your greed and interference has gone beyond the pale."

"I can pay him back..." Krylov was perspiring despite the chill night air, and at the utterance of Lukov's name, he had started to tremble. "I have the bulk of it and what I sold is being held in gold bars! I will have it sent to St. Petersburg tomorrow, with interest..."

"Lukov is not concerned about the money," she replied. "But what *does* concern him, is why the shipments of heroin ended up exploding in ports around Europe, rather than being distributed for free..." She paused. "But what the West now think is a direct attack was really just a way for you to help yourself to thousands of kilos of heroin and use the explosives to hide what you have taken. Lukov suspects... no, he *knows* what you have done."

"It was hundreds of millions of dollars of potential revenue that was going to be given away!" he argued. "Moscow wanted to attack the West... well they have! Thousands of lives, billions of dollars' worth of military equipment, billions wiped off the stock markets and now they know that Russia is to be feared! The Ukraine war has shown Russia as weak. They became bogged down in the mud and weather while the West continue to pump funds, equipment and ammunition into that despicable dog's war effort!"

"It was not your decision!" she screamed and shot off his right kneecap. The gunshot and echo through the trees drowned out the man's screams as he fell and writhed on the forest floor. "Do you know what you have done?" she screamed down at him. "You have jeopardised a GRU operation that Lukov had promised to fulfil! They are holding him responsible, and the heroin that he supplied to them for a healthy profit now has to be supplied again at his own expense." She paused, shaking her head, and allowing for the ramifications of his actions to sink in. "And that includes the ships that the GRU paid for. You have cost Max Lukov and the family billions of dollars..."

"I'm sorry!"

"Sorry?" she mocked him. "If Lukov cannot deliver what was promised then the GRU will have him killed. As you can understand, Lukov is not happy with that arrangement..."

"I will get the heroin back!" the man blubbed.

The woman kept the weapon aimed at him as he rolled onto his back. "And your street dealers will simply give it back to you?" She laughed. "I think not..."

"They will! I will get it all back! I will tell you where it is and where the gold is, too!"

"Oh, I know you will," the woman told him. "And you will tell me so much more besides..."

Chapter Twelve

The River House,
   Secret Intelligence Service (MI6)
Headquarters

Jim Kernow parked the Jaguar saloon in the underground carpark having shown his Security Service identification and the pass via a QR code on his mobile phone. Big Dave and Jack Luger each had a code, too. Neither man had official Security Service credentials, but that was merely part of their remit. The QR codes were processed hourly, so the uniformed security guards and the armed police officers on the street side checked the QR codes and after they had swept the underside of the vehicle with mirrors on retractable poles, merely waved them through.

"I'm well gutted," Jim said as he got out and locked the door. "Not a single Aston Martin in the car park..."

"You will find Vespers, that's vodka martinis, in the bar, though. Shaken, not stirred, naturally." A tall, smartly dressed and distinguished-looking gentleman told them.

"Which is where I suggest we head at this time of evening," he added, glancing at his watch. "Marcus Devonshire." The man smiled, offering his hand, and looking at all three of them in turn. "From what I hear, it's you lot over the river who have been up to all the James Bond antics these days, naturally with a lot less budget..." he smiled. "We tend to favour drones, computer hacking and using local assets these days. No sense in wasting an expensive education on all that rough and tumble stuff.

"Hold on," Big Dave frowned. "You have a bar?"

"Security," said Devonshire. "Our lovely boys and girls can't just put a few tables together in a *Wetherspoons* and talk shop at the end of the day."

"You'd leave far too many briefcases there for a start," Luger quipped.

"No lad, that's on the train home," Big Dave chided.

"Ah, the good old working-class *Box* wit," Devonshire replied sardonically. "Or half of it, at least..."

Big Dave laughed. "Go on then, show us how the other half live..."

Marcus Devonshire led them to the lift where they rose three floors and came out in a large foyer. The SIS coat of arms was displayed in green tiles in an otherwise cream floor. The soles of Devonshire's expensive shoes clipped on the tiles, while the other three men walked near-silently behind him. MI5 were often remarked upon by their shoes. A watcher's job was to follow people and because they could put in a lot of miles and needed to be quiet, many operatives favoured *Hush Puppies* over a pair of handmade Oxfords. Jim Kernow, although suited was wearing a pair of old, comfortable-looking leather shoes, while both Big Dave and Luger wore jeans, hiking jackets and trainers, and even though the place had a quiet feel to it, the few people they saw along the way made them feel underdressed.

"This is one of our satellite rooms," said Devonshire hovering at a door. Above the door was a green light and a sign that said: DO NOT ENTER WHEN LIGHT IS RED. The SIS officer opened the door, and the three men were met by a bank of monitors with three men and one woman seated at computer terminals. "Middle East," he explained. "Just routine. When it is something more auspicious like a drone strike or a coordinated operation, then this room will be a hive of activity and the red light will come on when the appropriate head brass are here to take command."

"How many control rooms do you have?" asked Jack Luger.

Devonshire shrugged. "Plenty," he replied somewhat defensively. "More than ten, less than twenty." He paused. "Ukraine and Russia are keeping us busy, as is the situation in Israel and Gaza. Syria, too."

"Impressive," Big Dave agreed.

"Oh, it's not unlike you chaps over at Thames House..." He paused, then added, "But you lot aren't really *Box* anymore, are you?"

"We are still very much with the Security Service," Luger said pointedly. "Our department was merely created so that we can handle pressing situations until the security leaks have been sealed over at Thames House."

"Good luck with that!" Devonshire scoffed. "I heard that the Royal College of Arms has been designing a new coat of arms for the Security Service. Water pouring from a jug into a colander, with a hand waving it away... *ibi ad secreta nostra...* there go our secrets!" He smiled with a somewhat irritating sympathy and said, "Maybe you chaps will have more luck as a smaller group. Like those instances when a business that has been around for decades gets too big or lacks direction and merely loses their way. Like Woolworths or Wilko..." He opened the door and led them out into the corridor, almost bumping into a smartly dressed woman. "Ah, this is Harriet," he said. "She'll show you around, perhaps get that drink for you if you're not too busy patching up the leaks across the river..."

Harriet was mid-thirties and attractive in a traditional sort of way. Her brunette hair was pulled back in a tight French twist, and she wore just a simple gold chain around her slim and elegant neck. Jack Luger noted the absence of an engagement or wedding ring, but he tended to notice these things. He was already taken by her light, blue eyes, and the smattering of freckles each side of her nose, which added a somewhat youthful appearance. She smiled at them as Devonshire turned the corridor and disappeared.

"How was that, gentlemen?"

Big Dave shrugged. "He's a dickhead..."

"You got that right," Jim Kernow agreed.

"It was certainly an interesting experience," Luger said more tactfully. "I can't say I'd be keen to repeat it."

"He's certainly one of a kind," Harriet smiled. "I'll show you what we have and then I'll take you for that drink," she said, changing the subject. "So, how's life in Five?"

Luger found himself staring at her legs as he followed her. "Busy," he said, averting his eyes just before she glanced behind.

"It's the same both sides of the river," she replied. "I've been with SIS for twelve years since leaving university, and there's never been a slow day."

They took a lift up another three floors and after fifty paces down the corridor, they reached a smoked glass panel

Die Trying

that stretched the length of the corridor on a gentle curve. She used her lanyard card against a control box and smiled as the glass cleared to reveal hundreds of monitors and a team of a dozen men and woman huddled over computer terminals.

"That's every traffic and high street camera in London, Manchester, Belfast and Birmingham," she announced proudly. "We can access most systems in every city throughout the country, given enough staffing and time."

"Big Brother is definitely watching us," Jim Kernow mused quietly.

"Is this legal?" Big Dave asked incredulously. "There's no such facility at Thames House."

"Not strictly," she replied pensively. "But we have a slightly different remit."

"You're meant to be spying on the enemy," said Big Dave. "Not on British citizens. And your remit is overseas. That's why you answer to the Foreign Office and the Security Service answers to the Home Office."

"That's a little hypocritical of you," she replied dismissively. "Given that remit, then there shouldn't be a trail of death, destruction and chaos spread across half the world by you guys. Simon Mereweather shifted the remit, Stella Fox barely had time to find the ladies toilet at Thames House, and it looks like Neil Ramsay has shifted the direction even more, but worse than that, he's created his own little band of merry men who don't even seem to answer to the Home Office anymore."

"What is this about?" Jack Luger asked, his tone about as unconfrontational as possible, but he had been irked ever since meeting Devonshire. Harriet mentioning former director general Stella Fox - his aunt who had been killed by the same gunman who put Ramsay in a wheelchair - had not helped. "We were invited here."

Harriet smiled. "I'm sorry. Neil Ramsay has ruffled a few feathers with his new remit, mainly because the remit has neither been made public and..."

"And SIS are acting like the fat, spoiled kid who can't play nice in the sandpit," Big Dave interjected.

"Perhaps a little," she conceded. "But you are a newly formed unit and nobody within the intelligence community knows a damn thing about you."

"I think we'd better cut to the chase," said Jim Kernow. "Or I could say, shit or get off the pot. You decide which euphemism for stop wasting our time you wish to use." The big Cornishman shrugged. He was the kind of man who said it how he saw it, and he did not have the inclination for games, or social interaction, even.

Harriet smiled. "Very well," she said. "Follow me."

The corridors of SIS headquarters in what was referred to as The River House were sterile and featureless. All glass was smoked, so as they passed windows that would otherwise have afforded the gleam of moonlight upon the Thames or twinkling streetlamps or lights from offices where people worked late, the effect was dull and somewhat detuned from reality. At a bank of office doors, Harriet opened one and ushered them inside. The room was a twenty-by-twenty windowless box. There were monitors on the wall, a large screen television and a desk with two telephones beside a computer terminal and monitor. A large printer and a seemingly endless supply of paper took up a table beside the desk and along with two comfortable leather chairs facing opposite one another with a low coffee table separating them, a conference table and eight chairs dominated the centre of the room.

Die Trying

"My office," she said as they stepped inside. "Please, take a seat at the table."

The office was large for one person, and the windowless design pointed to someone handling sensitive information and affairs, although the sparseness and lack of refinements meant that she was not in the higher echelons of the SIS. Luger studied her as she walked to the desk and picked up a file. He could catch glimpses of a good figure through her suit, the form of her breasts as she sat down at the table and opened the file in front of her. He caught Big Dave grinning him and shook away any thoughts of attraction. He was here for business and business only.

"Are you familiar with Max Lukov?" she asked.

"No," replied Big Dave, taking the lead. He had been with the team longer than the other two, and that was how seniority worked in an organisation devoid of rank. "But we're boots on the ground. I imagine if the man's worth knowing, then Ramsay will have a file on him."

"I admire your loyalty," Harriet smiled. "But if he did, then you would not be here." She dealt the photographs across the table with the dextrous fluidity of a croupier. "Forty-two years of age, Russian father and Georgian mother. She was a prostitute and when Lukov senior took a liking to her, he bought her from her pimp and whisked her away to a life of luxury in Moscow..." she said, with just enough irony in her tone to tell them that life had been far from a bed of roses for the Lukovs. "Lukov senior served in the Soviet army and the KGB and managed to hang onto both his job and life when the Iron Curtain fell. He moved over to the FSB and by the time Max Lukov had completed his army service, Lukov senior had used his knowledge of the KGB and the new Russian intelligence service to branch out into organised crime." She paused, watching the men study the photographs, before handing them printed bios of the man in question. "As you know, there has never been a Russian organised crime syndicate without former KGB or FSB in their midst. They knew the way things were done, they had the weapons and the right people to recruit. They knew all the secrets, too."

"So, Max Lukov is a crime boss?" Luger asked.

Big Dave smirked. He knew that the young man was by now quite smitten with the young SIS officer opposite him. "And he's the brains of the outfit," he jibed.

"Well, I can see who's the brawn..." she smiled back at the big Fijian.

Jack Luger fought hard not to scowl. "I was just speeding things along..."

Big Dave fought just as hard not to appear smug. He beamed a smile at Harriet and asked, "Has this got anything to do with the bombings across Europe?"

"Brains, too..." Harriet smiled. "Yes. Everything, in fact." She watched Jim Kernow as he placed the bio face down on the table. "Finished?" she asked somewhat condescendingly.

Kernow tapped his temple and said, "All up here, maid."

"Ok..." she replied dubiously.

Both Luger and Big Dave were still reading when Kernow said, "Lukov joined the family firm after leaving the GRU five years ago. Unusual that he should join a different intelligence service, what with Dimitri Lukov's time with the KGB and FSB. Do you have an angle on that?"

"We imagine that during his time as a head of the crime syndicate Dimitri Lukov wanted his son to have a unique insight into the military branch of the intelligence services.

Die Trying

Either way you cut it, the Lukovs had a unique insight into the military and both the KGB, FSB and GRU. There was nothing they would not know about special operations, and they would have a wealth of contacts."

"And his subsequent court martial?" asked Kernow.

"Bloody hell, Jim, how fast do you read?" Big Dave asked incredulously.

Kernow shrugged.

"He organised a large arms deal. However, he had also made many enemies, as had his father. The tables turned and he was made an example of. He was sentenced to ten years in a Siberian gulag but was released after two years when evidence was resubmitted." She paused. "Of course, that was all bullshit, because the people who banded against him all started to meet with terrible accidents."

"What sort of accidents?" asked Luger, finally finishing the printout.

"Oh, the normal everyday accidents. Gas explosions in the home, brakes failing in cars, falling out of windows." She paused. "Wrists, femoral and carotid arteries severed whilst shaving..." she chuckled. "Russian subtlety at its most profound."

"Nice," Luger commented. "So, he gets a free pass and joins the family firm."

"Yes." She paused. "But Max Lukov is predatory. He's a lion. And young lions eventually overthrow the alpha male. When the old man showed weakness a few times too many, and when Max Lukov was publicly put in his place by his own father, then he saw to it that his father met with a sticky end."

"He killed his own father?" Luger commented incredulously.

"Had him killed," she replied. "He used a female

assassin known to us. She lured him to a hotel room in Budapest and killed him."

"How?" asked Big Dave.

"Does it matter?"

"You can always learn something in this game."

"She handcuffed him to the bed and removed his appendages."

"Appendages?" asked Kernow.

"His balls," Harriet replied. "He bled out. When he was likely close to death, she sliced through his wrists, femoral arteries, and throat. She likes to make sure, that one. She's known as The Widow, and apart from that, we don't have much else on her."

"Then his killing was as much a message as it was an assassination," Big Dave commented flatly. "That much cutting is unnecessary, but certainly brutal. Something to gain the syndicate's attention. The king is dead; long live the king..."

"Who's going to mess with a man like that?" Luger mused.

"So, what has this got to do with us?" asked Big Dave.

Harriet took out some more photographs and typewritten sheets. She handed them out and noticed that Jim Kernow had finished his copies before the other two men had even turned the page. "What do you do with Box?" she asked amiably.

"I look after the boss, do what I'm told and keep my mouth shut," he replied.

"Oh..." said Harriet, somewhat taken aback by the man's bluntness. The minutes passed awkwardly until the other two men finished reading and studying the photographs, then she said, "One of our assets observed a meeting between Max Lukov and this female assassin. Our

Die Trying

communication taps had earlier transcribed a heated debate between Lukov and a known high-ranking officer of the GRU named Orlev. Lukov was chewed out royally. It seems that Lukov was tasked with organising a terrific supply of heroin. We can only assume that this heroin was part of the shipments seized in Europe and the UK. Lukov used a middleman, and it was something the middleman did that drew the wrath of the GRU. Find the middleman, find the link." She paused, looking at the three men in turn. "We feel that this fits Box's remit, so are offering what we have on file."

"Well, it sounds like the assassin will be finding the middleman soon enough," said Big Dave. "So, it may be more helpful to find the assassin."

"How you go about your job is not our concern."

"What do you want in return?" asked Jim Kernow. "Six don't give anything away for free..."

Harriet stood up and said, "How about a drink, gentlemen?'

Luger pushed out his chair and said, "I'm up for that."

"Lead on," added Big Dave.

"You'll have to leave the files here, I'm afraid," she smiled. "We don't like secrets leaving the SIS..."

"I'll remember it," Kernow replied.

"Really?"

He tapped the side of his head. "Up here for thinking, luv," he said, then pointed to his feet. "Down there for dancing..."

"Very well," Harriet said somewhat bemused. She smoothed down her skirt as she pushed back her chair. "The drinks are on us, of course."

Chapter Thirteen

St. Petersburg, Russia

The bodyguard held out his hand even before he checked her with the wand. She handed him the pistol and stood back impatiently. He handed the pistol to another man who ejected the magazine and emptied the breech. Both men wore surgical gloves, and the weapon was placed in a plastic zip-lock bag and sealed. The bodyguard then smiled at her. He was Lukov's driver and personal minder, and he enjoyed searching her every time it was called for. He was a perverse man and her skin crawled when he was near. He waved the metal detector wand over her, then decided that he would use his hands instead when it came to her breasts, legs, and crotch. He grinned as he saw the disgust on her face.

"Enjoying yourself?" she asked indignantly.

"I've had worse days..."

Die Trying

"I will kill you one day," she told him. "When all this is over, I will be the last person you see when your body turns cold, and your world turns dark..."

He smiled, giving her left breast a hard squeeze that caused her to wince. "But until then..." He stepped back from her and said, "Lukov will see you now."

The woman turned on her heel and strode to the impressive oak doors. Fifteen feet tall and divided into two, five-feet wide doors, the entrance to Max Lukov's domain was intimidating, and like her visits before, she was filled with both dread and the agonisingly incorporeal feeling of vengeance.

The second bodyguard opened the door for her, and she stepped inside, her heels clipping the wooden floor.

"She's clean, boss..." the bodyguard announced, then backed out and closed the door.

Lukov did not look up. He was reading through a stack of papers, and it had all his attention. Supposedly. She was aware of the tactic. She had learned all there was to know about human behaviour during her years working in her husband's business, and she showed her impatience by sitting down in the chair unprompted and studying an imaginary spot on her fingernail.

"Success?" Max Lukov asked, not looking up.

The woman remained silent until he tore his eyes away from the papers and stared at her. "Of course..."

"I have another job for you."

"No, no more. You said so..."

Lukov shrugged. "Very well," he said, pointing to the door. "You are free to leave..."

She stared at him, waiting for him to break his stare and for a while, both sets of eyes locked – both predators; both dangerous. But Lukov had the advantage, and he would always play his advantage. She knew this as well, and eventually she said, "I need to see him..."

Lukov smiled. "All in good time."

"Now."

"No."

"You can't expect me to kill; to have my head in the right place to complete the task." She paused, feeling sickened that she was showing weakness. "Please..." Lukov took out his mobile phone and dialled. She could barely hear what he said, his tone hushed and aggressive. He switched to FaceTime and handed her the phone. She found herself rushing to the desk and delicately taking the phone from his hand, ever mindful that she could not press a button or an icon and lose the connection. "Samuel! Samuel! It's mummy!"

"Hello mummy, when are you coming back?"

"Soon, my darling. Very, very soon..."

"I miss you, mummy!" The boy started to cry. *"I miss you and I want to come home!"*

"Soon, my darling. Soon..." She looked at Max Lukov and said, "Mummy has just one more thing to do. And then we will live together in our lovely little villa, and nobody will trouble us again."

"Please come back, mummy..."

Lukov held out his hand, clicking his fingers before resting his palm outstretched.

She smiled at her son and said, "I have to go now, my darling boy..."

"No mummy, don't...!"

Her eyes full of tears, that spilled out over her lower eyelids like a river breaking its banks, she handed Max

Die Trying

Lukov the phone and stared at him. "One more job," she said.

"Agreed."
"And if I fail?"
"See that you don't."
"But if I do?"
"Then the boy will die..."

Chapter Fourteen

SIS Headquarters, London

They rode the lift two more floors and stepped out onto a mezzanine. Below them plants grew from gravel beds and a small water feature added an air of calm in front of a coffee shop. Big Dave shook his head incredulously as they skirted the guardrail and headed for the bar.

"The Security Service really needs a bigger budget," the big Fijian remarked incredulously. "So much for Ramsay's town house and a Nespresso coffee machine…"

Harriet ushered them into a typical city hotel bar with glass and chrome and light-coloured wood. A group of three men huddled around a low table and regarded them cautiously as they were led to a circle of comfy-looking leather chairs near the wide window. Once again, the glass was smoked, and the lights of London appeared dully hewed.

"What's everyone having?" a waiter asked, appearing silently at Harriet's shoulder.

"Vodka martini, shaken not stirred," Luger grinned.

"Haven't heard that one before," the waiter replied with the thinnest of smiles.

"Oh, fuck it, then, I'll have a pint of lager," the young man replied tersely and sat back in his chair.

"Same, please," replied Big Dave.

"Orange juice," Kernow said with a shrug. "Driving..."

"And a G and T..." Harriet said. "Tarquin's gin and Fever-Tree tonic with lots of ice, and a slice of orange instead of lemon, please..." She looked at the men in turn. "You'll have to return the drink," she said. "It could become an information sharing exercise. Perhaps even a new direction for the two services, instead of remaining at loggerheads about remits and policies?"

"A cup of tea in the outer office might be as good as it gets," Kernow quipped. "Or a pint at the White Swan down the road."

"Well, it's just an idea," she replied breezily.

"Sounds good," agreed Luger, taking out his phone. "Do you want my number?"

"Perhaps," she smiled.

"Then, could I have yours?"

Harriet took out her phone and airdropped her number. Luger checked his phone and smiled, sending his number to her.

"Don't let us get in the way..." Big Dave commented.

Neither looked at him and the drinks arrived in time to prevent an awkward silence. The waiter placed the drinks down in front of them remembering their orders, and he left a bowl of cashews as well.

"What the hell is MI6's budget?" Big Dave said, shaking his head as he helped himself to a handful of cashews.

"It's not the budget," she replied picking up her frosted glass. "Fighting terrorism and espionage like MI5 do is more expensive than keeping an eye on it overseas. We also recruit and engage assets through good old-fashioned patriotism." She paused sipping her drink and nodding approvingly. "It's also less expensive putting a spy into somewhere than seeking out an enemy cell and performing round-the-clock surveillance while you wait for them to make their move or control the narrative. We also make good use of seized funds and turn any monies into fighting the UK's enemies."

"Creative accounting, more like," Jim Kernow commented.

Harriet did not reply, but even for a trained spy her silence was deafening.

"What's your angle?" Big Dave asked after he had washed the cashews down with a mouthful of Dutch lager. "This is all nice and civilised, but you are sharing information when usually you are determined to keep it for yourselves. So, forgive us for feeling dubious."

"You must be talking about my predecessors. I run the Russia desk and all I want is for it to run smoothly, and to the UK's advantage."

Big Dave drained his glass and said, "Well, thank you. I'll pass your thoughts on to Ramsay." He got up and Kernow followed, placing his empty glass on the table. "Still no paper copies for us to take?"

"It's not a party. You don't get a party bag to take home," she smiled. "Not yet at least. Maybe next time, after you reciprocate. I think SIS have shared enough for now."

Die Trying

Luger smiled and stood up leaving an inch of beer in his glass. They followed Harriet out to the mezzanine and took the lift down to the foyer.

Marcus Devonshire met them at the front desk wearing a mirthless smile, and Harriet bid them goodbye. "I'll see you gentlemen down," he told them. "Sorry I wasn't at the meeting but there was something more important to deal with."

Big Dave smiled to himself. He got the impression that picking lint out of his pockets would have been more important to Marcus Devonshire than spending time with people from MI5.

"So, how is it across the river in the cheap seats?" Devonshire asked as he walked swiftly in front of them.

"The service has its challenges at the moment," Luger replied. "Working for Ramsay is altogether a different proposition."

"You haven't been with the Security Service long though, have you?"

Luger tried to hide his surprise, but he failed, and Marcus Devonshire glanced around just long enough to see that he had rattled the young man. "I worked in naval intelligence, then signed up to MI5 just over a year ago," he replied. "As you no doubt already know..."

Devonshire stopped at the lift door and said, "It must feel a little like working for the local council, instead of government." He paused as the lift door opened and he stepped inside. He waited until they squeezed in, with Big Dave taking up almost half the lift alone. Devonshire pressed the button for the underground carpark and the lift door closed. "That bloody bean counter hasn't helped Five much," Devonshire mused. "She had no right heading the counter-espionage service. She was only in charge of Box for three months and ended up getting herself killed. Silly cow. It's big boys' games, big boys' rules in this job..." He shook his head. "But that's what you get for ticking boxes and putting a woman in charge. Should have learned under Remington. Anyway, good riddance to bad rubbish. At least the Security Service has a new leader at its helm, and an ex-military one at that. And that leaves that odd-bod Neil Ramsay with his little project unit while the incompetency is cleared up over at Thames House."

Jack Luger stopped the man mid-sentence, his right hand gripped around his throat. Devonshire's cheeks flushed red, and he tried to protest but let out only a rasp. "Stella Fox was a good person," he growled. "And she was my aunt..."

"He knows that fella," said Big Dave. "He's just prodding the tiger to get a response."

Devonshire attempted to grab Luger's wrist, but found it pinned to his chest by the man's left arm. His flushed red cheeks faded and curiously, his face went pale. "Well, he's poked the tiger now," Luger growled. "And the tiger might just rip his fucking throat out..."

"Easy lad," said Kernow, resting a large paw on the younger man's shoulder. "He's not worth doing time over..."

Big Dave put his hand in his pocket and pulled out some cashews that he had swiped from the bar. "He could have choked on these, but we couldn't clear them out of his throat," he offered. "Not even when we tried an emergency tractotomy with a Swiss army knife..."

Marcus Devonshire stared at the big Fijian in horror, then coughed and gasped as Luger released his grip on the man's throat. Big Dave popped the nuts into his mouth and chewed deliberately as the lift reached the lower ground level and the doors opened.

Jim Kernow patted Devonshire on the shoulder, rather less gently than the man was used to and said, "Thank you for your hospitality, Mr Devonshire, we'll see ourselves out from here."

Chapter Fifteen

Bayonne, France

King surveyed the apartment block and both the entrance and exit for the carpark. Lights flickered within, people crossing past the windows, briefly silhouetted as they lived their uneventful lives. King didn't really think that – you never knew what went on behind closed doors - but he was the one looking out for assassins while they heated their dinner or tuned into their favourite tv show.

The flat in question was veiled in darkness. But that was as it should be. He decided that he had been vigilant enough and kept to the shadows as he made his way across the carpark and into the stairwell. They were good people here. Hardworking, though ultimately struggling to make ends meet. But that sort of resident kept things tidy and in order and called the landlord when some tearaway graffitied the walls or smashed a window. Not like the block of flats

Die Trying

where he had grown up in Tower Hamlets. He found the key where he had left it, underneath a piece of concrete coving on the austere balustrade. There was nobody watching, and the apartment block did not have any CCTV. The French did not go in for keeping tabs *Big Brother* style like the UK seemed to. The key fitted easily into the lock and opened quietly. He and Caroline had taken out a long lease on the property and paid six months in advance, twice yearly. Landlords liked that. They never felt inclined to interfere and as they had explained, they worked away a lot and the landlord would be free to inspect the property whenever she wished. Inside, the layout was basic. One bedroom, an open-plan lounge and kitchen and a bathroom. But it was cheap. King could tell that he had not been the only one here recently and he checked the bathroom, then looked around the bedroom. The bed had been slept in and remade, and there was evidence of the shower being used, as it dripped intermittently. King twisted the tap and the showerhead stopped dripping. He frowned as he made his way to the dresser and felt behind it for the key that he had secured there with *Blu Tac*. Unlocking and opening the drawer, he already knew what he would find. Inside had been four passports, two Sig P226 9mm pistols and four magazines. A fifty-round box of 9mm ammunition and two bundles of euros secured with elastic bands. The box of ammunition was half empty and only one pistol and two magazines remained, along with his two passports and the two-thousand euros in twenties. His heart raced and he felt the elation rush through him and he almost cried out with the knowledge that Caroline was alive and well. She had beaten him to it somehow, and she had been here, slept naked here, showered here and she had left with exactly her share of their emergency stash. It could not have been anybody else. No opportunistic chancer, because nobody would have left half the things behind, and nobody would take a passport unless they matched the photo inside. King searched the flat in vain. There was no note, no explanation. She had simply used the bolthole and taken her share of the vital tools of their trade. Inside the wardrobe was a single outfit for King. Caroline's was missing, but he had expected that. He dropped the shirt, trousers and jacket on the bed and took the clean socks, underwear, and shoes out from the bottom of the wardrobe. There was nothing of Caroline left in the flat. He wracked his brains as to what she was up to, how she had survived and what she was going to do next, but for Caroline not to explain meant that she did not want him to know, and that meant that she meant to do it without him, and with that in mind, King knew what he needed to do next.

Chapter Sixteen

Cadiz, Spain
Five Days Earlier

She didn't know why King persisted in wearing his vintage Rolex. The man had no perception of time anymore. She had finished the salads and dressings and poured herself a glass of pinot grigio, and King an iced water with slices of lime. The boat rocked gently on the swell, but she was used to it now. Her sea legs had come in around Mallorca, and by the time they reached Marbella she was giving the motion little thought.

Caroline could see King lying on the beach and she smiled. He was forgetting recent events, living with the threat of a contract remaining on his head by facing life head-on. He had swum and enjoyed the chilly water and was now taking some time to warm up on the sand. She didn't mind – it would probably dictate what they did next. The Canary Islands as planned or knowing King they could shelve their intentions and end up sailing for the Horn of Africa. She smiled at the notion, thinking that there could be worse dilemmas to be had. She frowned as a woman headed towards him, a pang of jealousy rising within her. King was toned and well-muscled, rugged, and handsome and she was used to women glancing at him as they walked by. She wondered how long it would be before he gave her the short shrift, or whether he tried his hand at flirting with other women. It wasn't his strong suit, to be fair. He had always been more direct than that, and once commented that flirting was a waste of time. Like garnish on a meal. He had got over the practice a long time ago and saw it for what it was. A barrier, something superfluous.

The woman discarded her beach wrap and bikini top midway down the beach, which she thought odd. Why was she topless? She shrugged it off at first, but she had been told that the practice generally remained in the Mediterranean and wasn't as common on the Atlantic coast of Spain or Portugal. Still, it no doubt went on, but it certainly changed the dynamic in heading towards King. The pang of jealousy rose a little higher. Caroline snatched up the binoculars and focused on the woman. She almost giggled at the woman's completely flat chest, but checked herself in time, never wanting to purposely body shame somebody. But even still, she thought how little interest King would show in the woman's ironing board front. And she deserved that much at least. But as Caroline worked the magnification on the binoculars, she decided that there was something more manly in the hips and chest, although in an effeminate nature. She noticed the rolled towel in the person's hand and felt foolish and shamed at her jealousy and the vitriol with which she had judged someone simply walking towards the shoreline for a swim. They probably hadn't even given King a second glance. She put down the binoculars and finished clearing the mess away from preparing lunch. She just needed King to keep to his end of the bargain and spear a decent sized fish. Red snapper, preferably, as the lime and coriander marinade she had prepared went well with meaty, white fish and they had both developed a taste for snapper and they were easy to prepare and cook.

Caroline jumped at the knock against the hull. It sounded like a log impacting against the hull, but far too low in the beam. She thought briefly to the couple they had helped off Gibraltar whose rudder was broken by a curious – perhaps mischievous – pod of orcas. They had dropped sail, switched to the engine, and towed the craft to port. International news had run features on the killer whales as they performed similar attacks in the region. She climbed the stairs, taking the binoculars with her, and glanced down over the port side where the noise had originated from. The water was deep, and there was no sign of rocks, but she checked all-round the vessel. Maybe it had been an inquisitive shark, but she told herself that would be incredibly rare. She gave up on it and looked through the binoculars to see if King was coming back with their lunch anytime soon. To her horror, King was heaving the tender through the shore break and the woman/effeminate man was lying near where King had been relaxing, with a spear skewering them, and King's speargun discarded on the sand. She heard the gunfire and saw the two fishermen on the rocks fleeing and the gunman crouching on the other side of the beach. She had dropped the binoculars and was heading for the boson's locker where they kept an old shotgun and an even older 9mm pistol. The shotgun would be useless at this range, but she loaded the Czech-made CZ-75 pistol and took aim at the gunman in the rocks and rattled off a few rounds to see where they hit. Sand sprayed up twenty feet short and ten feet to the right, so she corrected her aim and fired five precise shots, making the gunman duck for cover. She then emptied the magazine, hoping to give King precious seconds to evade the gunman's aim and increase the range. She heard another knock against the hull and frowned as she looked down into the water and saw a diver swimming away from the boat, around fifteen feet deep. The facts spoke for themselves: they were under attack from all sides, and she could not wait and see what the diver had been trying to achieve, but she knew the most likely answer. The diver wasn't trying to board the vessel, and divers didn't just 'bump' into a boat. She snatched her diving bottle and harness out of the boson's locker and tossed it over the side, along with her mask. She weighed up what else she should take but could not chance remaining on board any longer. She swallow-dived over the side, aiming to dive down deep enough to retrieve the tank and mask on the seabed. She almost made it. The blast above her was immense and the concussive shockwave spun her over and she found herself pressed into the seabed in a foetal position, her ears ringing, and the air knocked from her lungs. She rolled over to make for the surface, but the tank was beside her and she unscrewed the valve and vented the mouthpiece, then bit down gratefully on the rubber and held her nose as she breathed. Eyes bleary from the seawater, she made out the mask on the seabed and slipped it over her head, tilting the bottom of it outwards and exhaling through her nose to clear the water with bubbles. With the mask in place, she saw that debris littered the surface and was falling slowly around her. She could see King swimming on the surface near the ruined tender, now slack in the water with all the air lost and the small outboard pulling the craft down. She started out for him, then something inside told her to stop. An instinct, survival perhaps, but she could not explain why she felt this way and she could not overcome the primeval lizard brain akin to a sixth sense. Still, she couldn't move, knew that to go to King went against the instinct that was controlling her. She sculled in the water with her BCU inflated enough for negative buoyancy. The thought had hit her that King could do this alone. It's what he had trained and lived to do. In fact, she was likely to hold him back because even though she was competent and capable, he was inclined to protect her. The thought that he should be at risk because of her filled her with dread. But she knew King and she knew that he had limits that he had put on himself because of her. King could take on anyone, but she knew that he had atoned for many things, and she knew that if this contract was ever going to be lifted, it needed to be eliminated at the source. And she knew that if she was with King, then he would not follow through killing a thirty-something, married woman with two young children. They had been to her home, and they had seen her children. They had delivered their message through her husband – bound to a chair for her to find, and he would have relayed their message to her, and the warning had still not been heeded. After killing for his country for most of his adult life, King had drawn a line. Perhaps it was a male thing? No women or children. Like a woman should be off limits. Well Caroline was having none of it. She was a woman, and she had no such misguided idealisms set in toxic masculinity. She would do what she had to do, and right now the woman living the two-point-two American dream, while secretly working for a clandestine intelligence unit tasked with her nation's dirty work was about to meet her match. King could hold off the imminent threat of assassins – the many heads of the Hydra - but Caroline would do what she had to do to kill the beast.

She had a vague plan, but it would not be easy. First, she had to cut King free. She turned and swam hard away from him, and she kept swimming for forty minutes until the air ran out and she ditched the tank, surfaced, and stroked for the shore.

Chapter Seventeen

Caroline had been wearing a bikini but had covered up for lunch in a pair of shorts and a shirt. She had swum a great distance and finally got out of the water near Rota. Shorts and cotton shirt wrung out and placed on rocks in the sun, she had finally collapsed on the sand and let the sun's rays dry her out while she stared at the sky, thoroughly exhausted. She was thirsty and drank her fill from one of the foot showers where the beach met the neatly paved promenade. Spanish beaches were such amenable places. The council ploughed and sieved the sand, so the first beachgoers of the day were met with neat lines free of broken glass, debris, and other things you'd rather not stand on barefoot. Wooden walkways led from the sand to foot washers and showers, with toilets nearby. Other countries could take note. After walking the length of the promenade, she carried on along the road and perched on some rocks while she watched surfers attacking the beach break with varying degrees of proficiency. She had watched many surfers in Cornwall, and had even tried it out a few times, along with stand-up paddle boarding and kayaking when she and King had owned a cottage together down there. One thing had struck her odd about surfers, perhaps it was their casual nature, or maybe it was simply unpractical any other way, and she was hoping that the Spanish locals were the same. Casually, she walked across the dirt carpark and checked under the driver's side, front wheel arch. Nothing. She ignored the next van because it had a purpose-made key safe that looked like a giant padlock hanging from its tow hitch. A tidy Volkswagen Golf was next, and she could see the empty board bag and hastily stripped clothes piled on the back seat. She checked under the driver's side wheel arch and struck gold. The keys had been wedged in there and she wasted no time in unlocking the car and adjusting the seat and mirrors as she sat down and started the engine. There was no sign of any surfers leaving the ocean, so she hastily checked the pile of clothes and the owner's wallet. Thirty euros in cash and two debit cards. The fuel gauge was half-empty, so she stopped at the first filling station and filled up. She hedged her bets and paid for the fuel using contactless on one card, then acted as though she had a change of mind and quickly bought a map, some snacks and bottled water paying contactless with the other card, before dropping both cards into the bin at the fuel pump. Like King, she swapped over the plates with a similar aged vehicle, using tools from under the spare wheel in the boot. She looked at the map and worked out whether she could make it in one go. Certainly, she would need a break, but theoretically she could just about do it, with the thirty euros acting as a cushion if she needed more fuel, but it would be close. In any event, she had to get to Bayonne before King.

Chapter Eighteen

The shower had felt wonderous as she stood under the hot spray and lathered her hair, soaped her body, and enjoyed the steam on her skin. She had travelled through Spain in the car and ran out of fuel in the Pyrenees. Using the entire thirty euros on a coach ticket she had arrived in France both hungry and tired and after the coach terminated in Biarritz, she had hopped a short way on a tram and a train without paying and walked the final five miles into Bayonne. After a restful sleep, she had showered and dressed and taken her half of the 'bug out' stash. Purposely resisting the urge to write King a note, she left the flat and placed the key back under the coving on the balustrade and hopped on another series of coaches to Berlin.

Without her to worry about, King would be able to face his enemies with no distractions. And without King to worry about the rules of engagement with his new-found conscience and sense of propriety, she would take on the woman behind the contract and use what she could as leverage. The woman's life would never be the same again.

Chapter Nineteen

London

Neil Ramsay watched the slick waters of the Thames in silence while Jim Kernow, Jack Luger and Big Dave picked at the pastries that Mae had bought at the nearby bakery. Ramsay's assistant had a matronly manner about her, and despite her protests, it was clear that she enjoyed looking after what she thought of - though would never voice - as her boys. She knew how Big Dave, Ramsay and Kernow took their tea, and that Luger enjoyed strong, black coffee, which she had perfected by using an espresso shot of Java roast and a Colombian lungo in her coffee pod machine. She had also fobbed off the young agent when he had expressed that he wanted her to share her secret with him, and she smiled and shrugged, but would never tell him that it was the tiniest pinch of sea salt that coffee afficionados claimed mellowed the roast.

Die Trying

"And this Russian middleman acted of his own volition?" Ramsay asked incredulously, realising just how dangerous disobeying the Russian intelligence machine and the country's organised crime gangs could be.

"It certainly looks that way," Kernow replied. "Russian intelligence contracted Lukov to supply drugs all over Europe, completely free of charge to get as many people addicted. Russia has huge resources, as we know. They could keep the flow of drugs going indefinitely." He paused, looking at the notes he had made after their meeting. "The middleman knew that this was an attack on the West and had a huge portion of the heroin removed and replaced by a tremendous quantity of Semtex. The way he looked at it, Russia got their attack, and his bombs destroyed the evidence."

"Not to mention he got the mother lode of drugs, too," Luger added.

"Find the middleman, find the trail," Ramsay mused.

"Easier said than done, though," Big Dave commented. "The Russians are pretty big on security up that way. I got out of there and into Finland not so long ago and it was touch and go then. The travel bans since the start of the Ukraine war will make it extremely difficult to operate there." He paused and shrugged. "And black people don't do so well over there, either. The black population is like nought point three percent or something ridiculous. Put it this way, people still stop and point like they're in the fucking zoo."

"That's problematic," Ramsay agreed.

"That's one word for it," Big Dave replied, somewhat perplexed at Ramsay's apparent lack of understanding.

Ramsay turned his attention to Luger and said, "You speak Russian..."

"Conversational, but not quite fluent," Luger replied. "Besides, I can't just fly in and move around freely."

"We'll work something out," Ramsay replied sagely.

Big Dave reached for his phone as it vibrated in his pocket. He checked the caller ID and said, "I'd better take this..." He spoke quietly and listened, then checked his watch before ending the call. "That was Detective Inspector Dermott from Devon and Cornwall police. He is the investigating officer in the drugs haul in Plymouth. He was with us when we discovered the explosive device..." Big Dave paused as Ramsay nodded. "Tommy Jury, the crime boss suspected of receiving delivery, was found on Dartmoor. Murdered. He described the killing and it sounds like a Russian mafia MO."

"In what way?" Ramsay asked tersely.

"Both wrists slashed, femoral arteries slashed, and throat cut."

"That's a Russian thing?" Luger asked in disgust.

"You'd better believe it, kid," Big Dave replied. "It's like belt and braces, but it's done in such a way that the victim knows that there's no way out, no second chance. Wrists first, one at a time. Then each femoral artery. Finally, the throat. Not behind the windpipe and sliced outwards like we are taught in the special forces for a quick and silent kill, but slowly from ear to ear. It's overkill, of course. Severing a single femoral artery would do the job in four to seven minutes." He paused. "The throat is cut while the victim is still conscious."

Ramsay shook his head, sickened at the thought. "I want you to go down there and have a look about, see if you can glean anything from this DI Dermott." He paused. "Get over to City Airport and I'll see that a helicopter is waiting for you." Big Dave recognised his cue to leave, and he stood up and nodded at the other two as he left. Ramsay turned his attention to Luger and said, "See Mae and get a flight booked for Tallinn, Estonia. Let her know when you're there for your orders."

Luger stood up and nodded. There was nothing else to say, and he was learning from Ramsay that the man was finished with him. However, having heard the killing methodology of the Russian mafia wasn't exactly filling him with confidence.

"What about me, boss?"

Ramsay waited for Jack Luger to close the door behind him, then said, "I'm impressed by your abilities and your memory, Jim."

"Thanks," Kernow replied somewhat sheepishly.

"I would like to add to your duties."

Kernow shrugged. "I'm on the winddown," he replied. "And I'm not like the other two. I don't want to be put in a position where I'd be forced to kill somebody."

"I'm sure we could avoid that."

"Could we, though?"

Ramsay thought for a moment, the memory of the Albanian woodland and the large man in front of him giving him no other choice and even as a lifetime pacifist with no specialist training, Ramsay's survival instinct had taken over. "Perhaps not," he replied heavily.

"I came on board as a driver and minder. I'm not a young man anymore."

"I understand," Ramsay said and leaned into the silence for an uncomfortable minute.

Kernow finished his tea and shrugged. "If something comes up that requires my attention, then I guess I can look at it."

"Good to know."

Kernow stood up and buttoned his suit jacket. "I'll be off to give the Jag a polish, then."

Chapter Twenty

Luger checked his phone as it chimed. He read the message and couldn't help smiling.

"Got lucky?" asked Big Dave.

"Perhaps."

Big Dave checked his watch as they walked to the end of the street and the taxi rank beyond. The taxi turnaround was quick this close to Westminster. "Whatever Ramsay has in store for you, watch your back." He paused. "Russia is the fucking Wild West. If the Russians get hold of you, then you disappear. It's as simple as that. Don't trust anyone, and don't be afraid to run."

"Great. You're really helping my confidence."

"So, who's the text from?" Big Dave asked casually.

"Why do you want to know?"

Big Dave shrugged. "Your eyes lit up for a moment. Maybe I'm jealous you've got some female attention. I'm having a dry spell, myself."

"It was Harriet."

"Harriet? You mean, last night's Harriet?"

"Yep."

Big Dave stopped walking. "That's... odd."

"Isn't it," Luger agreed.

"I thought she'd go for me. That little quip about brains *and* brawn."

"You wish!"

"What are you going to do?"

Luger looked at his watch. "I've got time for some lunch with her. A little more time than that, actually."

"I meant, what are you going to do when she decides I'm the better man..."

"Dickhead," Luger rolled his eyes.

"Seriously, though. Be careful..." Big Dave shrugged. "I've never trusted MI6."

Luger smiled. "I'm not naïve. She's playing good cop to Devonshire's bad." He paused. "I'm going to try and find out what she wants..."

Chapter Twenty-One

West Street, London

"I didn't think you'd come."

Luger shrugged. "Why on earth would I turn down lunch at The Ivy?"

"Rotter..."

Luger sipped from his glass of Laurent-Perrier *Grande Siècle*. He wasn't usually a champagne drinker, but Harriet had insisted that they share a bottle and if MI6 were picking up the tab, then he would take them for everything he could. He studied the woman opposite him for as long as he could without being inappropriate. He could tell that she had been born into money and class, the way she had called him a 'rotter' would have sounded dated coming from most people, but he found it quite endearing. He imagined her growing up in the Home Counties, educated in a private school, then a ladies' college and onwards to an Oxbridge university. He could have been describing Caroline, or even the mirrored image of himself. He had remained at his school's sixth form, then gone onto Cambridge before joining the Royal Navy. Class meant less these days, but you generally knew when you were with someone who played the same notes.

As was typical of The Ivy, their waiter arrived aided by two colleagues so that their meals and sides were served together. After they said that they did not require anything else, the waiter took the bottle out of the ice bucket on the stand next to their table and topped up their glasses.

"I take you out with money no object, and you opt for the shepherd's pie," she said with a chuckle. "It's the cheapest thing on the menu!"

Luger shrugged. "And the tastiest," he replied. And he was quite right. The Ivy was renowned for the dish. A mixture of beef and lamb, with a rich veal gravy and creamy, whipped potato, Luger had also gone for the *Mayfield* cheese topping. "I came here with my aunt before I joined the service," he said, gauging her reaction. Harriet was gorgeous and the food was excellent, but he had not forgotten why he was here. Still, he needed a segue.

"Were you close?"

"Yes."

"I know who she was..." She looked at him earnestly and added, "I'm sorry. It was a terrible thing to happen."

"Did your boss know that there was a connection between Stella Fox and me?"

She shrugged. "I imagine so. Nobody sets foot in the River House without a background check."

"And what did it say about me?"

"Schools, college, university, and a brief outline of your naval career. Weapons systems programming and naval intelligence. Mainly about the intelligence aspect." She paused. "And of course, your recruitment into the Security Service. But that's where it ended. We don't have operational details..."

"How's the lobster?" he asked, moving the conversation away from MI5.

"Delicious." She took a mouthful and chewed delicately and when she swallowed, her throat was briefly engorged, and he felt a little aroused at the definition of her jawline and neck. She dabbed her lips with her linen napkin and said, "I like it here. It's simple, but exquisite. Just lobster, garlic butter, and chips. But it's about as good as it gets." She paused. "You didn't really *want* a starter, did you? It's a little indulgent for lunch. I'll be asleep at my desk this afternoon!"

"No, I'm fine. We could share a dessert, get a couple of spoons?"

"I don't share dessert," she replied quite seriously. "And I never turn dessert down..." she smiled. "What about you, are you bogged down at a desk this afternoon?"

"I've a few meetings after three," he lied.

"It's a terrible place," she said lightly.

"I agree, offices are terrible..."

"No, silly. Russia!" She sipped some of her champagne. "That's where you're going, aren't you?"

He smiled. "What gives you that idea?"

"Last night's meeting," she replied. "Mr Lomu is, well, too black..."

"I expect he'd say he's not black enough," Luger chided.

"You *know* what I mean..." Harriet replied easily. "There are literally no black people in Russia, I think it's something like naught-point-nought-three percent."

Luger liked her voice, her accent. Nought instead of

zero, which he thought most people would say, sounded almost aristocratic. "They're not the most culturally diverse bunch, that's for sure."

Harriet nodded. "And that other fellow, the *memory man*, he's too old to go off on missions to Russia..."

"He wouldn't thank you for that," Luger replied.

"So, that leaves you," she stated flatly. "Because if someone was going off to Russia to find a link with this assassin and Max Lukov and a petty criminal found carved up with a couple of bullets in their kneecaps, then it would make sense for that person to be at the meeting, memorising the intel that we would never allow to leave in paper copy or by electronic means. We like to keep *our* secrets, a secret..."

"Ouch," Luger smirked, but he had nothing. She had seen right through Ramsay's delegation. "So, that said, when do you leave?"

"This afternoon."

"After your boring office work?"

"There is no office work."

"So, what time?" she asked, fingering the rim of her champagne flute with her index finger.

"Four."

She glanced at her silver Cartier watch and smiled. "Goodness, that doesn't give us much time..."

Chapter Twenty-Two

Toulouse, France

"We can't be certain that this man is after King. Or Caroline, for that matter."

"If the intel came from Ramsay, then it's good." Rashid paused. "I trust him."

"We don't know where King is, though." Jo Blyth paused. "This man may pose no threat at all..."

Rashid shrugged as he checked the man against the image on his phone. "Tomas Blanchet. He's an assassin. A gun for hire. He's been linked to Basque separatists, ISIS and an Albanian organised crime syndicate."

"We're not judge, jury and executioner," she said vehemently.

"Our job was to hunt assassins. Ramsay suspects that this man is a threat to King, and therefore the department, and that means the Security Service..."

"I know, I know, and that means the entire security of the UK..." she rolled her eyes sardonically. "It sounds like changing events to fit the narrative."

"Welcome to the intelligence services..."

"I'm not sure I'm comfortable with this," she said heavily.

Rashid nodded. "That man has killed seven people, that we know of. He operates in the dark web, and he has killed a prominent politician."

"You're meant to be selling this to me," she said acidly. "Politicians are not my favourite people."

"The dead politician was a French socialist who wanted better wages for the underclass. He was a husband and a father of four." Rashid paused. "Either way, Tomas Blanchet is an assassin for hire and when he kills it's just for money and nothing to do with ideals. I have more respect for terrorists than I do for assassins. At least a terrorist fights for something that they believe in. A cause and an ideal."

"Are we no better for killing him?"

"*We're* not, *I* am."

"Don't be so bloody silly!" Jo snapped. "If I'm watching him, if I distract him, if I keep watch for you, then I'm just as involved! Pulling the trigger is a physical act, but the build-up to that point is everything! There is no assassination without all of that!"

Rashid shook his head. "Then go back to the bloody hotel!"

"Hey!" she glared at him, and then her expression softened as she said, "What sort of person do you want to work with? Somebody who simply follows orders, or somebody with some intelligence and integrity? Because, believe me, when there are extremely difficult decisions to be made,

Die Trying

ones with huge ramifications, then you might want to work with somebody who sees all the angles."

Rashid looked away, his eyes back on the target. He exhaled deeply and cracked the window an inch or two, the sounds of the street flooding inside the van. "I get it," he replied without looking at her. "And you're right. I appreciate some push back from time to time."

"Push back? It's a balanced opinion," she said heavily. "I'm not a push-over. I have a first in sociology and history. So, I understand human behaviour and I understand the weight of decision. I also understand that mistakes, however small, can affect history. The butterfly effect if you will. What we do at any given time will have implications on the future."

Rashid nodded. She was right. Working with someone like her was better than some subservient, eager to please inexperienced recruit – or God forbid, someone with a bloodlust and the desire to prove themselves whatever the cost – and if he was quite honest, he found her integrity and intelligence as desirable as her good looks. He was about to make a gambit, but thoughts of his last work affair flashed in his mind, and he hesitated, then retreated altogether. Marnie had been a welcome addition to the team, on secondment from GCHQ, and she had been killed as a statement. He had vowed never to get involved with someone he worked with since that darkest of days, and he doubted he ever would.

"I get it,' he said heavily. "But if Ramsay has this man on his list of assassins it's because he suspects him as having taken King's contract."

"Or Caroline's."

"Exactly." Rashid paused, his eyes still on Tomas

Blanchet across the street. "But Ramsay's intelligence is usually spot on. He's an odd bloke, but he's a genius and I don't say that lightly." Rashid watched as a woman sat down at the table in the chair opposite him. The waiter sauntered over, took her order, and walked back inside the café. "Kind of public for a meet..."

"There's nothing more natural than sitting on a street and drinking coffee in France," Jo replied. "They could be friends, family, lovers or even holding a business meeting. Look around; nobody's taking any notice of anyone."

Rashid watched the woman slide an envelope across the table and the man took it and to his surprise, opened it and studied the contents. He seemed to be asking some questions, and the woman answered between sipping her latte. "That's quite blatant," he observed.

"Hiding in plain sight," said Jo. "I suppose the secret to going unobserved is to avoid doing things that sparks someone's attention." She watched as Blanchet folded the envelope and slipped it into his coat pocket. The woman slid a second envelope across the table. The brown envelope was approximately the size of a thick paperback novel. "Looks like he's an old-fashioned cash guy..."

Rashid pressed the redial on his phone, his eyes now back on the man as he held the phone to his ear. *"La transaction est terminée..."* he said, then ended the call.

"What are you doing?" she asked, somewhat perplexed.

"We're not cold-blooded killers," he said. "There was a shadow of doubt surrounding this one." He paused, watching as two men approached the table from either side and drew pistols on the man and the woman. Two police vehicles raced in and stopped abruptly, blocking their view. The man was already in handcuffs and the woman was screaming as a detective read her rights and a female uniformed officer secured her wrists with handcuffs. "I made the call last night."

"So, we were never going to kill him?"

"No," Rashid smiled, turning to look at her. "And you made the right call. You're going to be an asset to the team."

Chapter Twenty-Three

London

Jack Luger rolled over, perspiration glistening on his brow and chest, the sheet drying his damp shoulder blades and the small of his back, as Harriet rolled on top of him and positioned herself, a rider to his saddle.

"Not yet, Jack," she said softly, slowing the previously hectic pace. She reached behind her and gently cupped him as she rode him softly. "Only when I tell you..."

Luger wasn't inexperienced by a long way, but the hour he had spent in bed with Harriet had opened his eyes to lovemaking on a sensual level and what was possible when a woman with experience took control. He estimated that she had five or six years on him. She was both attractive and intelligent, and once in the privacy of his Primrose Hill flat, completely uninhibited.

Harriet writhed and clawed at his chest, then gave him

the signal he so wanted to be given, holding out for as long as he possibly could – or thought possible. In truth, once he succumbed to her guidance, he found a rhythm he had not previously experienced. The signal was in her eyes, the intensity of her expression and she gave a little nod before arching her back and moaning softly towards the ceiling.

Luger remained where he was as she rolled off him and cuddled into his damp body, her right leg resting over his waist, her firm breasts pressing into his ribs, pulsing to the rhythm of her own heartbeat. He did not want to emasculate himself by showering praise on her lovemaking, but he did say that it was fantastic, and she agreed with him. In truth, he felt a fraud. She had driven every delicious part of it. It was only then that he noticed the thin white line on her left ring finger. Sadness washed over him, suddenly jealous that someone else was experiencing the gift this woman entwined with him had, knowing that he would have gladly fallen in love with her, even just for her personable quality and her experience in bed. She had not worn an engagement or wedding ring last night at the River House, but he had not noticed a tan mark, either. Perhaps she had intended to create an illusion using just a little makeup or tanning lotion.

"Are you with anyone?" he asked casually, but not as casual as he had hoped to sound.

She smiled at him, then kissed him on the mouth. It was a kiss of gratitude, not passion. The tenderness had gone. She untangled her limbs and walked naked to the bathroom. "You're going to miss your flight," she said over her glistening shoulder.

Luger checked his watch. He was cutting it close. Gathering up his clothes, he could hear Harriet in the shower. Should he go in? The thought of her lathering with soap and hot water, the steam fogging the bathroom was an alluring one. Or did she want privacy? The deed done; business as usual. He hesitated, checking his watch. He needed to make the flight, but he couldn't resist the mental image of her. Luger tried the door, but it was locked. That answered it. He waited until she was finished and smiled awkwardly at her before stepping into the steam and taking a quick shower. When he stepped back out with just a towel wrapped around his trim waist, she already had her skirt on and was buttoning her blouse over her soft, satin bra.

"I had a lovely time," she told him.

"So did I," he replied, pulling on his boxers and trousers. "Perhaps we can have a drink together when I get back?"

"Perhaps..." she replied non-committedly.

Luger nodded, taking his cue, despite it being his own apartment, he said, "I have to go. I'm sorry to kick you out, but..."

"It's been nice," she said, then walked over and gave him a peck on the cheek. Luger noticed that the thin pale band around her left ring finger now glistered with eighteen carat gold. "You've got my number, so..."

Luger smiled, buttoning his shirt as he walked her to the door. He reciprocated the kiss with a peck of his own upon her cheek. The mood had changed quickly, and he couldn't see why. All he could assume was after the throes of passion had subsided, Harriet had a life and a lover to go back to, and this afternoon had been a mistake on her part. She left without looking back and closed the door softly behind her. Luger wondered whether he would see her again, but something told him he would, and it would only ever be on her terms.

Chapter Twenty-Four

B ayonne, France

When people were hunting you, you had to keep moving. Staying to fight could only be done when you had gained the upper hand and had established a defendable position. Anything else was both foolish and inevitably fatal. King knew enough about life and battles and gambling to know when to hold, fold or walk away. He had cleared out his half of the emergency stash, and with Caroline having taken the other half, and with them both using the apartment, he would be sure to end the rent agreement if or when he made it through this. The place had served its purpose and you never went back to a safehouse or locker after you had used it. He had sanitised the contact points – handles, the bathroom, kitchen taps, cupboards – and had used most of a bottle of bleach cleaning everywhere he had touched. He could only assume that Caroline had done the same. Bleach destroyed DNA such as hair and skin and removed fingerprints as well.

King thought about the CIA woman who had taken out the contract. He had sent her a message and she had ignored it. He had shown clemency and it had been interpreted as weakness. However he had intended it, and however it had been taken, he would show neither again. She had resources and she had the world's largest intelligence service's databases, contacts, and assets at her disposal. He did not yet know whether she was an official CIA officer and employee, or whether she was in fact an agent of the former director Robert Lefkowitz who had access to the CIA databases only by the holes in the firewalls that the former CIA director had created for his black-ops teams. These teams answered to nobody, and now that Lefkowitz was dead, King wondered just who these teams worked for, and indeed, if they could even be stopped. If King killed all-comers for the contract, and that felt like a stretch, would killing her even terminate the contract? He couldn't see that he was a threat to the agency, only to someone whose actions he had interfered with.

King washed up his empty cup and placed it on the draining board. He then used the bleachy dishcloth to wipe it over, then wiped the taps. He would not see this place again. King slipped the 9mm Sig Sauer into his waistband and pocketed the passports and money and headed for the door. He felt good for a night's sleep and a shower and a cup of tea, although he could have done without the UHT milk from the cupboard. And it was in this fleetingly rare moment of contentment that he opened the door and stared straight into the muzzle of a gun.

"Hands on your head and get back inside..." the man said in a broad Irish lilt. King, momentarily frozen in his

Die Trying

tracks, slowly complied and started to back away. "Not backwards! Turn around slowly..." King felt his shirt pulled up and the pistol snatched from his waistband. "Inside!"

King was already inside, so he could only assume that the man meant into the open-plan living area, and he walked out of the hallway and into the lounge-come-kitchen. He could smell the man's cheap aftershave and a heady mixture of garlic and body odour. The man looked dishevelled, and King suspected that he had spent the night in his car, waiting for King to emerge the next morning. Well, it had paid off. King was beyond cursing at his momentary lapse in concentration. But he was aware that this was the second time in a week that a man had a gun on him. He was either losing his touch, or he could not see the wood for the trees, and even as he crossed the room with the man behind him, he could see why his old mentor Peter Stewart had insisted on sending him to Hereford two of three times a year for a week or two of hell. It had helped keep his edge razor sharp.

King had few options. He had a knife in his pocket, and he could thumb the blade open with just one hand, but he had to get his hand on it first. "I thought you were somebody else," King lied. "I heard you outside and thought it was who I was meeting."

The man frowned. "You're expecting somebody?" he asked, glancing back towards the door, and edging further into the room. "Who?"

King shrugged. "Who sent you?"

"I said – who are you expecting?"

"Quid-pro-quo," said King. "You give me something; I'll give you something."

"You're not the one holding the gun, smartarse!"

King could see that the revolver that the man was

holding looked old and worn. Nothing wrong with that, but revolvers were loud. Way louder than an automatic, but that didn't matter much because the man was holding a virtually new Sig Sauer that was well-oiled and would not fail. King always carried a weapon made ready, so all the man had to do was pull the trigger. It was also far more powerful than the .38 in the man's right hand. King knew that the man would switch over the weapons, and that was the only opportunity he foresaw.

"Who sent you?" King repeated.

"One of your enemies," the man replied making King scoff at the statement. He couldn't help himself. "Something funny?" the man spat at him.

"Well, yeah. It was hardly going to be one of my friends. You might need to narrow it down a bit."

"Oh, you're a smart one..."

"Smartarse, wasn't it?"

"This is going to be *so* rewarding..." the man sneered.

King stared at him; his glacier-cold blue-grey eyes boring into him like an alpha wolf ready to attack. The man looked around the room. Outside, people could be heard on the walkway and down in the carpark, accompanied by car doors slamming and engines starting. King could see that the man was in a quandary. A gunshot would get everyone's attention.

"Should have brought a suppressor," said King. "Or a twenty-two. It's the little things that matter..."

The man spied a cushion on the sofa and backed towards it. He kept his eyes on King, the table between them, then tossed the revolver on the sofa and picked up the cushion. *A shiny new toy*, thought King. The man did not see King take a single pace forward to the table, and as he walked back, he hadn't appeared to notice the change in position. A moment later, he swapped the cushion and Sig over, and when he looked back at King, he was caught in a stream of thick bleach from the squeezy bottle that found his mouth, nose, and eyes. King leapt to his right, anticipating the gunshot, but the man was in a world of pain and panic, and he was clawing at his eyes as he started to choke on the taste and fumes. King added to the man's misery by kicking him in the left kneecap, a sickening crunch sounding like a snapped twig trodden on a cold day. The man went down, and King picked up the Sig, then walked around the flailing limbs and secured the revolver. Taking pity on him, King ran the recently boiled kettle under the cold tap and poured it over the man's face. It was enough to ease his pain, and panic, but not enough to counter the damage. The burns looked no different than if hot oil had been used instead.

"I can't see!" the man managed to cough out among snatched breaths. "I can't feel my mouth..."

"Another minute and I wouldn't have been able to feel anything at all..."

"It wasn't personal..." the man spluttered. "Just business..."

"Who sent you?"

"I don't know... I just get a text and bank transfer," he said, trying and failing to focus on King.

King knew that he wasn't going to get anything out of the man. He knew less about his employer than King did. At least King knew that Georgia Scott had a CIA background and worked in a deniable unit founded by the former intelligence director. Before he died, Robert Lefkowitz must have placed somebody at the head of that unit, if not Georgia Scott herself.

King looked around the room, wondering whether the

cushion would disguise the shot well enough to go unnoticed. He doubted it. The building was inexpensive, and the walls were thin. The glazing was single pane and he had heard the people talking as they passed by on the walkway. He needed to get the man away from here.

King refilled the kettle with cold water, keeping the pistol aimed at the man the entire time. He poured the contents into the man's face again, concentrating it around his bloodshot eyes. The man moaned, but he had stopped gagging and coughing. Patches of skin were ferociously red and sore-looking from the chemical burn.

"What are you going to do with me?" the man asked dejectedly, squinting through puffed eyelids, the whites of his eyes looking like freshly sliced strawberries. "I'll pay you my fee," he begged.

"And what was I worth?"

"A hundred thousand euros." The man paused. "I can find another fifty thousand as well..."

"Bank transfer?" King asked seriously.

"Of course!" The man delved a hand into his jeans pocket and King side stepped and pressed the muzzle of the pistol against the side of the man's skull. The man froze. "I'm sorry... I need my phone..."

"Okay..."

The man retrieved the phone and fumbled with the screen. "I can't see it..."

King snatched the phone and held it to the man's face, but it would not open. "Code," he said abruptly. The man told him, and he opened the screen, standing back a few paces and putting the table between them once more. "Which bank?" King asked, looking at the apps.

"A.I.B."

King opened the app and entered the details of his

Die Trying

offshore account and asked for the pin number in lieu of the man's deformed face and eyes which looked like recent piss holes in the snow. A security text arrived, and King responded. When he refreshed the app, the man's account was one hundred and fifty thousand euros lighter with the balance at just a few hundred, but King had not wanted to get bogged down concentrating too hard while holding a gun on his would-be killer. The funds would help, and he felt no guilt at stealing them from such a man. However, as it was an offshore numbered account, he couldn't simply withdraw funds from an ATM. It required a lot of paperwork inside an associated bank that could handle the transaction, and he needed his banking details and a whole host of personal identification.

King secured his prisoner's hands behind his back using the man's own shoelaces and forced him to sit on the floor while he sanitised the apartment again. When he had finished and keeping the muzzle firmly against the man's left kidney, he marched him out of the apartment, along the covered walkway and downstairs to the carpark. They covered the open area of ground in a few seconds and made their way along the pavement to the man's BMW. King looked around as he opened the boot, then shoved the man inside. Bullets peppered the open boot lid as he slammed it shut, and he turned to see someone dressed head to toe in black motorcycle leathers and a black helmet climbing onto a powerful sports bike and swinging a machine pistol over their shoulder on a sling. King then noticed a second motorcyclist aiming a pistol.

There was no cover, but he knew that he would not make it back to his own car before the motorcyclist reached him, and with two mobile opponents working together, he could not stand and take aim without being an easy target himself. King scrambled to the driver's door, the roar of a motorcycle behind him, and the sharp report of a semi-automatic pistol echoing over the engine noise. Bullets peppered the rear of the car and the rear window shattered. King floored the accelerator; not even sure what size engine was under the bonnet, but he needn't have worried as the vehicle surged forwards, the traction control correcting the start of a wheel spin and bringing the rear wheels back under control. With an automatic sports gearbox, it was as simple as driving a go-kart and King was hammering down the road temporarily gaining on the two sports bikes. Temporarily being the word. The motorcycles roared behind him, one of the riders firing their pistol with their left hand, but King had done this before, and it was harder than it looked. The rider dropped back, tucked the pistol back inside their leather jacket and concentrated on catching up.

The street gave way to open road and the flaking paint of unkempt town houses was replaced by unkempt country houses with the ubiquitous flaking paint. The grass lining the road was waist high, with rusted mesh fencing separating the road from overgrown fields. The road had as many potholes as smooth sections. Which was good for King in the BMW and bad for the two sports bikes, the riders weaving drastically from side to side as King gained distance on them. A series of bends gave King an even further lead on them, but as he found himself travelling too fast for a good line on the next sharp bend, he overshot and took a gentle right onto a different road that had a smooth surface and bright white lines down the centre. He suspected that he had made a terrible mistake, and when he saw a bright, clean sign for Biarritz it confirmed it. A quick glance in the mirror told him that the two motorcycles were gaining on him, and a few seconds later at the next bend, the two motorcycles had doubled in size in his rear-view mirror.

King had a good view of the road ahead and could see it was clear. It was as good a time as any and he slammed hard on the brake and the motorcycles shot past him on either side. King hit the accelerator and the three-litre straight six-engine howled as he took it to the redline in every gear. The rider to the left glanced over his shoulder and realised too late what was about to happen. King swerved and the front bumper slammed into the rear wheel of the motorcycle and the rider was thrown high into the air. King had to swerve hard to avoid missing him but felt the rider thump against the bumper and scrape all the way on the underside. In his mirror, the rider rolled limply across the tarmac and rested still. King kept up the pressure, accelerating straight for the other motorcycle and got within a foot of the rear wheel before the rider dropped down two gears and wound on the throttle. The 1000cc Ducati howled and surged forwards, gaining on the BMW, but King kept on the accelerator and as he reached the next bend, the motorcycle slowed and the rider leaned it hard over, but King had faith in the BMW's handling and traction control and as they swept through the apex, the bonnet gave the rear wheel the merest kiss, and the motorcycle entered into a wobble that gained momentum and inertia and as King screeched through the bend, dangerously close to the verge, the rider lost control and was bucked from the saddle. The motorcycle continued wobbling drastically down the road and the rider rolled fifty metres before resting still on the side of the road. King veered to the left and ran over him, the torso thumping underneath, and the wheels bouncing off the legs. Ahead of him, cars were slowing for the accident, but King accelerated onwards and turned off at the next junction, and immediately right, which led him into a closed retail park with dilapidated buildings and several burned-out vehicles which had been jacked up on blocks with their wheels removed.

He sat for a while with the engine switched off and just the sounds of the engine ticking cool. His adrenalin was subsiding, which would help him make measured decisions. Decisions on the fly were reactionary. He needed to work out his next steps. His visit to America had had the opposite effect to its purpose. Instead of cancelling the contract, Georgia Scott had gone all out in proving that she would not be threatened and would hand out retribution ten-fold. King wasn't used to abject failure, but he had known it, and he had always overcome it eventually. His old mentor Peter Stewart had once said to him, *shit happens, but that's what bog roll was for... clean up and get off the pot...* The Scotsman had certainly had a way with words, and a wisdom that seemed to become more profound after half a bottle of Scotch. With a whole bottle inside him he was Gandhi and the Dalai Lama combined.

Right now, King had a lead. The Irishman in the boot would provide answers. Eventually. It was just going to take the right amount of persuasion. King got out and drew the pistol from his waistband. Using the boot opening button on the key fob he stood back and aimed at the boot space.

"Friends of yours?" he asked. There was no answer, so King stepped back further waiting for the man to make an escape attempt. "Who were the ninja warriors on bikes?" King edged closer until he saw the man, then tucked the pistol back into his waistband and closed the blood-splattered boot lid. He could see the bullet holes around the numberplate and rear lights nearest the man's head. *Well, at*

Die Trying

least the guy's eyes wouldn't sting anymore, he thought.

Chapter Twenty-Five

Moscow

She was fresh off the plane and because of the sanctions in place against Russia she had been forced to fly from London to Cairo with Egypt Air and then from Cairo to Moscow with Etihad. It had added nine hours with four more hours sat waiting in the Cairo departure lounge. She was now tired and irritable, and she had a train booked to St. Petersburg in two hours. Any longer, and Lukov would become suspicious.

She checked the address against the note on her phone, then deleted the note. This was the place. She would have paid handsomely for the information, but the man had wanted her body, her sex instead. Men always did. So, she had taken him to bed, but before he could have his way, she sliced his balls off with a cutthroat razor. She had stopped the bleeding after she had tied him to a chair, and she had asked him questions and cut him repeatedly until he offered up the truth. They always did in the end.

She was known as The Widow. She had never intended to become a killer, but sometimes the world worked for you and other times it worked against you. She had once had a good life. A loving husband, a wonderful son, and an idyllic home. Or so she had thought. How thin that veneer had been. Her husband had been in business with the wrong people. Their house had been a business asset and the money they spent happily had not been theirs. She had returned home one day to find her husband and their au pair slaughtered and her son missing. A month later, after she had lost all hope and was in the depths of despair, Max Lukov had sent her a message and told her that she now worked for him. So cruel to make her mourn for a month, but so necessary because she would have done anything to get her son back. He would pay her a living wage and keep her son alive. If she refused, then she would never see her son again. Her first kill had come soon afterwards. The man was to be seduced and murdered. That man was his father and with his death Max Lukov was now head of the family business – an organised crime family in northern Russia. She knew nothing of killing, but with the man seduced and tied to the bed, she had met little resistance. Her instructions had been clear. The man had to be castrated and his arteries cut. With enough vodka inside her, she had summoned the guile and courage to complete the job.

With her son held hostage Lukov knew that he had his pet wolf tamed without the confines of a cage. Holding her son would keep her in check. He seemed to enjoy controlling her faux freedom, revel in knowing that she would never stray. She could come and go as she pleased but was forever at his beck and call – and his mercy. However, she was determined to make this open prison condition his downfall. Every time she could, she would disappear and search his crime and business empire for her son. She had ruled out many places, and her list was only getting shorter. She had killed many of his men, but never with the same methods she favoured or indeed had become notorious for. When possible, she had left signs of the GRU or other mafia families to further grow Lukov's paranoia.

She crossed over the street and made her way down the alleyway beside the building. Litter and the stench of urine told her that the alley was not used as a regular thoroughfare, just a toilet for the homeless or late-night revellers on a long walk home. The rear of the building backed onto waste ground with burned out vehicles and piles of rubbish and building waste that had been fly-tipped. It wasn't a good part of town, and that was why Lukov had chosen it. He did not want nosey neighbours, the police or town planners on his doorstep. Although he had undoubtedly paid off his share of town planners and police officers over the years.

She found access at the second floor window and made short work of the climb, easing her fingertips into a quarter inch of gap in the render and free-climbing to the ledge, where she pulled herself up effortlessly and perched on the windowsill while she worked the shattered glass out of old, dried and cracked window putty and tossed the shards onto patches of grass that had taken hold in the gaps in the potholed concrete below. Easing her extremely lithe body through the single broken pane, she reached out to the beam and monkey-climbed hand over hand across the room and slid down the wall at the far end, the toes of her trainers slowing her fall and she landed lightly, in a crouch to cushion the impact. The door was open and led out onto an open metal staircase that overlooked the entire floor.

Die Trying

Machinery lay dormant, suspended from producing whatever counterfeit clothing had been on the line by the flick of a control switch on the wall. She could imagine the workers shuffling in and out at the beginning and end of shifts, the operation running around the clock. She had noticed that trafficked people shuffled, pride seemingly a factor in one's gait, walking tall and confidently no longer an option. Many of these workers would have been paid poorly, and some would not have been paid at all. Sex workers could still be useful after their looks faded, or their minds and bodies had simply had enough of what perverted men could do and then shifted to a manual labouring position within the Lukov family crime machine. Others would have paid traffickers for a route to a better life but had merely been horse-traded mid-way. The world could be a cruel and unforgiving place for people without a voice, and right now, she felt gagged into silence. Lukov had held her prisoner with her son as easily as the poor souls who had worked here while the traffickers held onto their passports. In many cases, they had been cajoled because of threats to their families back home.

She wiped the top of a piece of machinery with her fingertip. It was thick with dust. Either the place had been busted by the police when evidence could no longer be ignored by corrupt officers, or the venture had ended because of supply and demand, but whatever the reason it had ended suddenly and a long time ago. Lukov had no end of use for slave labour and the poor souls were likely needed elsewhere or sold off to other crime syndicates. Human lives as easily traded as sheep.

She did not have to look around for long to know that this place would not give her any clues to her son's whereabouts, but it was another location off the list. There was nothing for it but to return to St. Petersburg and continue looking for a trail, a clue that would start her on the right path. And there were only two things that kept her going in her darkest moments. Her son for one. And the lengthy and painful death she planned for Lukov for the other.

Chapter Twenty-Six

Arlington, Virginia

"I must say, your message intrigued me."

"I thought it might," replied Caroline. She moved her handbag and patted the seat next to her.

Newman shifted the weight onto his good leg and eased himself down. He rested the stick between them, Caroline suddenly remembering the rapier blade sheathed within. Just like the man beside her, appearances were deceptive.

Young, tall, and handsome, Newman had been a promising CIA field agent until King had cut him down with an assault rifle so he could get a clean shot at an assassin with Caroline in her sights. Slow-flowing water had passed under a few flimsy bridges since then, but Newman and King had finally buried the hatchet. Though somewhat tentatively.

"You know why I'm here," she announced.

"I guess."

"Alex has done good work that has benefited both our countries."

"Without a doubt," Newman agreed. "But he's no angel..."

Of course, he isn't," she replied indignantly. "How could you be in this game, and with his past. He's done things people should never have been asked to do. But he's made amends for a lot of things, and when I first met him, he was instrumental in saving countless American lives on US military bases." Newman frowned and Caroline shrugged. "Classified Top Secret but use your imagination. It was in a worst-case scenario context."

"I see," he replied, but there was a lot left to the imagination.

"Our two services crossed swords a while back and we both suffered as a result. In fact, it's had repercussions ever since." She paused. "We're not enemies. We are the greatest of allies. But we *are* personalities, and we seem to have a situation where someone won't be pushed and the other won't be pulled."

"That is certainly one way of putting it. Diplomatically, for certain." Newman eased his right leg out, the result of a split-second decision, but certainly a decision that could change Caroline's fate. "I know the person in question," he said. "But why should I help you?"

"What she has done is beyond the pale," she said, watching the American frown. "An English colloquialism. You may say she's gone off the *reservation*..."

"And King operates with a clear mandate?" he smiled dubiously. "There was ruminations a while back that it was a British agent behind the death of a president, but those rumours were hastily quelled for fear of irreparable relations with our greatest ally."

"I wouldn't know about that," Caroline replied blankly.

"Even though it was the President who first engaged the CIA to teach MI5 a lesson?" Newman paused. "Back when he was a congressman, of course. But perhaps these were simply rumours, too?"

"I wouldn't know about that, either." She paused. "Would that be the same president who funded a global metallurgical empire on supposed scrapped military vehicles and debris after the Gulf War, but really with stolen Kuwaiti gold? An Iraq war hero, whose men all perished in a blue-on-blue massacre when he travelled away from the frontlines? The same president who used his political career to further his own net worth by a factor of ten?"

"Well, he didn't get my vote, that's for sure," Newman shrugged. "I get that you have a vested interest. But if you were not involved with the man, and you were here in an official capacity, which I know you are not, then I would urge you to accept that King has become a problem, that if removed would get the CIA and MI5 relations back on an even keel."

"Well, it's a good job that I'm not here in an official capacity, then you don't have to say that load of rubbish," she said icily.

"It is true, though," he persisted. "This could all be over if..."

"What, if Alex put his head on the chopping block?" she raged. "Don't be so bloody ridiculous man! But there are multiple assassins engaged in the contract. It will only get messier, and I was drawn into it. Someone placed a limpet mine on our boat while Alex was on the shore, and it was detonated before he returned. So, it looks like the parameters have changed. It looks like I'm a target now as well." She paused, her attractiveness doing nothing to belay the coldness in her eyes. "And I'm certainly not putting *my* head on the chopping block for anyone, or any cause..."

Newman considered this as he looked out across the cemetery and the gravestones and memorials. He always felt moved in places such as this, and never more so than at Arlington. The air seemed to be filled with an aura of duty and bravery and sacrifice. It was difficult to remain unmoved.

Caroline felt the same way, although Newman would never know. She felt the same sentiment when she entered a cathedral or a gothic church. A feeling of insignificance, of being part of something far bigger than oneself. It was with this notion that she had arranged to meet Newman in such a place of national significance. It could work both ways, of course. Newman was a patriot first and foremost, so getting him to go against a fellow CIA operative could be out of the question. However, ending this now would set the two agencies – however they may be masked by deniable units – back on track and working towards shared interests and common goals.

"I can make a call," Newman relented. "I will try to dissuade her. That's about all I can do. I'll give you that much."

"It's not a conversation for an open line," Caroline said flatly. "Or one remotely committed to cyberspace."

"I *do* know fieldcraft," Newman replied testily. "I worked in the field exclusively until your boyfriend put five bullets in me..."

"Considering the skill and ruthlessness of the assassin, he might well have saved your life, too."

"Perhaps," Newman said, standing up and putting some

weight on the cane. "But if she won't listen, then I don't see what else I can do about this. We're on the same side, after all. I may not agree with her methods, but Robert Lefkowitz saw something in her, and the world we live in sometimes calls for extreme measures."

Caroline got to her feet and gave him a hug, then looked at him with her hands still clasping his shoulders. "I really appreciate your candour," she said sincerely. "But this is different. This is ego and survival. Only it's me and King who are surviving, and it's Georgia Scott who is nursing a bruised ego." She paused. "I'll wait for your call."

Chapter Twenty-Seven

Dartmoor

The AgustaWestland 109 banked hard under full throttle and Big Dave felt the burger and fries that he had eaten at London's City Airport gain a little too much height in his stomach.

"Jesus, Flymo! Do you have to fly all the time like you've got a gunship on your six?"

In the righthand seat next to him Flymo was beaming a smile from ear to ear. From a lower-working class background and broken home, raised on the streets of Brixton, Flymo had merely joined the army for three meals a day and a bed for the night. But the young man had possessed a gift in hand-eye coordination and visual perception. During basic training a sergeant had put him forward for some aptitude tests and he had joined the air corps while other recruits had gone into various trades and infantry regiments. Flymo had been the first black lieutenant in the air corps who had gone through the ranks. He had flown every model of helicopter in service and was eventually selected for the Joint Special Forces Aviation Wing and later No. 658 Squadron AAC, flying the Special Air Service's operations out of Stirling Lines, the SAS base at Hereford.

"Just doin' what I do best, man!" Flymo hollered into the intercom. Both men wore headsets and mics, as even in the luxurious cabin of the executive Sikorsky the noise from the rotors overhead and the engines behind them would otherwise be intolerable. "You might want to hold on for the landing," he added with a chuckle.

The big Fijian gripped the panic handle with one hand and punched his friend firmly on the shoulder with the other. There were times when he had been glad of the man's flying skills, after all – he had earned his moniker from hovering lower than the lawnmower brand of the same name – but flying from A to B should never be as scary as this. The helicopter nose-dived steeply, and at the last minute, Flymo balanced both the rudder, cyclic and collective and the craft's nose rose like a striking cobra and when it came back down, the three wheels touched gently on the grass.

"You're a bloody show-off..." Big Dave commented flatly as Flymo powered down the engine and rotors but kept a firm grip on the controls to prevent the craft from tipping over until the RPMs had dropped significantly. "I'm never so relieved to get out of an aircraft than when I'm flying with you."

"I'll take that as a compliment..."

"Don't."

"Well, that's funny," Flymo replied. "I've often picked

you up and found it difficult to imagine you being more *relieved* to see me."

Big Dave ignored him as he opened his door and said, "I've got to go, there's barely room for me in here with your ego getting so damned inflated." He took off his headset and tossed it onto the seat. DI Dermott was waiting a safe distance away on the grass, looking bemused at the dramatic arrival. "How's it going?" Big Dave greeted him.

"Fine. I'd certainly like to have your transport budget."

"Well, *I'd* prefer a train ticket home, but we can't always get what we want," he replied lightly. "Sitting next to that man isn't all it's cracked up to be."

"I can imagine that from the landing display. Will your man be coming with us?" Dermott asked, looking past Big Dave at Flymo as he ambled towards them.

Big Dave turned and followed the detective's gaze. "I guess so. How far is it?"

"Not far," he replied. "This was a flat area that we thought ideal for a helicopter to land on." He paused. "The place where we're going is on a steep slope covered with granite boulders and large holes in the ground hidden by bracken. Bloody hazardous, I've already lost one officer with a suspected broken ankle, and another one to take him to A and E."

Dermott led them to an old Land Rover Defender in police livery. The vehicle had seen better days, but it would have been used exclusively for police business on Dartmoor and Exmoor and pulled out of the vehicle pool for days such as these. This was a harsh environment, and any replacement would end up looking the worse for wear in a matter of weeks.

Big Dave could see the police cordon and vehicles halfway up a large tor. Two more land Rovers and three

Die Trying

quadbikes had parked in a semi-circle and a tarp had been erected on poles.

"It's not a pretty sight, but I suppose you lot have seen some horrible things, too," DI Dermott commented flatly.

Big Dave did not reply. He doubted there was little that could shock him anymore. Two tours of Afghanistan and countless operations all over the globe had steeled his resolve, or perhaps worn him down. Flymo was a pilot and even though the man had witnessed terrible things, he had fortunately had very little exposure on the ground in conflicts. "You don't have to see this," said Big Dave.

Flymo shrugged, but the big Fijian already knew that the man wasn't likely to wait in the vehicle. He climbed into the rear with Big Dave while Dermott rode up front. A female uniform police constable drove without saying a word. After two hundred metres of rutted track, they climbed a high verge and headed towards the tor over the short, windswept, and sheep-grazed grass. Gorse, bracken, and heather scraped underneath the chassis of the Land Rover as the driver picked her way between the boulders and up the slope.

"Why in the hell would someone murder someone all the way out here?" asked Flymo.

"I think you've answered that," DI Dermott replied. "Little chance of getting seen, much less of being caught in the act."

The vehicle stopped and the men made their way the fifty or so paces to the crime scene. Forensics and pathologists – Big Dave did not know which – were picking through the scene, some concentrating on the body and others only on the surrounding area.

"If we get any closer then we'll need coveralls, hoods

and over-socks as well as face masks and gloves." Dermott paused. "Do you want to get closer?"

Big Dave stared at the naked corpse. It had tattoos down each forearm and a gold earring in the right ear. Even from ten feet away he could see the wide, open gashes on the wrists exposing the tiny white bones and tendons. Both femoral arteries were cut, too. The blood had soaked the peaty soil and grass.

"The throat was cut from ear to ear," a pathologist said, addressing DI Dermott only. "Several slices, right back to the spine." She paused. "Which you can see as both a white and cream contrast from here..." she pointed. "What's interesting, though, is that upon close examination under the cadaver's back, a tiny incision would appear to have penetrated the vertebrae and I suspect, nicked the spinal cord. Which means the victim would have been paralysed while the killer made the cuts. It's a strange MO and not one I have personally come across before. It would have rendered the victim completely helpless. I will, however, examine the cadaver further when I get it back to the lab, search the databases and make some enquiries with fellow pathologists just in case someone has come across such methodology before. To my mind it's either a professional hit, or the beginning of a serial killer's campaign. It's too technical to be anything spontaneous."

"Could it have been a woman?" Big Dave asked.

"It could have been *anyone*," she replied curtly. "Why a woman in particular?"

Big Dave shrugged. "I could drag this guy up here and do whatever the hell I wanted to him."

"Agreed," she replied. "You are a giant."

"None taken..."

"I'm not meaning to offend." She shrugged. "But you're what, six-four, six-five and eighteen or nineteen stone?"

"About that."

"So, yes, you could overpower most men."

"But the victim is five-nine, five-ten and I'd estimate around eleven or twelve stone. He looks like he has good muscle tone, pretty fit." Big Dave paused. "He would have probably put up a good fight against most men. But not many women would have stood a chance in overpowering him."

"None taken," she chided back at him.

"But a woman who knew how to paralyse someone with a tiny incision?" Big Dave shrugged. "Well, he would have been putty in her hands."

"Still had to get him up here though," DI Dermott interjected. "Dead weight is dead weight. People can lift two-hundred and fifty pounds in the gym, but half that weight in dead form is quite a task. Most women couldn't do that."

"Again, none taken..." the pathologist chided.

"Were there any tyre tracks?" Flymo asked. "Seems a vehicle would be needed, for a woman *or* a man."

"Loads..." the pathologist said. "Forensics are taking plaster casts, but it looks like motorcycles and the green laning bunch have been busy out here so getting a good cast may be difficult."

"*Green laning?*" Flymo asked.

"People with old four-by-four vehicles who go down country lanes and across the moors," Dermott explained. "Actually, not all old vehicles, either. Some people have all the new toys."

"Bloody country folk," Flymo commented dryly. "They need more towns down here..."

Dermott ignored him and said, "Well, they will take

casts of what tracks they can, and then the real detective work will start, but there will be a lot to go through and at least a dozen dead ends." He paused. "But the idea of a woman killer makes sense to me," he agreed. "There are drag and scuff marks in the mud, so the victim could well have been incapacitated elsewhere, driven here and dragged out the vehicle."

"The MO is Russian for sure," Big Dave commented. "We have experience of Russian contract killers and the Russian mob. This kind of killing is a message." He paused. "But who to?"

"To whom..." the pathologist mused quietly, then flushed red when the Big Fijian looked her way. "Sorry, force of habit..."

"Keeps you single, I'd bet..."

"Ouch..." she smarted. "That and the long hours, the nature of the work and my love of Scandinavian cinema."

"That ought to do it," Big Dave said lightly. He turned to DI Dermott and said, "You have my number; text me the photographs you have of the crime scene. I have a feeling we'll find this MO in the files somewhere. And I agree, this looks too neat and tidy to be a first-time job," he added, addressing the comment to the pathologist.

DI Dermott nodded. "That sounds about right. My constable will give you a lift back to the chopper," he said.

Big Dave shook his head, glancing at Flymo beside him. "It's ok, we'll tab out of here. It will give me another chance to appreciate *terra firma* before getting in the air with this nutter..."

Chapter Twenty-Eight

The Baltic Coast, Russia

The forest was sparse and cold. May was a spring month, but not in Russia. Not this far north at least. The ground was still firm under foot and the chill off the Baltic Sea reached the marrow in your bones. It was easy to forget in two months the heat would be oppressive, and the mosquitoes would drive a person crazy.

Lukov had brought with him five bodyguards. Enough to protect, but not too many to intimidate. It was a fine line to tread. Orlev of the GRU could come with a whole army if he so desired. But to meet the man on his own – that could well be his downfall. The forests were fertile with human remains out here. In the fifties and sixties, the KGB brought many 'enemies of the state' to the forest for enhanced questioning, and none of them returned. Lukov did not want to suffer the same fate, but he knew that Orlev had chosen the meeting place to unsettle him.

Lukov watched the Mercedes SUVs bounce along the logging track. The Russian military intelligence service had come a long way since he had first served with them. Back then the vehicles had been the Gaz Volga and various Ladas. These Mercedes with their blacked-out windows and oversized alloy wheels looked like drug dealers' rides, not military intelligence, although ironically, Orlev and his thugs were not much different. He watched as Orlev stepped out, followed by his righthand man, Sergei Bostock. The men wore civvies of jeans and long, black leather jackets. Orlev's bodyguards all wore tracksuits. They were heavily armed carrying shortened versions of the military's AK-12 assault rifle. Every one of them was a hardened former Spetsnaz commando. Lukov counted ten men, and there were still several waiting in the cars. This may very well end badly for Lukov, but he had an ace up his sleeve. One false move and the two snipers he had installed in the trees had orders to shoot Orlev first. They were close, too. The line of sight in the forest had been difficult to get a clean shot past one-hundred metres, but at that range, neither man would miss.

"I'm going to keep this simple for you to understand," Orlev said coldly. "I want to know what has happened to the money paid to you to grease the wheels with distribution, and where my missing drugs are." There was no warmth in the Russian general's eyes or his tone. His expression cold and grey in the dimly lit forest. "Do not disappoint me, Lukov."

Lukov bristled. For the man to speak to him like this in front of his own men was unacceptable. He would have to disperse these bodyguards before they had the chance to

Die Trying

talk amongst themselves – or worse still, to his other men. "The new shipment has arrived, and we are solving the delivery problem now that the authorities are watching out for major drugs trafficking," he assured him quite belligerently. "I do not see why we have to go through the theatrics of meeting like this..."

"Because if the answer was not satisfactory, then you would not be leaving here," Orlev said matter-of-factly. "You would be digging your own grave, and then you would be lying in it."

"You seem to have forgotten something," Lukov scoffed. "Something important, and something obvious. You have too much to lose," he said. "We both do. This is business, and business, my friend, is not as simple as the military or the GRU where all the decisions are made for you. We had to use other crime syndicates in the UK, and they let us down. They have been dealt with. The rest of the heroin is now..."

"The second shipment of the heroin was an extra expense!" Orlev spat at him. "The other European nations are now on high alert! You may have recovered the missing heroin from your thieving associates, but the cost of supplementary shipments has angered the people at the very top." He paused. "And the bombing, to cover your thief's tracks, has upset the balance. They know we're planning something. Our surprise has been lost."

Lukov knew that it had been a mistake to involve Krylov – the man had been greedy and aspired to become a family leader like Lukov – and he had used other crime syndicates with similar aspirations. Lukov had dispatched The Widow and she had dealt with both men efficiently. He would make it his business for her to kill Orlev before this was over. He would not be chastised like this in front of his men.

"These freelance fools have been killed," the Russian mafia boss replied. "We have secured most of the product and money taken, and I will make up the rest. As a sign of my commitment and belief in the operation. The shipments are enroute, we have designed a method of smuggling the product and the operation will continue as planned. The European leaders will soon dismiss any plans of a Russian military offensive."

Orlev stared at him and said, "I want details of the shipments."

Lukov scoffed. "You want to cut out the middleman."

"It would certainly save time and inefficiency."

"The GRU talks about efficiency!" he laughed.

"Be careful what you say next, Lukov..." Sergei Bostock said coldly. "Remember who is paying you..."

Orlev laughed. "I do not want to *cut out the middleman*, as you say..." The GRU soldiers spread out a little more, the muzzles of their weapons a little further from the ground. "But I feel that it may be time for you to have your wings clipped..."

It was over inside three seconds. The soldiers aimed and fired, and the five bodyguards went down, the nearest one coming to fighting back was to discharge his pistol twice into the ground as he fell. Lukov waited for his snipers to shoot Orlev, but the gunshots never came. Instead, two camouflaged soldiers emerged from the trees, each man carrying the head of his snipers in their hands, dangling by the hair, their blood dripping on the ground. The two men tossed the heads into the throng of steaming bodies. The two soldiers were equipped only with Spetsnaz folding combat shovels. The shovel blades had been sharpened to a razor's edge on one side with a serrated edge on the other, with a wickedly sharp triangular point. The unit was notorious for their 'killing shovel', in the same way the British Ghurkhas were famous for their curved knives, known as the kukri.

Lukov stared at the man who had once served under him. In a different Russia. A long time ago. He clapped his hands slowly and said, "So, there you are. You can cut out the middleman..."

Orlev laughed. "You will not fail me again, understand?"

Lukov stared at the bodies of his men on the cold ground. Nobody in his organisation would see him plead for his life, so it wasn't a complete loss. "I will not fail again, comrade..."

Orlev smiled and left without a word, followed closely by Sergei Bostock. The men with the rifles followed, getting into the four black Mercedes. Lukov watched the convoy of drug dealer or football player SUVs bounce and weave through the forest, waiting until they were out of sight before he fell to his knees and wept. Not for his men, but for the humiliation and his pride. And for relief.

Chapter Twenty-Nine

Tallinn, Estonia

Jack Luger liked to get a feel for a city by people watching. A beer or a chilled glass of champagne, or a coffee depending on the time of day or location, and you could watch and learn about people and culture and how the city ticked. Naturally, he would take in the sights and the architecture and history of a city if he had the time, and in his year spent travelling between leaving the Royal Navy and starting work with MI5, Luger had seen a great deal of Europe, Africa, and Asia.

Tallinn was no mere Cold War relic. There were influences from Scandinavia directly across the Baltic Sea from this seaport town. Colourful houses nestled between tall towers, some straight from Helsinki or Stockholm, with towering arabesque minarets and great edifices of Russian architecture. It was very much a place where East met

West, with the West slowly winning through. Well-known coffee house chains had sprung up alongside concrete relics of Soviet-era political and committee design, and phone shops seemingly on every other street corner. Vaping was big, too. Pop-up vape shops occupied vacant commercial units, promising half-price products for a short time only, and seemed to be on every street.

Luger checked his phone again, then sipped some more of his coffee. Estonians did coffee well, and he had noticed that people with time on their hands drank coffee from independent stores while people who appeared to be on the go used the franchise coffee outlets. He suspected that despite global market trends, Tallinn had a good chance of pushing out the soulless franchises before long. Especially if the quality of the Americano and almond croissant in front of him was anything to go on.

"How's the coffee, here?" the man asked. Luger had not noticed him approach. "Warm or hot? Many places never seem to get it hot these days..."

"Hot enough," he replied, satisfying the code phrase as the man sat opposite him. The waitress bustled over, and the man ordered a tea. 'English breakfast tea', as one always had to outside of the UK. "I'm Luger," he told him.

"Carter."

"Fairly cloak and dagger stuff this," Luger ventured, more of an icebreaker than anything else.

"We're on the line, here," Carter replied. He nodded his head to his left, adding, "Russia is right over there and since the Ukraine War, it's like Check Point Charlie once more." He paused, staring intensely at Luger. "Sure, people come and go over the border, but if they detect a Brit or a Yank, then the big old machine that is the FSB – the KGB by another name – will follow and watch, then intercept.

They're blatant, too. They don't hide. That's part of the fear they create. My understanding is that you wish to find someone and talk to them. Well, you'd better be sure of yourself, young man, or you'll be sweating and pissing yourself whilst tied to a chair and wondering whether they'll ever stop hitting you..."

Luger waited for Carter's pot of tea and jug of milk to be put down along with a cup and saucer. When the waitress had left them alone, he said, "Well, we'll just have to make sure they don't see me going in."

"I have a plan for that," said Carter. "And an exfil plan, if you survive your little jaunt."

Luger sipped his strong, black coffee and shrugged. "Can't I just hop over the fence?"

"I very much doubt that," Carter replied tersely. "Anyway, the border was instigated more by Estonia. When they joined the EU and NATO in two-thousand and four they worked hard on security measures after mounting tensions. Since Ukraine, Russia upped its security presence on their side. Nobody's hopping over anything, anywhere. Besides, most of the border runs through the lake. And I don't imagine you'd fancy the swim very much..." He paused. "Gunboats with fifty calibre machineguns, sonar buoys and marines on the shoreline. And that's just on the Estonian side. Bloody cold, too."

"Seriously?" Luger asked. "Not the cold, the gunboats and sonar buoys."

"Seriously."

Luger finished his coffee and ignored the remains of his croissant when Carter joined him. An expensive education and strict upbringing had taught him not to eat in front of another if that person did not have food of their own. "Shall we get to it, then?"

Die Trying

"My, we are eager, aren't we?" Carter paused. "There is nothing so disturbingly gratifying, yet painfully lamentable about a young man who will willingly risk his life when all good advice has been ignored. *I told you so*, doesn't even begin to come close."

"Bloody hell, Carter," Luger said shaking his head, somewhat perplexed. "It's slipping into Russia to follow a lead, not going over the top at the Somme!" He paused. "Besides, I'm just following orders."

"For Ramsay?" Carter scoffed indignantly.

"He's my boss."

"A rather dubious battlefield promotion."

"But a promotion, nonetheless."

"Who do *you* work for?" asked Luger.

Carter smiled wryly. "I'm just the man on the ground."

"SIS?"

"Lord, no," Carter scoffed.

"Five, then."

"Close, but no cigar."

"And GCHQ don't have field agents," Luger commented. "Not the type who do this, at least."

"I'm just an embassy man," replied Carter. "And we'll leave it at that..."

"But you were with one of the services, right?"

Carter looked at him intently for a moment then said, "Don't fuck up in this game, lad. Mistakes, however small, could find you pushing papers across a desk in the loneliest of places." He paused. "And never put all of your trust in MI6 or MI5, because sooner or later you could get sold down the river..."

Chapter Thirty

London

They had strolled through Horse Guard's Parade and into St. James' Park. Ramsay rolled his wheelchair himself, eager to burn off his lunch. Jim Kernow had quietly informed the team that they must never aid him unless he asked for help. He had borne the brunt of Ramsay's temper, but he had patience. The man's life had been turned upside down and he had taken such little time off work to adjust.

Big Dave walked beside Ramsay with Kernow trailing a few paces behind. He took his role as driver and minder seriously and having retired from the police service Ramsay had seen him temporarily reinstated and diverted to diplomatic protection status, allowing him to carry a Glock 17 pistol in his role as Ramsay's protection officer.

"MI6 says that the MO of the female assassin, who killed petty mafia criminal Piotr Krylov near St. Petersburg, matched someone they had on file. This woman worked for Max Lukov before, and we know that Krylov was tasked with the shipment of heroin rigged with plastic explosive. What do you think about Dartmoor?" Ramsay asked. "Connection, or coincidence?"

"Given the MO, Tommy Jury was most likely killed by the same person," Big Dave replied. "It's not just the methodology, it's the details that stand out. The length of cuts dictates the person's strength and size. A deeper, longer cut would be done by someone taller and stronger. Most people using a knife as a predetermined weapon will make sure that it is honed to a sharp edge. They'll check it against their thumb for sharpness, maybe slice a sheet of paper. The knife will be sharp. Once the blade gets sharp enough, it's sharp enough..."

Ramsay nodded. "So, it's the killer, not the blade that determines the size and depth of the cut? I didn't know that."

"Obviously the length of blade would make a difference, but in both cases, and in the file that we read in the River House it looks like it was a similar length blade." Big Dave shrugged. "I've shared a few texts with the pathologist," he explained.

"I bet you have," Ramsay replied. "When are you meeting for a date?"

"When this is done," Big Dave said with a cheeky smirk. "Because I doubt that you're sending me anywhere near Exeter now."

"That's where she lives?"

"Yes." He paused. "She works out of Exeter, too. She covers Devon and Cornwall Constabulary's entire region."

"Good. Some stability would do you good. Maybe you could aim towards settling down in the country with this pathologist lady and leave this madness behind? You could buy a Labrador together."

"Never. You're stuck with me for a while yet."

Ramsay stopped wheeling and looked out across the park towards the lake. Big Dave noticed that he was breathing heavily. He wasn't surprised; Ramsay had never been prone to physical exercise. Although he was slim, it was nervous energy and forgetting to eat as he puzzled over his work that kept the man trim. Ramsay had been forced to change many things since his injury, not least physically manoeuvring himself around in a wheelchair, but his sense of pride in not allowing people to help him showed everyone what a determined character he was. When he was number two to Simon Mereweather, and when he was part of the team, he had idiosyncrasies that many thought would hold him back in his new role as director of the operations unit, but he had shown them that he could evolve and adapt quickly.

"I'm pleased to hear that," Ramsay said somewhat thoughtfully. "I want you to meet Caroline. She's got something that needs finishing."

"Meet Caroline? Are we assuming she's not dead?" Big Dave turned and looked at Ramsay. "What's going on?"

"Caroline is alive. I probably should have mentioned that," he said without any sign of emotion. "She just got in contact with me, and she needs some help."

"Tell me where and when and I'm there," the big Fijian beamed, unable to hide his elation.

"It may get messy," Ramsay replied. "It may not be nice."

"Like I said, tell me when and where."

Chapter Thirty-One

King had dropped the BMW several streets from the train station in Bayonne and bought a ticket to Bordeaux with cash. With the train leaving two hours after rush hour, he had been able to find a quiet space with his back against the bulkhead, a good view of the carriage ahead, and a convex mirror above him and to his right which afforded him a view of the next carriage and lavatory behind him.

He had wiped his fingerprints off the revolver and left it in the boot of the BMW with the body of the Irishman. King suspected that the weapon was likely linked to other crimes, and he had not wanted to risk using it for the simple fact that he had a new 9mm pistol with him with twenty-five rounds of factory ammunition and he could not vouch for anything about the assassin's weapon. The six .38 rounds had been a mix of both shiny nickel and old tarnished brass cases and copper-coated lead and soft lead bullets, which indicated either home-loads or a desperation in sourcing ammunition. The rounds would have varying performances and may even be dangerous to use for the shooter. As much as it pained him to give up a weapon, he wasn't in a desperate enough position, and the French police may even close some investigations with the body of a contract killer and his weapon in the same place.

The journey to Bordeaux took only two hours and a saver deal set him back a mere eighteen euros, and he reflected on the way that Europe had an economical and working transport system, even though he could not remember the last time he had taken a train in the UK for a direct comparison. As he settled back in his seat and brushed the crumbs of a brie baguette he had purchased at the station off his jacket, he realised that the last train he could remember catching had been in Indonesia during a tricky mission while working for MI6. Time had simply flown since then, or maybe he had reached an age when one truly noticed the speeding of time. So many countries, so many missions, and so many lives lost. Both enemies and friends alike. Was he ready to retire? Let the smart youngsters like Jack Luger and Rashid pick up the mantel? Probably. But he had tried twice, and both times he had been pulled back in. Perhaps it was not meant to be. Perhaps he was meant to die on the job. Besides, who needed the quiet life?

Chapter Thirty-Two

Washington DC

Newman chose the meeting place, and he arrived an hour early to check it for listening devices – or worse. The booth was perfect for their needs. A clear path to the exit, a tinted bay window from which they could observe the street, yet largely remain unseen. And the coffee was good, so it was all working out.

Georgia Scott arrived noticing Newman already had a drink and she asked for a double espresso as she passed the counter and made her way to the booth. "A phone call would have sufficed."

"Not when you hear what I have to say."

Scott looked at him dubiously. "Get on with it, then."

"The contract on King..."

"Forget it," she said, hesitating as her coffee arrived. She waited for the server to leave and said, "I won't be threatened. He and his bitch came out here and threatened my husband. They expected that to work. For me to fold. Well, where has that gotten them? I don't fold. It's already cost her her life, and he'll learn that soon enough."

Newman regarded her for a moment, then sipped some of his coffee. She was under the assumption that Caroline Darby was dead, and he didn't think it would hurt to let her carry on believing that. It would help Caroline, at least. "What do you expect?" Newman replied. "I've collided with King a few times and all I can say is that your husband was lucky. I'm surprised all they did was tie him to a chair and say some stern words. They paid you a courtesy." He shook his head, somewhat perplexed by the woman's obstinance. "The Brits are our allies, Georgia. This is distracting for everyone involved."

"It's not distracting for us..." She sipped some of her espresso and pulled a face like it had really hit the spot. An essential pick-me-up for the afternoon in a long working day.

"There will be fallout."

"I'm not scared of the Brits. You shouldn't be either. They're barely significant these days."

"If you really think that, then you're foolish."

She glared at him as she said, "Be careful Newman..."

"What? You'll take a contract out on me, too?" Newman scoffed. "Robert Lefkowitz did a great deal to stop this situation before. He would not be happy about this."

"You barely knew him!"

The remark smarted him. He had a great respect for his former boss and had been honoured to take up secret tasks unbeknownst to the CIA controllers. Although he later found out at the man's funeral that Georgia Scott had been in a similar role for years before Newman. "I knew enough," he said, hoping his expression had not betrayed him. "And I know he would tell you to stand down and look for an alternative to this madness."

"It's too late for that." She paused, finishing the rest of her espresso in two sips. "The Brits lose an agent, and we all move on. They'll still suckle at our teat because they know what's good for them."

"You've underestimated them," he warned her. "They'll be back..."

"Really? Well, not both of them..." she replied acidly, getting up from the table. "I'll let you get the cheque." She made to turn but looked back at him. "Enjoy your retirement. I think we're done with you Newman. Being a cripple is one thing, but being soft is quite another..."

Newman shrugged. He wasn't going to give the woman the satisfaction of rising to her insult. He still had his CIA desk, and fieldwork hadn't worked out so good for him since his injury. He was pretty sure that he was done with the likes of Georgia Scott and secret departments with unsanctioned agendas, ultimately unregulated and answerable to no one.

Chapter Thirty-Three

Caroline watched from across the street. She wore oversized Gucci sunglasses which she had bought in the duty free at Charles de Gaulle Airport in Paris and had pulled her normally free-flowing hair back into a tight ponytail. She looked chic, but suitably disguised. From the booth in another ten-a-penny coffee house she sipped between a double espresso and a glass of iced water. The air buds she wore could well have been playing her favourite playlist, but instead picked up the conversation from the digital microphone she had dropped in Newman's jacket pocket. The transceiver she had slipped into his other pocket had brought her here. Inside, she was seething at what the woman had just said, but she wasn't going to let rage take over her emotion and judgement.

"Eyes on," she said quietly into the microphone on her wrist, disguised as a *Fitbit*. "Exiting... three... two...one... now," she said as Georgia Scott stepped outside the coffee house and slipped the strap of her handbag over her shoulder.

"Got her," Big Dave replied.

Die Trying

"Don't lose her."

"Go and get the vehicle, I've got her from here."

Caroline left a ten-dollar bill under the saucer and made her way out of the coffee house. American streets were quite unique. Usually, the pavements were far wider than those in the UK or Europe, and they were almost entirely straight. There were parking spaces along both sides of the street, although nobody crossed the road to park against the traffic flow. An almost entirely American thing, but usually involving strict penalties. There always felt like there was more room in American towns. Which was good for moving around your day, but poor for surveillance drills, and she could already see the six-foot-four, eighteen stone Fijian trailing some fifty metres behind Georgia Scott, keeping himself close to the store fronts, which were equally as wide and straight as the pavements.

After Caroline had left the bolt-hole apartment in Bayonne, she had contacted Ramsay and told him of her plan. Georgia Scott's band of assassins had blown their world apart, but Caroline's body had never been found. Equally, she had not been seen since. She was invisible. She had requested Ramsay's help and he had arranged for the funds and equipment to be left in a luggage locker at the Smithsonian train station, and he had told her to expect a friend to assist her. Caroline had worked well with Big Dave many times, and she was relieved when she saw him at her motel in Falls Church. She had already hatched her plan, and considering what they were going to do next, the big Fijian was probably the best man for the job.

Caroline got into the GMC Yukon hire car – a great behemoth of an SUV with an engine that could probably jumpstart a power station – and drove down the road, away from Georgia Scott and Big Dave. There were no roundabouts, and a U-turn would probably have a cop down on her in minutes, so she turned left at the lights and took another left until she could come back on the road with the traffic. She could see Big Dave ahead of her, and now just twenty metres in front of him, Georgia Scott walked purposefully along the pavement studying the screen of her phone. Caroline checked all three mirrors and studied the road ahead. There was a food delivery lorry parked outside a restaurant around eighty metres in front of them, and a space directly behind it. Fifty metres ahead of her builders were filling the load bed of a large pick-up truck from a shop undergoing refurbishment. It was about as good as it would get, and she said, "The food delivery truck, it will block the view ahead and the builders' pick-up will cover us from behind."

"Looks good," he whispered into his mic. *"I'll start to close the gap..."*

Caroline overtook Georgia Scott and pulled into the space between the two large vehicles, but in truth the GMC was every bit as large as the builders' truck. She ensured that the central locking was off, and she slipped over the front seats and into the capacious rear. She had in her left hand a small, hard plastic case. In her right, a silenced .22 Ruger pistol. The gun would get Scott's attention. A .22 was as quiet as a firearm could get, and the suppressor made it almost undetectable among the ambient noise of a city. Even in a quiet suburban sprawl such as this. That gave the weapon credence. It had been chosen specifically for the task. In Caroline's experience details mattered.

Timing was everything and Big Dave had experience rounding up the infamous playing card list of most wanted in Iraq, just after he had passed selection and training with the SAS. He had abducted many key players using every-

Die Trying

thing from snatch and grabs, poisoning and ambushes to elaborately faked meetings of senior members to encourage some of the most wanted to simply walk into their trap. Another troop had put together a fake rape-rally with the promise of young virgins, and a whole host of names had turned up, some high up in Saddam's morality police. The men on the cards had been detained and hauled off in trucks while in a 'tragic' chain of events the rest of the men who were not on the most wanted list but simply liked to rape young girls were trapped inside the building when a smoke grenade set fire to some bedsheets. There were no survivors...

Caroline used the passenger-side mirror to judge Scott's distance, her heart racing as she saw the woman's features clearly in the reflection. Behind her, Big Dave filled the rest of the mirror. Suddenly, he grabbed her by the shoulders and pushed her towards the SUV. Caroline opened the door and kicked it wide, before scooting over the seat and leaning against the door with the pistol aimed right at Scott as she was thrown inside. The door closed and Big Dave opened the driver's door but was forced to wait while he adjusted the electric seat from Caroline's driving position. It seemed to take forever before he could fit inside. Scott's expression went from surprised to angry in a flash when she saw Caroline behind the pistol.

"You...?" she seethed.

Hands on the headrest in front of you..." Caroline said, jamming the suppressor into the woman's ribs while she patted her over. "Have you got a weapon on you?" she asked curtly.

"No."

"If I find one, I'll put a bullet through your kneecap."

"The CIA are not permitted to be armed on US soil."

"But US citizens can carry a weapon with a concealed carry licence." She worked her hands around the woman's back. "I mean it, if I find any weapon I'll take your kneecap off!"

"There's a thirty-eight in my bag," she conceded gruffly.

Caroline took the woman's bag and kept it close to her. She handed Scott a pair of handcuffs. "Try these on for a fit."

"Fuck you!" Caroline aimed the pistol at the woman's knee. "Okay! Okay!" She slipped the bracelets around her wrists and snapped them shut. Caroline reached over and squeezed them tighter, the ratchets clicking and Scott wincing as they tightened. "What are you doing?" Caroline said nothing as she opened the plastic case and selected a hypodermic syringe. Before the woman could protest, she stabbed her in the thigh and administered the full dose. "God, no!" Scott complained.

"Just a little something for the ride." Caroline put the syringe back in the case and turned her attention to Georgia Scott's phone. "Thumb print or facial ID?"

"Facial ID..."

Caroline tried to open the phone knowing it would go to the passcode, she then held the phone to the woman's face when prompted. The phone opened and Caroline opened settings and changed the security features. She glanced at Scott, who was becoming drowsier by the second. She checked her watch, then unscrewed the suppressor and slipped it into her jacket pocket. After she lifted the woman's eyelid, she put the pistol into her other pocket. "She's out," Caroline said matter-of-factly.

Big Dave nodded, keeping his eyes on the road and the rear-view mirror.

Chapter Thirty-Four

The Baltic Sea

The Baltic Sea had a curious lake-like quality to it. The swells were mere ripples and stacked to the horizon as if someone had dropped a rock in the centre and the ripples had made it to the shore. Reeds grew in the shallows and ducks and gulls bobbed together on the minute swell, a confused menagerie of seabirds and waterfowl. The shallow water ran from clear to green and further out to sea, a deep and foreboding black. Above, the sky was clear and blue with dark rain clouds on the distant horizon, which had given the sea its blackness.

Luger shivered with the piercing wind. Despite being the month of May, there was a chill that could turn the shade to mid-winter. The wind factor increased along with the boat's revs and by the time they reached fifteen knots, he had fastened his coat to the top button. He looked at the fishing rods, already tackled and resting in the holders, whipping in the wind like flimsy aerial transmitters. "If the land and lake borders are so well protected, then arriving by sea should make no difference," he shouted above both engine noise and wind.

"Hence the fishing gear," Carter replied. "Baltic pike. The only sea in the world where pike can be found. Granted, the salt is less concentrated here. It's brackish but gets saltier the closer you get to Sweden and the opening to the North Sea." He paused. "They're big, too, those pike. Like barracuda. Pike sport fishing is big business both here and in Lithuania."

"Great," Luger replied without enthusiasm. Fishing was the last thing on his mind.

Carter stared at the horizon. "As long as we stay in Estonian waters and do not stray into Russian territory, then we can go about our business."

"Sport fishing?"

Carter laughed. "Not exactly," he replied. "Help yourself to a rod. Lures are the best for Baltic pike. Big, shiny, silver lures with three sharp hooks. Last one to catch a pike buys a round when you get back."

"Back?"

"From Russia, of course." Carter paused, picking up a fishing rod. "We're heading out for you to catch a lift…"

Chapter Thirty-Five

Baltimore, Maryland

Details mattered. Caroline had removed the SIM card from Georgia Scott's phone and switched it off. She now had control of it when she needed it, which would be soon enough. Big Dave had earlier switched the licence plates on the GMC, and although it would not foil a police search – and he had never driven more carefully because of this – it would confuse any attempt to trace them via CCTV and toll roads. Certainly, enough not to have any comeback on them, or the hire company. Both Caroline and Big Dave had switched off their phones, removing the SIM card as well and now carried burner phones to communicate with each other.

They found a suitable place in the suburban business districts where lockups, warehouses and industrial units were available to buy or rent. Businesses turned over quickly during this administration, and seemingly more so in Baltimore. Caroline had never visited the city before, and could see it was honest America – hardworking, if not high-achieving. A busy port town where it was not uncommon for people to be born into, live and die in the same place with no judgement from one's peers, because that was their life, too. It was also one of the most dangerous cities in the United States, coming in at number two with fifty-two murders per hundred-thousand people, or one a day.

The lock-up looked dilapidated. Two empty doors down, a car body shop looked like it was in business merely to cut-and-shut insurance write offs. From the pile of licence plates in the open doorway, it also looked like the place in town to bring a stolen car and attempt to legitimise it. Caroline studied the building while Big Dave got out and strolled around it. Either side of the building grass had grown in patches where the light could warm the ground. The alleyways had become a dumping ground for debris and litter. Rusted oil drums and bald tyres were scattered along with wooden pallets. Empty beer cans lay pressed into the dirt, where they had been trodden in place by people with no better place to be.

Caroline could not see an alarm, but if the place was vacant, then there was little point wasting the electricity. If somebody squatted inside, then this was the sort of place where a few dockers could be hired for the cost of a night's drinking and move them on with baseball bats. When Big Dave emerged from the other side of the building, he nodded to her, and she brought the van over and backed it to the doors. She popped open the tailgate and Big Dave took out a set of pneumatic bolt croppers and made short work of the chunky padlock. He discarded the two pieces of padlock and dropped the chain to the floor where it coiled

Die Trying

like a snake at his feet. The doors were rusted but gave when he yanked hard on them, and as the daylight penetrated the darkness, dust was blown into the air and filled the shards of light making them appear tangible.

Big Dave stepped around the rear of the vehicle and pulled Georgia Scott's unconscious body out of the vehicle, while Caroline took out a chair that they had purchased at an office supplies outlet. They both looked each way down the street, which was little more than a track, long since forgotten by the city's planners and highway authorities. The road would be the last choice for anyone, no sense in using it for a shortcut, and the businesses on this road were either barely worth visiting, or on their last months of trading. All it needed was tumbleweed blowing down the street.

Caroline placed the chair in the centre of the space and Big Dave dropped Georgia Scott in the chair, holding her firmly in place while Caroline fastened her ankles and wrists with duct tape. She fastened a short length to her mouth, then stood back to admire her handiwork. Lastly, she placed a pillowcase over her head.

"Do you think this will work?" asked Big Dave. This wasn't the worse thing he'd done, but it felt like it was getting damned close. During his military career, he had not found the killing difficult. The first time he had killed a man it had been in an intense gun battle, and it had been either him or the enemy. It had been as simple as that. Subsequently, he had killed and fought his way through his military career and become a mercenary when he had been cut loose due to government cutbacks and found no other way of paying off his debts and finding a way to eat. Since being recruited into MI5, he had done many things, but there was something so premeditated about what they were doing now, that when he saw the woman slumped in the chair, bound, and gagged, it did not sit easily with him. For Caroline, it was personal. She and King were lovers, she was invested. For Lomu, he couldn't help thinking that there might be another way.

"I hope so…"

"What if she doesn't talk?" he asked flatly.

"She'll talk."

"You sound like you're certain."

"I have to be," she replied. "Alex is dead if this woman doesn't lift the contract."

"He's tough. He can get through it. He always does."

"Until he doesn't," she said flatly. "One on one… hell… even three on one, but not infinite. God only knows how many contractors she's put on this." She glanced at their prisoner as she started to stir. "I guess we'll find out how this is going to go down soon enough…"

Chapter Thirty-Six

The light was fading fast, just a glimmer of gold to the west, somewhere over Denmark he guessed. Luger looked at the diving bottle and BCD. The weights were integrated into the BCD vest, and the dry suit looked several sizes too large, but that had been intentional to accommodate his clothes underneath.

"This is the plan?" Luger commented flatly.

"Yes," Carter replied indignantly. "Here, let me help you into it."

Luger started with the dry suit, which was an all-in-one affair. "What about my shoes?"

Carter picked up a rubber bag. "You put them in here, along with the money that you've been assigned, your telephone and weapon."

"Weapon?"

Carter nodded and showed him the Makarov. "It was a good choice for going into Russia. The serial numbers have also been removed with acid." Luger nodded, his heart racing and despite the cold, he was now perspiring as he slipped his shoulders into the suit and pulled the headpiece over his head and secured it across his chest with the zip. The rubber was tight around his neck, wrists, and ankles. "Swim down thirty metres and they'll pick you up."

"As simple as that?"

"Dead simple."

"If you could have left out the *dead*, that would have been great."

Carter shrugged it off and helped him on with the tank. Luger tested the regulator and second stage demand valve, his heart still racing. The ripples on the surface had turned to a two-foot swell and the boat rocked constantly because the swell did not come in sets, just a constant onslaught that rocked the boat up and down and from side to side as the tiny craft lifted and dropped with the swell.

With his hood up and his mask on, Luger stepped into the pair of fins and Carter pulled the straps tight. "Straight down?" he asked to clarify.

"Straight down, thirty metres," he replied. He watched as Luger checked his watch. They had three minutes to spare, and Luger breathed deeply. Carter watched as he sat on the side of the vessel and put the mouthpiece in. "Oh, hang on!" he shouted, with Luger just starting to lean backwards. "You'll need this..." he said, pulling out a double-sided light on a Velcro webbing strap. "This is a strobe light," he explained. "Otherwise, they'd never have found you..." He fastened the strap around Luger's forearm and activated the light, which flashed and blinked a hypnotic, brutally bright white and red LED. "All set?"

Luger stared at him indignantly, then launched himself backwards and into a classic diver's entry. The water enveloped him, and he felt only the chill on the exposed skin around his mask and regulator. The dry suit was extremely buoyant, so he bled off some air from the BCD, or buoyancy control device, and felt himself start to sink more quickly. The strobe was an annoyance, and he used the dive computer attached to a long tube to register his descent to a rate of sixty feet a minute. At thirty metres, he took a deep breath which slowed his descent and added some air to his BCD until he maintained negative buoyancy and merely hovered in the void, illuminated around him in intermittent flashes of red and white and total darkness.

He saw the movement, his heart racing as he was taken back to his first viewing of *Jaws* and the primal fears unlocked forever more in the ocean. With every flash of white, the object grew closer and once he calmed himself, convincing himself that sharks - although present in the Baltic Sea and represented by many species - should not be his primary concern, he breathed slowly to control his breathing and wait for the object to grow closer. After two more white flashes, the object became two and then three, and three torch beams switched on, illuminating all around him.

The first diver to reach him switched off the strobe and pressed his mask close to his own before pinching his gloved thumb and forefinger on a universal 'OK' gesture. Luger responded in kind. The second diver attached a leash around Luger's left wrist and performed the same gesture, which Luger nervously reciprocated, and the three divers finned back the way they had come, their torch beams sweeping the blackness ahead of them. Luger watched the man on his left study a palm-pad of some sort and after a few minutes, they had descended another thirty metres and travelled three hundred metres from where Luger had hovered in the void.

The torch beams caught the great hulk of the submarine's hull and Luger felt trepidation as he followed, merely a passenger in what happened next. One diver left open the hatch towards the prow of the great vessel and the other diver swam Luger into position. The first diver contorted himself around the opening and lowered himself inside. He then received Luger and once he was seated in the enclosed space, the second and third divers entered and the last man in closed the hatch. There were three lights inside the chamber and once the last diver had taken his place on the bench, holding himself in place, the first diver pressed a large, red button and the water started to slowly subside. Luger took his cue from the divers, who started to remove the masks and regulators. He removed his own and unfastened his BCD, taking the weight of the tank off him now that the water washed around his knees. After another minute the chamber was empty of water, just the walls running, and the ceiling dripping seawater on their heads. Luger could see two men looking in through the glass porthole in the hatch in front of him, and the chamber opened with a gush of air hitting him in the face. He climbed out of his dry suit and placed it beside his BCD and tank.

A man of around forty with a neatly trimmed beard and carefully combed hair extended his right hand. "Commander Sean Trevelyan," he said. "I'm captain of the boat..."

"Jack," he replied as he shook the commanding officer's hand. He purposely left out his own surname. He wasn't here to make friends and the less anyone knew about him, the better.

The commander nodded and said, "You are welcome to use my quarters. Tremaine will show you there and give you a cup of tea. Dinner is in an hour." He paused. "And then we'll get you to shore."

Luger thanked him and followed the young rating. The

Die Trying

width of the vessel was far greater than Luger had expected it to be, with multiple floors reached by metal grate stairwells. Every man and woman he passed seemed to be carrying out their tasks efficiently, and in virtual silence. They passed bunks with curtains drawn and Tremaine turned and put a finger to his lips indicating that the crew were sleeping.

"There's not enough bunks for everyone, so we hot-bunk. Someone leaves for a shift, and another takes their place in the bunk. Some of the crew just bed down in the torpedo bay and storerooms," he whispered. "But that's life in the silent service."

"It's something else," Luger commented flatly. He had been aboard a submarine for a day testing a new weapon system and he had hated every minute of it. Now he remembered why. The 'captain's quarters' were snug with just a single bed, a desk and chair. There was paper on the desk with pens and pencils and around the cabin were photographs of Commander Trevelyan and his wife with their young child. Luger had served aboard frigates, and he had spent a lot of time away from home, but he was a single man and at least on a frigate you could see the sky and distant shoreline. Down here, being a family man, it must have been hell for the three to six months that they were typically away. Luger didn't know how they did it, he was feeling claustrophobic already.

He looked up as a knock sounded on the thin, plywood door which was already opening. Luger recognised the man as one of the divers. "Hi, I'm Nick," he said. "I'll be taking you ashore."

Luger shook the man's hand. "Jack," he said.

"It'll be a three-man team," Nick told him. "We'll leave the same way, out of the escape hatch, except this time we'll be using micro-breathers and ascending from just fifteen metres..."

"What's a micro-breather?"

"A disposable can of air with a mouthpiece. Gives around fifteen minutes of breathing."

"Oh..."

"It's okay, nothing like what we just did. That was way harder." Nick paused. "Then on the surface we inflate the Gemini and get on board."

"That's an inflatable boat, right?"

"Got it in one. Then you take off your dry suit and try not to crease your tuxedo on the run up the beach," he smirked.

"Very funny." He watched as Nick left, closing the door behind him, then he looked into the tiny mirror on the slim cupboard beside the commander's bed and said, "What the bloody hell have you got yourself into?"

Chapter Thirty-Seven

Bordeaux, France

King had found a little bistro near the train station and ordered a cold beer and steak frites. The French got steak and chips right because they did exactly that. A piece of bavette char-grilled and served rare, seasoned with salt and pepper and a little thyme, and then served with a pile of crispy fries cooked in duck fat. A paste of bone marrow and roasted garlic was smeared on the steak as it rested before serving, and King had a small pot of Dijon mustard on the side. The meal was divine, and the hoppy, nutty beer washed it down well. For the first time in what felt like an age, he felt comforted in the knowledge that even though she wasn't safe, at least Caroline was alive. But she had her own idea on how she would approach this, and he would just have to wait and see what that was.

After the excellent meal King returned to the cheap

hotel room he had paid for earlier in cash and rested on the bed to take stock. Georgia Scott would need to have access to the CCTV systems in the traffic network and cities throughout France, as well as inside the public transport system for the assassins to have got onto King so quickly. He could not see any other way, and that access would have to have been gained through an AI programme of some description, much like the system that Ramsay had developed and tested when they had hunted agents of the Iron Fist. King suspected that he had been 'pinged' through facial recognition, and he knew that even if he hid his face, the system that Ramsay pioneered could identify a subject by height and weight calculations, as well as the gait of stride and body movements. King would simply set off electronic and virtual 'trip wires' as long as his face remained uncovered, and he made his way anywhere on foot. He needed a vehicle and had spotted a Range Rover in the street outside that would suit his needs. Range Rovers were notoriously easy to steal, and he could access the wiring through a small hole which he would cut in the plastic part of the boot lid with his knife. Hacking into the vehicle's computer could be done via a simple app that he had already downloaded onto his mobile phone. Not intended to aid villains, but aimed at the automotive aftermarket sector instead, the app would reboot the tracker's software and cancel the previous security code. The vehicle's computer would transfer the locking code, and he could then lock, unlock, and open the ignition code using his phone. King had the app stored in his own storage cloud and had installed it to his newly acquired phone on his train journey from Bayonne to Bordeaux. He had checked the street for CCTV, and it looked clear, and the hotel itself was such a basic affair that security had not been a priority of the owner.

Tomorrow he would have a car, and he had a plan to leave the city, but not before he had made the opposition aware and instigated them to follow. He would be the bait to tease out the rats, and he would deal with them appropriately in a place of his choosing. But for tonight, he was happy to remain anonymous and would be grateful of a good night's sleep.

Chapter Thirty-Eight

Latitude: 59.762077N Longitude: 27.893595E
The Baltic Sea

Jack Luger sat beside the three SBS commandos, the water swirling around his feet as the chamber filled with water and the air hissed its escape through the vents above his head. The other men appeared calm. In front of them the Gemini inflatable boat and its twenty horsepower four-stroke outboard with near silent running ability was compressed and wrapped inside a rubber duffle bag no larger than that of a folded six-man tent. Each man carried their weapons in a rubber dry bag. Luger had seen the men checking their compact Heckler & Koch UMP .40 sub-machineguns and 9mm Sig Sauer pistols before sealing them against the seawater they were about to enter. Luger knew that the weapons would work if they got wet, but Nick had briefly explained to him that in a firefight, a gun heated up quickly, the water evaporating and the salt

Die Trying

residue that was left would be enough to cause feed problems and stoppages. He didn't know why he was thinking about this as the water enveloped him and the red light above their heads switched from red to green, but he supposed it was enough to take his mind from the imminent opening of the hatch and the elements beyond.

One of the SBS commandos opened the hatch, while Nick caught hold of Luger's shoulder and guided him out into the blackness. They would not be using the strobe lights because they would be too close to shore when they breeched the surface. Instead, the first SBS commando used an underwater torch to sweep a beam of light through the abyss and played it on the surface some seventeen metres above them. Nick steadied Luger while the other commandos got the large rubber bundle out of the hatch and pulled the cord on the CO_2 canister and the bundle raced to the surface amid a million air bubbles that raced along with it. By the time Nick and Luger reached the surface, the bundle had inflated fully, and the small Gemini inflatable boat bobbed beside them on the surface. As briefed, Luger removed the regulator mouthpiece and swapped it for his snorkel. He blew out a great breath to clear it, then deflated the weighted BCD before removing it and allowing it to sink to the seabed. Nick helped him aboard, and he turned around and hauled the commando into the craft. The other men tossed their weapon bags into the boat and clamoured inside. Nick had already started the engine, although it was barely audible. Luger did not know, but the submarine was no longer below them and was gliding silently to the extraction point some two miles to the north, where it would wait at seventy metres with its communication buoy on the surface.

The Gemini motored along at a swift pace, the swell no

more than a foot or two and moving with them towards the shore. Luger held onto one of the soft canvas handles with his right hand, his feet tucked up close to his chest. Spray splashed his face, but the dry suit protected him from both the wet and the cold. The Baltic Sea often froze over during the winter months and pieces of ice could be found as late in the year as April. The water was searingly cold at a little over 2°c and would not rise much above 3.5°c in this region during the summer months. Luger had the strange sensation of his cheeks burning with the cold spray, his hands still thankfully gloved. Ahead of them, distant lights twinkled on the shoreline and the rising tension was insurmountable. When he next looked at the other men in the boat, they were cradling their sub-machineguns and wore bullet-proof vests with utility harnesses and had balaclavas tugged down over their faces.

Close to shore Nick cut the engine and they glided in with nothing to hear but the gentle lap of waves on a shingle beach. Two of the men leapt over the side, the water up to their chests. They gently pulled the boat towards the shore, then when they were in the shallows, one of the men raced up the beach taking up a covering fire position while the other stepped in up to his knees and pulled the boat the rest of the way, securing it to the beach with a small anchor attached to rope, not chain. He too, then ran up the beach and took cover.

"Out you get," said Nick stepping out of the boat. Luger stepped out and waded to shore. He made his way to the rocks where one of the SBS commandos was using the rocks for cover and started to unzip and tug off his dry suit. Nick helped him and bundled it into a rubber dry bag. Luger was left standing in jeans and a hiking jacket and Nick handed him another dry bag with his shoes, phone, and weapon.

Die Trying

"You're on your own, now mate," he said. "We'll find a LUP and wait for contact. If we don't hear anything, then we return to the sub in seventy-two hours. Mark it," he said, showing Luger his watch. Luger checked his own Omega Seamaster and nodded. "Good luck."

Luger tucked the Makarov pistol into his pocket. There were no spare magazines, so he had only eight of the strange, bulbous looking 9.2x18mm bullets. He had never used the weapon before but had familiarised himself with it on board the submarine. The fact that he had been given the weapon and just eight bullets signified something macabre to him, like it was a last resort means to an end. Seven bullets for the enemy, and one for himself. The thought made him shudder, but he could not get hung up on such sentiment. He was here to do a job, and that was that. What would be, would be. Hopefully, he would never have to take the pistol out of his pocket. But he wasn't a fool. He knew how the Russians treated spies and terrorists. He just hoped he had the courage to do what was necessary.

The road to access the beach was little more than a rutted track. From what he had seen of the beach, and knew from the year-round temperatures, this wasn't a summertime resort and was probably accessed by just a few fishermen year-round. After a hundred metres the track met the road, and he had enough sense of direction and familiarity with the map he had studied to know that he should take the left and keep the coast on his left. He was cold, despite it nearing the end of May, and he felt exposed on the road. His contact would meet him near the forest, and he would know that it was his contact because the lights of his vehicle would flash three long beams and two short. In the distance vehicle lights approached and Luger quickly got off the road and hunkered down into the drainage ditch running alongside the road. The earth was hard, the frozen ground less than a foot below the surface not yet thawed. He ducked his head and tucked up his collar, and the lights bore down on him and passed just as quickly. A thump of eighties rock was audible over the sound of a rough engine, and pungent cigarette smoke was left hanging in the air along with rich petrol fumes.

Luger stood and stepped out of the ditch. He checked his mobile signal. Nothing. He was a hundred metres from the edge of the forest, and he approached as per his instructions, on the opposite side of the road to make himself clear to his contact. After fifty metres, a swathe of light blinded him. Three long dashes, followed by two dots. This was it. No mistake.

Chapter Thirty-Nine

London

The cards on the table in front of him presented little challenge. He could finish solitaire in minutes. He had devised an algorithm on his computer as a teen, and those rules for play were imbedded in his mind. There was little challenge to be had, but the process of compartmentalising the processes, of layering the suits and moving the colours to release cards, then replace and move on, gave him time and the ability to think. Some people played golf, others fished beside drizzle-soaked riverbanks, and Neil Ramsay solved puzzles.

He had been troubled ever since the invite to the River House. MI6 seldom shared. They sold, they bartered and stole information, but they never really shared. The relationship had often been likened to siblings and Ramsay could see why. MI6 was the petulant first child, the spoiled and righteous one who always sought to get their own way, while MI5 was the stoical second child, who had the maturity to sit back and wait for the emotional storm to blow over. The second child got things done quietly. In truth, he had been intrigued. He had hoped that it could spark a new era of cohesiveness. He had hoped that after MI5 had sorted out its security issues, then he could reintegrate the unit with a healthy relationship with MI6. But he knew it was not to be. He tried the line again, but it went straight to voicemail indicating that the device was either switched off or completely out of signal. He did not curse, because he never really had. Never found it helped. And he did not get frustrated. He simply laid the two of diamonds on top of the three of hearts and reshuffled the pack. A man's life was on the line and as he dealt the cards, he wondered whether he had got everything wrong about this case from the start.

Chapter Forty

Baltimore, Maryland

Caroline had never tortured someone before. She knew the principles, and she had been taught how to resist interrogation. Up to a point. The tactics that she had learned had been to delay for as long as possible – the idea being to give her team enough time to get away, or even a rescue. The methodology in training had been to layer her answers. Firstly, give away nothing but lies. Secondly – after appearing to be broken – give away the cover story in the hope that it would be believed to be the truth. In practice, everything could change in a heartbeat. Nobody could withstand barbaric torture indefinitely. Everybody had a point of submission. Caroline knew all of this, and she knew that Georgia Scott would, too. However, as much as Caroline would fight for her and King's survival, she wasn't about to get all medieval on the woman bound to the chair in front of her. It simply wasn't who she was.

"You can't win," Georgia Scott sneered at her. She looked tired, worn but she wasn't even close to broken. "Just end this now. Accept that you're beat and move on…"

"I'm not the one tied to a chair," Caroline retorted.

"I must say, this is the nicest interrogation I've seen." Scott paused. "Not even so much as a slap, let alone waterboarding."

"It's early yet."

"Even your companion's heart isn't in it. Is that why he's taken off?"

"No," Caroline said coldly. "He's got a job to do…"

Scott stared at her, but there was a flicker in her eye. "Where?" Caroline did not reply. She had brought another chair with her and now sat in it facing the American. "What's he doing?" Caroline said nothing. She had bought a large, white coffee in a go cup and sipped it through the hole in the lid. Each time Scott asked about Big Dave, she simply looked at her and sipped her coffee. The woman was worried. She may have been brave, possibly cavalier with her own life – maybe even her husband's - but when it boiled down to it, she had two children and she had an imagination. And someone like Georgia Scott, who had seen some terrible things and likely ordered terrible things to be done, that imagination was an extremely active and vivid one indeed.

Caroline had almost finished the coffee. Big Dave was certainly on an errand, but it was on his own terms. He had gone to a nearby diner to sample a few American classics. Neither of them had eaten in a while and Caroline knew how voracious the man's appetite was, and she expected the servers and line cooks to witness something truly special.

Die Trying

She put the cup down on the ground, making a mental note to take it with her. DNA testing was always something they had to consider. Fingerprints too, which was why she was wearing a pair of paper-thin calf's skin leather gloves. "You will call off the contract," she said eventually.

"No, I won't."

"You'll have a limit," Caroline told her. "I can find it."

"You're not about to kill my kids," she said. "You're not the type. I can tell."

"We got to your husband once..."

"Fine. Do your worst. Do what you want to the cheating bastard. I'm filing for divorce, so you'll make me more money and save me a whole lot of lawyers' fees."

"He's having an affair?" Caroline asked dubiously.

"He's a vain ex-college football star turned realtor. He has keys to expensive houses and an ego. You do the math..."

Caroline shrugged, almost feeling bad for the woman. "I don't want to hurt you," she said. "But I will."

"Just let me go and fly home." Georgia Scott paused. "Sorry, but Uncle Sam wins this one..."

"This is not a case of America verses Britain, this is personal. King got in your way, and you didn't like it." She paused, then raged, "This is just ego! Like your cheating husband! Now, call off your fucking contract!"

Georgia Scott did not so much as flinch. Caroline could see that this was going nowhere. She could break the woman eventually, but short of gouging out her children's eyes in front of her, this woman wasn't going to give easily. She got out of her chair, picked up the tape and wound a long length around the woman's mouth and the back of her head. She wasn't giving her any chances, and she checked her bonds were good and tight before putting the hood back over her head.

"You can't say that I didn't warn you," Caroline said, and briefly felt pleasure when the woman grunted and moaned under the hood, testing her bonds, and almost tipping her chair. By the time she was inside the SUV and had started the engine, she felt guilty at putting the woman through such mental anguish, but quickly shrugged it aside as she thought of the attempt on her and King's lives, and their dream yacht scattered all over the seabed off Cadiz. She paused at the end of the rutted track, mindful of some vagrants eyeing the luxury vehicle. One of the men was already on his feet, staggering towards her with an iron bar in his hand. Caroline floored the accelerator and raced away, catching the man in her mirror as he threw the iron bar after her and it clattered on the asphalt. It was time for Plan B.

Chapter Forty-One

Baltic Coast, Russia

The MI6 contact was an overweight incessant smoker of around fifty named Ivan. Luger suspected that using the name was the British equivalent of using Smith or Jones. He did not for one moment thing that Ivan was the man's real name. Luger wondered what the man got out of his arrangement with MI6. It certainly wasn't money for a new vehicle. The old Volvo estate had certainly seen better days, and inside the heaters were on full and the smoke from Ivan's pungent cigarettes escaped via the merest sliver of open window.

The Russian had said little. He was going to take Luger to a police officer who was on his pay role. He had been at the crime scene, and he had snapped some pictures of Krylov's corpse on his phone and would allow Luger to copy them – for a price. After which, they would speak with

Gransky, a local criminal who had business dealings with Max Lukov, and who knew Piotr Krylov. Ivan had said that if Krylov had told anybody about his scam at Lukov's expense, he would have told Gransky.

"How much further?" Luger asked, glancing at his phone. No signal. Not good when he relied on it for his extraction. He didn't like the idea of laying up someplace for seventy-two hours with no shelter or food for the Plan B element. Something he could not afford to miss. "Do you have a cell phone signal?" he asked, hedging his bets for a SIM card switch later if necessary.

"Yes, yes... no signal. Signal is poor out here. Better in town..." He dropped the cigarette butt out of the narrow crack of the window and relit another using the vehicle's cigarette lighter. The inside of the vehicle was still thick with smoke. "In town, we can get a good signal. After we drink and meet with my police contact. There are whores in town, too. Some of them have all their teeth!" he laughed raucously.

Luger nodded. The cabin illuminated from his phone, and he checked the screen. A one bar signal, and a message in the In-Box at the bottom of the screen. He thumbed it open and froze.

Do not trust the asset. I repeat: DO NOT TRUST THE ASSET. This is an MI6 mole hunt. You are being set up. KILL him and exfil by your own means. DO NOT return to the rendezvous. Good luck - R

Luger slipped the phone back into his pocket, his hand shaking slightly. He glanced at the man next to him and said, "Pull over up ahead."

"No, we don't want to get caught out here. There are bandits on the roads at night, and police officers who want bribes."

Die Trying

"Pull over, I need a piss."

"The town is close," Ivan persisted. "Very close."

Luger snatched out the pistol and pressed it against the man's temple. "I said, pull over..." His hand was shaking but the man could not see this. His cigarette hung limply from his dried lips and fell into his lap. He did not seem to notice. "Now!" Luger snapped impatiently.

Ivan slowed the old Volvo and mounted the grass verge. To their left, the Baltic Sea shimmered in the moonlight. To their right, the forest looked dark and foreboding. The sort of woods where writers and illustrators exiled the evil dwellers in fairy tales, relying upon fear to keep folk out. Already, Luger preferred the idea of heading towards the shore, but there would be no safety there.

"It is not true," Ivan stumbled over his words. "I am to be trusted..."

"Who said that you're not?"

"Your text," he replied, bringing the vehicle to a halt. He clunked the automatic gearstick into park and applied the handbrake. "You did this when you read the text."

"Why would you not be trusted?"

The man shrugged. "Suspicious minds," he replied meekly. "You trust me, I show you. It is not far now. We go to town and meet my police friend." He paused, struggling to swallow with such a dry mouth. "And then we talk to Gransky..."

Luger thought about Ramsay's text. He had been clear what was expected of him. But to kill a man on the strength of a text? He had killed before in self-defence, but to kill a man in cold blood? This wasn't who he was. It seemed so surreal. But he had also seen and been briefed on how the Russians worked. Terrorists dragged to court with missing eyeballs and beaten black and blue, their arms broken and held together in crude casts. He knew that he would be tortured as a foreign spy, most likely shot in the back of the neck, and buried in the forest. Russia wasn't interested in trading captured assets with the West anymore. "Open your door," he said. "I want to drive..."

Ivan opened the door and started to get out when Luger squeezed the trigger. The inside of the car lit up as bright as day for a split second and then filled with the pungent smell of burnt nitro powder. What people forty years out of date called cordite. Ivan slumped out of the car, his left foot shuddering as his nervous system shut down. Strangely, Luger felt more guilt at giving the man false hope, and somewhat more selfishly – getting the man to open the door so that the inside of the vehicle would not be splattered in blood and brain matter. Luger de-cocked the pistol before pocketing it. He got out of the car and walked around the boot, then pulled the body clear and worked his way backwards into the treeline. He struggled until he was twenty metres deep into the forest and propped the body into a sitting position against a tree, facing away from the road. He couldn't see any reason why it would not remain in place, and it seemed somewhat more dignified than dropping the body on the ground. At least, until a bear or wolf or other predator got the scent.

Luger returned to the vehicle and sat behind the wheel. Tapping his fingers on the padded steering wheel as he thought things over, he started the engine and drove back onto the road, switching off the lights and using just the half-moon's light to guide him down the road towards town. Ivan had been adamant that the town was just ahead, and after what Luger estimated to be a mile he pulled into the side of the road and parked the car in the treeline. He got out and closed the door softly, taking in the silence. The thin strip of forest to his left, between himself and the shore was no less eerie than the dense forest to his right, and as he made his way on foot his instincts became more attuned with his surroundings and his eyes grew sharper in the gloom. The half-moon was largely covered by cloud now, and only occasionally lit the ground around him. His right hand felt for the pistol, and he was briefly comforted by its presence, although it probably would not deter a determined and hungry brown bear if his aim was anything but perfect with every shot.

The road wound to the right, heading away from shore. Luger maintained his progress, then stopped when he saw an orange hue glowing on the horizon, and he assumed it was the town they were so close to. He estimated it to be around five miles, which he recalled from studying the map would be about right. Sisto-Palkino was nine miles from his infiltration point. He was about to return to the car when he noticed a faint, red light in the foreground. And then another. Pinpricks of red in a dark, grey canvas. There were more, and he wondered whether they were fireflies. He knew nothing about them, but he had always imagined them in humid summer evenings in America's south. Or perhaps that was just down to the literature he had studied in school. But what he *did* know was that a firefly was born as larvae and that was something that happened in spring, and like all larvae, they went through chrysalis and emerged in summer. Fireflies would not be glowing in the sky in a country barely escaping a frozen winter. Even the earth underfoot was as hard as concrete. Luger watched the tiny red dots penetrating the night and then when a heavy bank of the cloud released its grip on the moon, Luger could see the glint of moonlight on several vehicles parked at the side of the road. Once the moonlight had confirmed his suspicions, he could smell the pungent cigarette smoke on the wind, as if Ivan were seated beside him once more.

So, there it was. Ramsay's fortuitous text had saved him from walking into an ambush. Ivan was a double agent and MI6 had found its mole. Anger surged within as he thought of Harriet blindsiding him with her looks, her talk, and her sex. But why? Was it merely a doomed man's gift, the pathetic last request before facing the firing squad? MI6 had already placed enough intelligence in front of them to warrant a visit to Russia. They would have known that Ramsay would send one of his agents, and the fact that Carter worked in the Embassy in Tallinn meant that they had used a joint resource. Devonshire and Harriet would have been able to sit back and wait to see if MI5's agent made it to Sisto-Palkino and was suitably aided by Ivan and his contacts, or simply 'stumbled' into local police and FSB agents. Luger thought back to Harriet and the shower she had taken in his apartment. She had been in there a while, but that's how most women were. Had she had enough time to go through his things, perhaps check his phone while he was in the shower? She was MI6, so getting into his phone wouldn't have been a problem – that's the sort of thing their sister service excelled at. Had he let slip something important? He didn't think so. She had seen right through him and knew that he was going to Russia, but there was no way he would be going on a direct flight. Not since Ukraine. No, he would infiltrate by another means, and if Ramsay had used the embassy's resident spook, then it was safe to assume that MI6 would know about it.

Luger turned and double-timed back to the Volvo. It was only when he had completed a three-point-turn and driven away without any lights showing, that he wondered whether Ramsay suspected any of this, and had anticipated

Die Trying

the deception before Luger had even arrived in Estonia.

Chapter Forty-Two

Washington DC

"It won't work."

"It'll work."

"You'll be stopped as soon as you hesitate."

"Why would I hesitate?'

"Because you won't know where the hell you're going!"

Caroline shook her head. "Not if you're with me."

Newman stared at her incredulously. "You're crazy," he replied. "Crazy to think it can be done, and super crazy to think that I would agree to going with you."

"It'll work with you beside me."

"If I was caught then I'd be tried for treason," he chuckled. "And you'd be shot dead *while trying to escape* or wish that you had been by the time the CIA have interrogated and bargained with you. Hell, MI6 would probably do the job for them!"

Die Trying

Caroline mulled on this. If she was caught, then it did not bear thinking about. She would be off the grid, the FBI wouldn't be involved – would probably never even know – and without a law enforcement agency involved, then she could kiss her Miranda rights goodbye and look forward to a secret underground prison in North Dakota or Wyoming or some other mid-west state. Human rights were not at the top of the CIA's list when it came to spies, terrorists, or radicals.

"I'll take the risk," she said eventually.

"I won't." Newman paused. "Why the hell would I?"

Caroline stared at him for an uncomfortable moment, then said, "She's depth charged your career."

"Your boyfriend's aim did that for me!" he scoffed, watching two children on skateboards trundle past them. A dog walker seemed to have a problem with the two children despite being fifty metres from them and on a different path through the small park.

"I'm pretty sure he hit what he aimed at," she chided. "Oh, too soon? Alright, you got injured, but you still had a career afterwards. Now she's cut you loose from her unit and you can bet your bottom dollar she'll see that you're finished with the CIA."

Newman frowned, then closed his eyes with the realisation. He reached into his jacket pocket and retrieved the tiny listening device, no larger than a kidney bean. "You..."

"Sorry," she shrugged. "But like she said, she's done with you."

Newman closed his eyes, shaking his head. He delved into his other pocket and retrieved the tracking device, eyeing Caroline warily as he put the two devices between them on the bench. "That was low."

"It was necessary."

"Supposing that I was crazy enough to agree, what if she arrives while we're there?"

Caroline checked her watch and said, "Speaking of that, we don't have much time." She paused. "She's about to become a MISPER…"

Newman frowned, then stared blankly at her. "A missing person?" He shook his head despairingly. "Oh, what the hell have you done?"

"I'd say that we have four hours to do this, tops."

"I should call the FBI right now."

"Should or will?"

Newman tapped his cane on the ground. It had a brass tip that made the cane sound like a tap shoe on the concrete. Caroline knew that the cane contained a hidden secret. She had seen the rapier sword blade contained within, had witnessed the man use it first-hand. "I haven't decided."

"You have," she told him. "You're just conflicted and like being begged. But I won't do that. Georgia Scott is as much a problem for you as she is for me. You know things about her, and she certainly seems the type of woman to cover her tracks. Permanently." Caroline stood up and handed him a piece of paper with an address scrawled on it. "Be there in two hours. I have a couple of things to do first."

Chapter Forty-Three

The Gulf of Finland

In 2014 the Russian Federation and the Republic of Estonia agreed to establish a maritime boundary passing through the Gulf of Narva and into the Gulf of Finland. The boundary is a modified equidistance line with each point roughly equidistant from the respective Party's coast. The agreement, however, has not been ratified by either government due to long-standing political tensions. This failure to 'rubber stamp' the agreement has led to light security measures in good times, and heavy military presence in the bad times. The Ukraine war had now driven security back to Cold War tensions. The maritime boundary spans sixty-six nautical miles from estuary to sea and is defined by nine turning points for commercial shipping. It begins in the southeast at the land boundary terminus in the Narva River and ends in the northwest at a provisional tripoint location with Finland. Luger had entered Russia in the darkness in a silent-running rubber boat. He had studied the small fishing boats pulled up on the beach, and he had seen a Russian Navy gunboat patrolling offshore. He knew that he would not get far stealing a small day boat and motoring out to the twelve-mile limit, and he had already been told that Lake Peipus (Peipsi on the Estonian side) was heavily protected and that left the bridge crossing at the Narva Friendship Bridge, connecting the E20 European Route to the towns of Narva in Estonia to Ivangorod in Russia. However, because of heightened tensions between NATO member states and Russia over Ukraine, the Friendship Bridge was now far from friendly.

Luger continued to drive down the road parallel to the border fence. The fence was in fact two fences ten feet apart and around twenty-feet high. There were guard huts every few hundred metres with young, unenthused Russian conscripts smoking with their AK-74 assault rifles hanging from their shoulders on slings. They paced about, eyeing the traffic but otherwise seemed bored and not very vigilant. They did, however, have assault rifles and the armoured vehicles parked alongside the huts were fitted with large, belt-fed machineguns on swivel mountings. Luger supposed the more experienced soldiers were fighting in Ukraine, but nevertheless, he did not want to risk testing these men's abilities. On the Estonian side, by contrast, there was little military presence and he assumed that despite the escalation in tensions between Russia and NATO states, Estonia was not risking prodding the big, powerful Russian Bear. The Estonian's US-supplied Humvees looked far superior to their Russian counterparts, with .50 calibre Browning machineguns mounted on central turrets, and Estonian soldiers looking like they had stepped out of a US army surplus store. They were, however, less in number and parked well back from the border fence.

After another few miles the fence ended at the lake and there was a large military presence in the form of gunboats. These powerful-looking armoured boats made a lot of noise and created a great deal of wake as he watched one trundle into port and another race out at a tremendous pace. Like the armoured vehicles, they were armed with machineguns on the prow, only with dual barrels and armoured shields on each side. There were also what looked like mounted field guns on the rear, indicating that they had long-range, explosive ordinance capability. The boats were different to the British navy's equivalent – a little old-fashioned looking and their jet-black, billowing diesel exhaust fumes were raising the sea levels in the Maldives as Luger watched – but doubtlessly an effective deterrent to smuggling and attack. Luger discounted stealing a craft and making a break for it. There would be an Estonian contingent on the other side of the invisible maritime border to avoid as well.

Luger turned around in a layby and drove back the way he had come. He passed a used car showroom with a well-stocked forecourt and pulled in. There were the usual everyday models, but he was surprised to see how many of them were Fords, BMWs and Japanese makes, along with a few chunky-looking vehicles that he did not recognise but assumed were Russian and Chinese. To the side, a multi-vehicle transporter was stacked with second-hand Mercedes, Jaguars, and Audis. He supposed with sanctions in place, these vehicles had come in from devious routes, and many countries, particularly in the Middle East, India and Asia had not imposed sanctions and still continued to trade. The second-hand car market was probably never stronger than in Russia right now.

Luger smiled, the transporter giving him an idea. A crazy one, but then again, these were crazy times.

Chapter Forty-Four

Langley, Virginia

"The wig makes a big difference."

"It's not a wig," replied Caroline. "It's a three-hundred dollar cut, colour and blow dry."

Newman had to agree she looked different. In fact, she was a pretty good imitation of Georgia Scott. The chestnut brunette made Caroline look more serious, and she had paid a lot of attention to the CIA woman's make up, including the wing eyeliner. He had been used to seeing Caroline's mousey blonde hair scraped back in a practical ponytail and the transformation was impressive. She had paired the look with Scott's style of business suit and blouse. Even Caroline's breasts looked smaller. "Minimiser bra," she said, catching him looking.

Newman flushed as he looked away. "I'll engage with

security," he said. "But we're still talking thumbprint ID and swiping the card on the lanyard."

"No problem," she replied, sticking the gel imprint copy of Georgia Scott's thumbprint over her own right thumb. She checked herself in the mirror of Newman's 70's Cadillac, studying the card before looking back in the mirror. "What sort of person is she within the agency? Would she talk to the security guard, or be pissed off that he's wasting her time?"

"I guess from what I've seen, if we are engaged in conversation, she probably wouldn't break the dialogue to ask how a uniformed guard's day was going."

"Georgia Scott..." she said looking at the mirror. "How's that for accent?"

"Fucking terrible!"

"What?"

"Too harsh... that's Philly, maybe New Jersey."

"That's what she sounds like!"

"To you, maybe. Try it more softly."

"Georgia Scott... I'm good, thanks... Can I get a soda...?"

"Now you're Legally Blonde." Newman shook his head. "Jesus, we're screwed..."

"Oh, for God's sake!"

"Who's that? Emily Blunt?"

"That's my *own* bloody voice!"

Newman couldn't help but smile. This was madness, and in the midst of madness, you sometimes needed some respite with a little humour. "Try softening it just a little. Scott's a little Maryland, a little New England. She rounds her vowels, but she went to Harvard. She's not backwoods."

Caroline closed her eyes and said, "Georgia Scott... How are you today...?"

"That's pretty damn good," he said. "Engage with me,

keep the conversation going and don't stray politically. She's not a Republican, and she's not an all-out Democrat, either. Like most of us in this business, I suppose." Caroline nodded. She wasn't terribly political, either. She just spent her life clearing up the political mistakes. "What happens if we are directed towards retina scanning? It'll all be over, and they'll arrest me if I'm with you." He paused, studying the lanyard around her neck, then staring at her intensely. "Hey, your eyes aren't even the same colour as hers! Jesus, this is going to be a bust!"

Caroline took a small, plastic box out of her handbag and said, "These are copies."

"A likeness, yes. But not copies."

"No... copies." She paused, slipping one into her right eye with her fingertip. "It was tricky, but she complied in the end..."

"What the hell have you done?" he asked somewhat incredulously.

"Relax. It's not what it sounds like. It's a clear non-prescription contact lens made from a gel extracted from seaweed. When baked with an ultraviolet light the colour and shape of the eye is... I suppose... photographed, for want of a better word."

"Will it fool a retina scan?"

"Sort of," she replied. "It does and it doesn't, depending on the system and programme concerned." She paused as she fitted the second contact lens and blinked it in place. Her eyes watered and she dabbed a tissue at the corner before saying, "Fingers crossed..."

"Fingers crossed?" Newman frowned. "That's all you've got?"

Caroline scoffed. "Believe me, we've gone on less in the past."

"I know, I've seen how you guys' work..."

"I'm not even going to say *I'll take that as a compliment*. That was a pretty barbed comment." She slapped the dashboard with her hand and said in her best Georgia Scott imitation, "Right, let's do this!"

"You owe me after this," he said. "Presuming this works..."

"I'll put you on my Christmas card list."

"No, it's ok, we're not that close." Newman started the Cadillac and put the gearstick into drive. The trees were green with buds and early leaves and the sun and blue sky filled the journey with hope. Langley could look so stark in winter and early spring, and the wind could cut you in half from the Potomac River and Chesapeake Bay, but Newman knew that those days were over for another four or five months and it lifted his mood considerably, despite their intentions. "I guess I should say good luck, but considering this is nothing but an act, perhaps I should say *break a leg*." He paused, as they queued for the first gate. "Although why anyone would wish someone to break bones is beyond me. It must be a British thing. Those are the sayings that make least sense."

"That's because you need a well-rounded education to go with it," Caroline replied curtly. "Actors on the stage would wish colleagues good luck by breaking a leg, meaning to bow to applause during an encore. No applause, no encore, and that meant that your performance was poor. You only get to break firm posture with a thespian bow by stunning your audience. Hence, *to break a leg*, meant you earned your bow."

"Jesus, can't you lot just say good luck?"

"Well, don't ask me about the superstitions and phrases concerning *the Scottish play*, then..."

Die Trying

They left George Washington Memorial Parkway and at the end of the private road the guard checked the licence plate against his list using a small tablet. He then studied Newman's lanyard and parking permit and waved them through. They went through security a second time then parked in Zone B, two rows back from the director's saved spot and the chief of staff's. Both slots were occupied, meaning that the two most powerful people in the CIA were at their desks. There were many more anacronyms that Caroline was unfamiliar with, but they all had their own parking space around the director's spot, so she assumed they were extremely important. She got out of the car confidently and walked towards the entrance, turning, and waiting for Newman like he was holding her up.

"Just go on in, don't let me stop you," Newman said acidly as he walked with the aid of his cane. Caroline stared at it, noticing that it was black ebony instead of dark oak and he added, "I don't take *Mr Stabby* into the building. It would never get past the metal detectors."

Caroline nodded. She had left the .22 Ruger in the car along with her coat and carried her phone in her suit jacket pocket. She looked back at the entrance where a group of young men and women were heading inside. The extra people may well keep security busy, so she led the way with Newman hobbling to catch up with her. "It's all down to logistics," she said. "Foreign policy will dictate where the agency is deployed and in what capacity. Election years mean less bold assignments because of potential political fallout if the operation is compromised."

"Agreed," Newman said, catching on quickly, as they stepped inside the foyer. He led the way through the first metal detector. "The Middle East desk will always have its challenges, especially now that public support for Israel is waning. People are learning that Hamas is not the Palestinian people, but inescapable tyranny because of social degradation by the Israeli government." He showed his lanyard and said, "Good morning, Karl..."

"Good morning, Mr Newman," the guard replied. "How about the game?"

"What a sham," he replied as Caroline showed her tag. "The White Sox will be all over us if our batters go out like that..."

"Yankies in two weeks, depending on the Sox," the guard shook his head as Newman placed his thumb on the scanner. "No chance in hell if you ask me..."

Caroline pressed her thumb on the red coloured glass and said to Newman, "Devlin wants reports on Hamas and the IDF ceasefire. They'll break it, I expect, but we need to be ready for the fallout..."

"That goes without saying," Newman replied, patting the guard on his shoulder as they walked, and a young woman stepped up behind them to be scanned. "I'll give Devlin something after lunch." He paused as they reached the first flight of stairs and said quietly, "Just as soon as I find out who the fuck this Devlin guy is..."

To Caroline's surprise, there was another security cordon on the second floor, and they repeated the charade, this time Devlin getting the blame for something in Taiwan and rising tensions with China. Two identity card swipes and two thumbprints later and they walked out into a vast marble foyer with the Central Intelligence Logo in full technicolour in the middle of the floor. To their right, the memorial wall was marked with black stars, each one denoting a CIA officer killed in service. To the left of the wall the stars and stripes hung limply with the CIA's flag on the right side. Inscribed in perpetuity between the flags were the

Die Trying

words: *In honor of those members of the Central Intelligence Agency who gave their lives in the service of their country.*

"See the book below in the glass case?" Newman asked as they walked past. Caroline nodded and he said, "The first hundred stars have the names in there, but the other forty stars have no name attached for classified reasons."

"It's chilling," she said sombrely.

"I find it inspiring." He stopped suddenly and looked at her. "I can't do this," he told her emphatically.

"We can't stop here!" she hissed at him.

"Floor four, sector three, office seven..."

"Don't do this..." her glare softening as she pleaded.

Newman closed his eyes, then glanced back at the memorial wall. "I have friends up there," he said.

Caroline stared at him, but she could see that it was too late. Newman was already walking away, the brass tip of his ebony cane tapping on the marble. Caroline turned around and walked confidently across the foyer and took the stairwell. The sides were glass supported by stainless steel frames, and the treads were the same marble as the foyer. Her heart was racing as she took the stairs – not wanting to risk conversation in the confines of a lift – and she could feel her legs turning to jelly as she reached the fourth floor. A few calming breaths soothed her, but she was already searching for sector three as she walked the wide corridor. Sector three loomed ahead, partitioned by double glass doors and a retina scan and keypad to the right side. It was now or never, all or nothing. She had come too far and right now, the thought of making Scott talk by threatening the woman's children seemed the more favourable option. But she had decency at her core, and children was a line she would not cross. In lieu of a husband that the woman loved and who didn't cheat, this had seemed the best option, especially as she already knew Scott to be a woman who would not crack until too many lines of morality had been crossed.

"Now we see how good you really are, Neil," she said under her breath as she bent down and closed her left eye, leaving her right eye wide open to be scanned. Ramsay had written the programme and the best optologist in Harley Street had developed the gel and ultraviolet light method to indelibly capture the image of the eye. However, testing was one thing, and using the method for real when her life depended on it was quite another. Especially as the French *Carte des Yeux* system had unequivocally detected data corruption.

The light was bright red, and she was aware of a black line first moving across her vision laterally, and then horizontally. The red light flicked off and she straightened up, the door hushing open and her stomach turning cartwheels as she felt the elation flush through her. Office number seven was on her right and the nameplate simply read: Georgia Scott. Caroline tried the door, and it clicked open. The office was a twelve-by-fifteen-foot box without a window. There was a printer, computer console and a fax machine just in case someone from 1998 tried to get in touch. A large, flat-screen TV was fixed to the wall opposite Scott's desk, and filing cabinets and box files contained secrets that even the CIA director would know nothing about. And he probably preferred it that way.

An initial search led to nothing, and she stood back and started to think outside the box. She looked through some of the box files, then underneath the printer and in the paper tray of the printer and fax machine. Caroline turned her attention to the cabinet behind the desk. There were framed photographs of Georgia Scott with various dignitaries – some that Caroline recognised, but many that she did not – and some photographs of her in the field. Caroline recognised Camp Bastian and Kandahar from her own time there in army intelligence. There were trophies for marksmanship with the FBI and two commendations. One for bravery and one with no citation at all. The notion grated on Caroline. There but for circumstance, went a woman she could have embraced their similarities, or been pleased to work with. They could even have become friends.

Caroline rifled through the books. Many of them were self-improvement books, or military history. Some were accounts of former FBI and CIA intelligence officers. She wondered whether they had been gifts from people she had worked with, or if she had been compelled to purchase and look for inaccuracies, plausibility, or downright lies. After ten minutes of rifling the shelves, she found that one of the books fell open at a certain page. She noted the page number, closed it, and opened it a second time. Success. She scan-read the two pages but found nothing. She left the book open and picked up each book, watching the pages fall open. There were marks on the pages underneath certain words. Caroline took a picture of the marks and zoomed in on the phone. It was the sort of grime that built up on an office worker's fingers throughout the day – ink, coffee, makeup, the otherwise unnoticeable grease from one's hair – and it had left a fingerprint underneath the word. Caroline wasted no time checking all the books where the pages fell open. She photographed the marks or ink smudges and felt somewhat overwhelmed as she realised that it was needle in haystack stuff. But she had gone on less to work with in the past. She had scoured shredded papers in Afghanistan and painstakingly overseen the strands put back together to form a paper trail that helped lead to top Al Qaeda leaders. She checked her watch and wondered if she would get out of the compound on foot. She had seen people cycling into the carpark, so not everyone arrived by car, which was unusual for America. When she was sure that the bookshelf offered no more clues, she checked behind the picture frames and citations. Nothing. She studied the map and the key and coordinates. There were similar finger smudges and she photographed these and looked out for pin marks, of which there were seven and she photographed these also. Deciding enough was enough, she pocketed her phone and let herself out.

At the end of the corridor, she saw a group of men and women gathered around a water cooler and she took out the phone as she walked and become engrossed in an imaginary conversation.

"Georgia...!" a woman called after her.

Caroline held up a hand and said, "This can't wait... I'll be back in a few minutes..." without looking at the woman and skipped down the stairs with lots of *'a-ha's* and *um's* and a heartfelt *right away, sir'* into her phone, and felt a wave of adrenalin rush through her. She placed her phone on the conveyer as she walked through the metal detector, then swiped the phone and continued her imaginary conversation, suddenly struggling with what to say. She started to nod and say, 'yes, sir' a lot. Once down the stairs to the first foyer she regained some composure and glided through security, deciding to wait directly outside in view of the security guards for a full five minutes, pacing around pensively and nodding occasionally, before striding off towards the carpark. Newman's old Cadillac had gone, and she barely faltered as she walked a path, eventually catching up with a man and a woman heading the same way on the footpath beside the private road. Her heart skipped a beat at the main gate when she saw for the first time that one of the guards carried an assault rifle and watched her carefully, but she walked straight past, and she assumed that perhaps he had found her attractive enough for his stare to linger. The couple turned around and headed back, lighting cigarettes, and talking animatedly. She was on her own now and knew that even though she had not had a choice, she had done what many British did in the US and underestimated the sheer scale and size of the place. She was essentially in the middle of nowhere with a massive walk ahead of her, with the George Washington Memorial Highway in the distance and looking like an impossible walk with multiple lanes of heavy goods vehicles and cars racing past.

Newman's red and white Cadillac pulled in at the end of the private road and he got out and waved at her. The guard practically ignored her as she walked beside the barrier and got inside the classic saloon. She hated to admit it, but she was pleased to see him.

"Sorry, I just couldn't do it," he said, slipping the gearstick into drive. The large, but essentially underpowered engine purred into life, and they took off lazily and accelerated smoothly onto the highway.

"I get it," she replied. She wouldn't have willingly acted against her own service either. She was just pleased that Newman had gone so far. "The memorial wall was quite special," she admitted. "Thank you for getting me as far as you did."

Newman nodded. "So, what now?"

"I'm going to appeal to Georgia Scott's better nature. If she has none, then I know that Ramsay will be able to run the numbers and names that I have collected against her phone and come up with something."

"Where is she?" Newman said sombrely.

"Safe."

"That's not good enough." He paused. "You need an exit strategy, and you need to release her. And then there's the conundrum that she may well decide to screw you over to a larger, more savage degree. You may end up worse off than you were when you came here."

"That's a chance I have to take," she replied.

"So, tell me where she is."

"I can't do that."

Newman pulled off the highway and they entered Langley's commercial centre from a long, curving slip road. "I need to know if she is safe and well," he said.

They stopped for a red light and Caroline opened the door and slipped out of the car without a word. Newman opened his door, the light flicking to green and the drivers behind him taking no time at all to sound their horns. When he looked for Caroline, he saw her disappearing down an alleyway between a coffee house and a sandwich store on the other side of the road. The horns kept sounding and drowning out a stream of expletives as he closed his door in annoyance and surged ahead at the lights.

Chapter Forty-Five

Bordeaux

King was struggling for a plan. He was being hunted, but short of knowing the person behind the contract, he had no way of knowing who was after him, or where the next threat was coming from. He had been reactionary from day one, and he had been low on resources. He knew that he was being tracked by facial recognition software, and there was little he could have done about that, especially as that same software would recognise everything from his height and build to his gait. He had not suspected identification software until it was too late, and he imagined that he already had a hostile combing the city for him. But what he *could* do, was make a stand. He could use the software to drop a few breadcrumbs for his would-be killers, and if he could find somewhere suitable, with a strategic advantage, then he could fight until the fighting was done.

He had paid for another night, even though he was leaving. In his experience it always paid to leave false trails, even though assassins had been onto him from that day in Cadiz. He had made the call, deliberating whether he should, but he needed some breathing space and he needed help. Ramsay had curtly said that he would *see what he could do*, but it had not been a categorical no. King knew that help would come, and that meant that he could finally see past the trees. An hour later King checked his email to find the draft folder had been edited. This simply meant that Ramsay had used it to reply, without sending anything into the ether. Ramsay had access to all the team's email accounts – specifically a chosen account for this reason – and communication was completely secure, just as long as nobody else had the login details. King had opened the email and studied the pictures and details. An Airbnb gite near the town of Lacanau on the west coast of France. Not far from Bordeaux, and certainly a scenic and secluded drive through the forests, but also susceptible to an ambush if they got ahead of him. The gite sat atop a small hill with a church on a hill opposite and a small village sprawling over a hill a mile distant. There were trees and fields all around the property. Judging by the photographs it had been midsummer when the brochure had been put together because the pool was playing host to two splashing children and the fields were dotted with large, round haybales and the cut grass looked scorched by the sun. King checked the map and saw where he could get onto the main toll road enough to flag his image on whatever software Georgia Scott was running through the French traffic control system.

King left Bordeaux by the south of the city and made his way northwest into the countryside. The Range Rover was a powerful V8 model and made swift work of France's superb road surface. King sat back with a pair of Tom Ford sunglasses he'd found in the glovebox and felt the sun warm his face as he drove the forest road. Following the afternoon sun, he had it with him for the next hour of so. He glanced behind him, satisfied that the Renault he had picked up earlier that morning in central Bordeaux was still with him. He had taken the morning to make himself known. Walking several streets before driving and then alighting the vehicle near traffic control systems, picking up a few groceries in various supermarkets – always the larger ones with CCTV systems – and using public carparks, returning after he had spent thirty or more minutes on the streets. He carried the Sig P225 9mm tucked into his waistband with his shirt tail covering the weapon, he also stopped by at a tobacconist and bought a sizeable folding knife with a locking blade. He had then dropped into a culinary store and bought a butane, self-igniting blow torch.

King pulled into a smalling filling station and stretched as he got out, keeping an eye out for the Renault, which crawled past and accelerated when they noticed King watching them. Two men, both around thirty and with hard eyes and chiselled features. For some reason, or perhaps just assumption, he thought them to be French and ex-forces. He had worked with the French Foreign Legion in the past, and the two men reminded him of the men whom he had worked with in Tangiers. As usual, King had parked facing outwards with the front wheels straightened so that he could make a quick departure if necessary.

King did not waste his money on fuel. He would ditch the Range Rover and pick up another vehicle in Lacanau, most likely beside the ocean in this resort so famed for surfing and kitesurfing. Surfers were still haphazard with their vehicle security, and he would still bet that half of the surfers parked there had their keys stashed under the wheel arch. Instead, he bought some water and a *pain au chocolat* and made sure that he walked unhurriedly back to the Range Rover. Changing the vehicle would be a risk now that he had flushed out his would-be killers, but he had to make it believable. He would soon make himself visible again, but only when the time was right. Keeping the Range Rover could get the attention of the police, even though he had swapped the number plates with a similar year, a check on *l'ordinateur de la police nationale*, the French equivalent of the PNC would show the plates as not matching the vehicle and further checks would find a Range Rover matching the description reported as stolen in Bordeaux.

King got back inside the Range Rover and headed west. The forests were thick with tall pine trees and vast swathes had been cut and gravelled to create firebreaks every mile or so, the firebreaks at least a hundred metres wide. He knew from experience that the pine forests on this stretch of coastline could become oppressively hot in the summer months, and fires could be easily sparked by some broken glass or piles of forest litter and leaf debris that could smoulder and spontaneously combust. It was beside one of these firebreaks that the Renault had pulled in and waited for him. King instinctively gripped the butt of the 9mm pistol which he had slipped into the door pocket. Part of him wanted to smash into them and finish the two men right there and then, but he needed to be certain. These men could be French intelligence agents or police detectives who were after King for any number of transgressions, and although he would never go quietly, he wasn't about to kill innocent law enforcement officers. No, he needed more than suspicion, and the only way he could get that was to present himself as a target.

Chapter Forty-Six

Langley, Virginia

Caroline had slipped into a quiet booth of a coffee house and used the Wi-Fi to email the photographs to Ramsay, along with the MSISDN – the unique data and IP address - of Georgia Scott's phone from which he would lift the call list data. Once the sequencing of numbers had been run through – always a zero at the start, followed by sevens and then the designated pattern codes used by European mobile phone networks, Ramsay was confident that he could find matches with the numbers in Scott's phone account's history. Scott had deleted her call lists, but Ramsay had not been phased by this in his email, as data could never truly be wiped.

The big GMC pulled up outside and Caroline got out of the booth and left enough for her coffee plus tip. She checked her phone instinctively, but it had only been an hour since she had sent Ramsay the information.

"How did that go, then?" asked Big Dave. "You're still alive, so it either worked or you didn't go ahead with it."

"It worked." She leaned back in the comfortable leather seat and closed her eyes. "Jesus, I need a drink."

"I expect Georgia Scott will need one by now." He paused. "And not a gin. Water would be my best bet..."

Caroline flushed red. She hadn't meant to be so flippant, and with Big Dave reminding her that the woman was strapped to a chair with no food, water – or even a way to go to the toilet – she felt appalled at herself. She checked her watch and grimaced. "Take me right there," she said. "Wait, let's find a deli and get a sandwich and some water."

"Yeah, I could do with something to eat."

"For her..."

Big Dave shrugged. "Supposing Neil gets something off her phone, what's the exit strategy?"

"I'm working on it."

"Because she could simply offer a new contract."

"You think I don't know that?" she snapped.

"Neil said to come here and assist you, I thought that there was more of a plan than this."

"The plan was getting her to terminate the contract," she replied, her tone softening. "I wasn't to know that her husband was cheating on her. He was to be my leverage. I was never going to *harm* her children."

"She got to where she is by not being nice. She got to where she is by lying and deceiving people." Big Dave paused. "What's to say she isn't lying? She could have just made that up about her husband to throw you off."

Caroline stared straight ahead. She was too close to this, too invested. A contract on King was a contract on her. This

Die Trying

was the reason you never got involved sexually or emotionally in this game. She had lost her fiancé, Peter Redwood to a suicide bomber she had been following, and she should have learned then. She had vowed never to get involved with someone she worked with ever again. Was her relationship with King clouding her judgement? The only answer to that was a resounding yes. Of course, Georgia Scott could have been lying about her husband. She had certainly upped the ante when both she and King had sent Scott a message through him. The lie had rolled right off her tongue and Caroline had merely accepted it when she should have tied *him* to a chair and beat the living hell out of him in front of her eyes. She would have soon got the truth then. She had underestimated her enemy, and now she was far more embroiled in this than she had ever intended.

Caroline's phone chimed and she studied the screen. Ramsay had a couple of hits on the number sequencing and information on the numbers where Scott's messages had been sent. She looked up as Big Dave pulled into the side of the road next to a deli.

"Look, a pound of sliced pastrami in a sandwich."

"Scott doesn't look like she'd eat a pound of beef in one sitting. Or in one month, to be fair."

"For me," he replied indignantly.

"Just get her a ham and cheese sandwich and a couple bottles of water," she said offhandedly as she studied her phone. Another text from Ramsay and another hit on a number. There were also two numbers that Ramsay said had been attributed to attempts on King's life in L'Albir, Spain before the end of their last assignment. This was great news, because it not only showed who had been taken out, but who still posed a threat, and if Ramsay's aggressive malware did its job, then the location of would-be assassins when their phones connected to a phone service.

Caroline watched the traffic as she waited. She kept an eye on the mirror and tell-tale signs of someone watching them, but the traffic was moving freely, and she did not spot anyone or anything suspicious. Big Dave's comment had irked her, but she was not annoyed with him; merely with herself. Newman had pointed out the obvious long before her teammate had. She had made the mistake of playing nice in a dirty game. She did not really know why she had, but it had simply boiled down to Georgia Scott's children, and to her annoyance, the American had known that her children would be her trump card. She had already taken her husband off the table with nothing more complicated than a school-girl's lie. It had rolled off her tongue so easily, and Caroline had believed it. Even tied to a chair in a lockup, Georgia Scott had got the better of her. Caroline had taken a tremendous risk in raiding Scott's office, and even if Ramsay discovered every possible phone number and Caroline called off all the contracts on Scott's behalf, both her and King would always be looking over their shoulders waiting for Georgia Scott to renew the contracts on their heads. And simply because she could, and there wasn't a damned thing that MI5 could do about it.

"I got you a grilled cheese," said Big Dave as he got back behind the wheel.

"A grilled cheese what?"

"Sandwich. They call a toasted cheese sandwich a *grilled cheese* out here. they don't even use the word sandwich" He handed her two paper bags and put the bottles of water in the cup holders.

"And what in God's name do they call that?" she asked, looking at the meal for four in his hand.

Die Trying

"A Ruben," he replied. "It's a grilled Swiss cheese sandwich with corned beef, sauerkraut, and Russian dressing and sandwiched between rye bread." He paused. "And it's not corned beef like we know it, it's proper salted brisket. Not the tinned crap from Argentina."

"Good luck eating that while we drive..." she said as Big Dave pulled out into the light traffic, his great right paw wrapped around the sandwich and the greaseproof paper wrapping it. The automatic gearbox changed up through the gears and he grinned as he took a bite. "Okay, so you're well-practised," she conceded.

They finished their sandwiches at the same time, despite Big Dave's being three times the size as hers and the fact that he was multi-tasking. The drive to Baltimore took a little under an hour, and another fifteen-minutes to get to the run-down part of town where they had chosen the lock-up. The Francis Scott Key Bridge lay twisted and broken across the river, work platforms and tugs working amid the mess in the shipping lane. Caroline looked at the timber-clad houses as they drove past. Small grassy patches at the front of uniformed and perfectly square homes with stars and stripes flags hanging out front. An austere, colourless, and largely poverty-stricken part of the city that looked no different from parts of Philadelphia, New Jersey, and Maryland. She wondered when the scenery changed, most likely as far south as Florida or as north as Connecticut. The Eastern Seaboard was not her favourite part of the United States.

Another two messages came in and Caroline studied them. "Well, he's either wrong, or a bloody genius."

"Ramsay?" Big Dave asked.

"Yes."

"He's smart," he said. "I've never had reason to doubt him."

"I agree." She paused, studying the numbers that were now listed in front of her. A text from Georgia Scott's phone cancelling the contract could mean that this would all be over. Or was she really naive enough to believe that? She had begun to realise that this may never be over. "He's more suited to a desk, though."

Big Dave shook his head. "No, I've seen him front and centre enough times." He paused, looking at the screen of her phone. "Ramsay has a lot of fight in him. I don't know anybody who would have so quickly overcome the barrier of paralysis, the pain, the life adjustment... the sheer bloody challenge that he has had. He only came back to work because MI5 was in a compromised state, and he knew that he was needed. He saw that there was a challenge ahead, and only sacrifice and commitment would put things right."

Caroline nodded, looking at the lock-up door across the rutted track. She had heard Big Dave's take on Ramsay, but she was blinkered, distracted. She was so close now. She copied and pasted and sent the numbers to Georgia Scott's phone, then after composing a short message, she spent the next few minutes sending the message to seven contacts, and just to be sure, she sent the same message to the numbers already deemed inactive because of King's and Rashid's actions. All she could do now was hope that the assassins did not take too long to switch their phones back on, and that they believed the message and obeyed the order. "That's it," she said. "Only time will tell..."

"No, it's circumstance," said Big Dave. "Time has nothing to do with it."

Caroline frowned. "It's done," she said adamantly.

Big Dave took a bottle of water out of the cupholder and

opened it. He drank most of it down thirstily, then opened the sandwich they had bought for Georgia Scott and took a bite out of it as Caroline frowned at him. "You'd better go and see her," he said, handing her the .22 Ruger, then taking another bite of the sandwich. "A change in circumstance is the only way this will ever truly be over for both you and King." He paused. "Sacrifice and commitment is the only way you're going to put this thing right."

Caroline stared at the gun in her hand. The bulbous suppressor gave it a purposeful look, and that look could not be doubted. She knew that the big Fijian was right, and the realisation was damning. She could feel a twist in her gut, and she wiped the corner of her eyes where tears had started to form. She didn't know if Big Dave had noticed, but she didn't care. She opened the door, tucked the weapon under the flap of her suit jacket and closed the door behind her. The walk across the rutted track felt longer than was possible, and she felt herself slowing down with the dread inside her infecting her limbs. Unlocking the padlock, she glanced back at the vehicle, but the tinted glass masked Big Dave from view. Caroline looked back at the open door then stepped into the darkness. She closed the door behind her, allowing her eyes to grow accustomed to the gloom. The gun felt heavy in her hand, but it was the weight of emotion she felt most as her hand tightened on the hard, plastic grips, her finger slowly, irreversibly taking up tension on the trigger.

Chapter Forty-Seven

Lacanau, France

King had left the Range Rover on the seafront and helped himself to a Volkswagen Passat in a carpark used primarily by surfers and kite-boarders. He had found the keys under the driver's side front wheel arch, its owner oblivious to the theft as he surfed the pristinely clean beach break. It was an older car but had a powerful engine which had surprised him on the long stretch out of the seaside town. Lacanau was a town a few miles from the coast, with Lacanau-Océan, being the town on the seafront, although both were referred to as the same. Between the two towns, pine forests enveloped hidden campsites and cabin resorts all the way to the lake, which was one of France's largest freshwater lakes and a busy tourist area for water sports, parascending and even commercial fishing for perch and pike, and small crayfish.

Die Trying

Parking facing outwards he had walked around the property and inspected its security features, which were next to none. A hundred metres of private drive connected it to a side road that led from a small village and to a clearing in the forest that had been turned into a picnic area with swings, picnic tables and some rather dubious-looking toilets. There were signs everywhere against barbeques and fires with hefty fines imposed if ignored. King had cursed at first. Ramsay had chosen a remote property with only one escape route by road. But then, King had seen the logic, because it meant only one escape route for the men who were after him, and King would have to see what he could do about that.

He had made sure that the two men had seen him abandon the Range Rover, and he had taken the time to drive right past them in the Volkswagen. He had lost them in the forest, and they had not been on his tail when he arrived at the gite. He couldn't make it too easy for them.

The gite itself was large and spacious with high ceilings, whitewashed walls, and slate floors. Upstairs old, worn wooden floorboards meant that simply walking from A to B was a creaky, noisy affair. Good for detecting enemy movement; bad for moving stealthily oneself. The windows were narrow and shuttered and when he opened them the bars in place made the bedrooms death traps for escape. He checked downstairs and it was the same story. The house was secure against burglars from the outside, but inescapable from the inside. Certainly, somewhere you would not want to be if a fire broke out. There were two doors. One at the front and one at the back, and both were solid oak with a Z of wooden planks reinforcing them on the inside, with more than a hundred large doornails hammered in from the front. Nobody was kicking in these doors anytime soon.

King found the log store and tool shed at the back of the house. He helped himself to what he would need and crossed the lawn into the forest and headed for the quiet forest road, and the only route of escape.

Chapter Forty-Eight

The Russian border with Estonia

He had chosen the spot well. With a sentry hut a hundred metres to the north and another two hundred metres to the south on the shore of the lake, he had three hundred metres of fence to choose from, with a clear area the other side. The Estonian border guards were barely visible to the north with a single Humvee parked way back from the fence and a patrol boat moored at the shore of the lake. The Estonians had likely been warned by fellow NATO member states about the escalation in tensions, despite the Russians doing exactly that. However, the security escalation seemed to be on the surface only. Most Russian infantry troops were now issued with the AK-12 assault rifle, but these guards were all equipped with AK-74 rifles, and some of them looked to be so worn that they could well have been first issued in 1974. The uniforms were old, too. Camouflage had moved on since the Soviet Union were occupying Afghanistan, but it looked like the Russian Federation was using up its surplus stock on these guards, which indicated to Luger that they were throwing countless resources at the war in Ukraine and the rest of the military were suffering because of it. He made a note to file a report on this to Ramsay, should he manage to return.

Luger had bought the motorcycle from a nearby dealer. For what he planned, he did not want to steal an uninsured bike from a hard-working Russian and leave it in no doubt worse condition than he found it. He still had to steal a vehicle and needed to be quite specific on that. The motorcycle had been left parked near the border behind a low wall near some wheelie bins that looked to have missed collection for a few months. It wasn't the sort of area someone would happen across easily.

The trouble now, was timing. Timing was everything.

Chapter Forty-Nine

The River House, London

Devonshire sipped from his glass of single malt whisky and watched the lights of London flickering across the Thames. He looked up as Harriet sat down at the chair next to him. They were seated at four and eight o'clock, with the lights at twelve. She did not look at him as he spoke.

"Ramsay's errand boy didn't get captured," said Devonshire. "Not yet at least."

"So, Ivan *is* clean?" she asked quizzically. She had been the one to bring concerns of a mole inside the Russian machine to Devonshire.

"We're not entirely sure," Devonshire replied.

"Meaning?" she asked hopefully before sipping her gin and tonic.

"There was a large police and FSB presence in the area.

Our police informant relayed that the FSB was alerted to an enemy agent suspected in the area."

"So, Ivan *did* inform the authorities, at least?"

"It looks that way, so in that respect, it was a success." Devonshire sipped some of his Scotch and sighed. "But the MI5 officer has not been found."

Harriet felt a flutter inside her. Partly at the recollection of their time together in Luger's flat, and partly because the situation was about to escalate. "He twigged?"

"Or someone else did." Devonshire looked at her. "You didn't tip him off, did you?"

"Of course not!" she snapped. She had wrestled with her fling with Luger, not entirely sure that he was going to be the MI5 officer who made the trip, not until Carter had informed them from Estonia. Carter was a washout, a disgraced Special Branch officer turned security guard and police adviser in a post he had not wanted with little chance of getting back to London. It had been the only way for him to keep his pension. Ramsay had requested assistance from the British embassy and Carter had been sent. Harriet had suspected that they would use Luger, but once it was confirmed she had felt conflicted. Her only recourse had been to double down and get behind her boss.

Devonshire shrugged. "One had to ask..."

Harriet sipped her drink, more for a distraction than to slake her thirst. If Devonshire did not know who tipped off Jack Luger, then he was in the dark as much as she was. But someone had. Someone had worked out MI6's apparent generosity in sharing information, and that could only have been Neil Ramsay, because the rest of MI5 was screwing down their security leaks and being supervised by MI6. And if Ramsay suspected MI6 of sabotage, then they would be ready for them next time. Devonshire had spoken many times in hushed conversations about taking control of MI5 and creating a new combined intelligence service with MI6 at the helm, and now their sister service would be onto the fact. What had been intended as a political embarrassment for MI5's new operations unit had just backfired.

"And what about Ivan?" Harriet asked. "If he tipped off the FSB and met Jack Luger at the rendezvous point, then how in the hell did Luger get away?" The question stung as she heard the callousness of her own words, and she could not help secretly feeling elated that the young MI5 officer had got away.

"Ivan was discovered in the woods with a single bullet wound to the head. The police found his car near the border." Devonshire paused. "One can't help feeling pleased that MI5 carried out our mole hunt for us. But it *is* a double-edged sword. We now have a situation where the newest offshoot group in British intelligence now know that we used them and were willing the life of one of their intelligence officers."

Harriet drained her glass and looked for the waiter to catch his eye. When he came over, she asked for another gin and tonic and a double single malt for Devonshire. She had learned to buy her share of rounds and her large monthly bar tab had not hurt her career ladder. "So, Jack Luger is back in Estonia?"

Devonshire shook his head. "Who knows? Carter hasn't heard anything, but why would he? The man would simply fly out or perhaps take a flight out of Lithuania." He paused. "He wouldn't need any help from the embassy, and he will have probably worked out that Carter should not be trusted, because to get his career back on track, Carter let us know that MI5 were colouring outside the lines again."

Harriet nodded. "Or there could be another result from this..."

Devonshire looked at her and frowned. The drinks arrived and he waited until the waiter was on his way back to the bar, briefly wondering how many nuggets of information the man held. He made a note to tighten security and perhaps suggest a new turnover of staff. "And what would that be?"

Harriet took a sip of her gin and tonic. The second one always tasted better. "We willingly shared information that we had acquired with the Security Service, or rather, their off-shoot band of rebels. You and I both know that our goal was to see them shut down, but they can only speculate on that matter." She paused, swilling the ice in her glass, and staring thoughtfully through it towards the lights on the other side of the river. "They used an embassy asset. That had nothing to do with us, whatsoever."

"Indeed."

"And if that asset turned out to be dirty?"

Devonshire leaned forward attentively, glass in hand. "Then we blame him?"

"The best accusations are those left unsaid," she smiled. "We control the narrative. Carter informed his contact, who he knew to be a double agent." She sipped some more of her drink and said, "We could thank MI5 for flushing out a double agent in our own embassy, and Ivan, who turned out to be a triple agent we thought we had installed effectively into Russian organised crime. We'd only have a little bit of egg on our face for that, and it would soon be forgotten. MI5 would come out of it cleanly, maybe have their wings clipped, but at least we avoid an all-out battle with the Security Service and this off-shoot clearly operating beyond its remit."

"And Carter?" Devonshire asked, then added, "I mean, his testimony would turn that sequence and version of events on its head."

Harriet shrugged. "Accidents *do* happen..."

Chapter Fifty

Lacanau, France

King had made some preparations and walked around the property as he headed back to the house. The tool shed had contained gardening tools, weedkiller, buckets and petrol for the strimmer and mower. The maintenance man mixed up his own two-stroke fuel, swimming pool chlorine and PH adjuster, and weedkiller mix using plastic containers and King had made use of these, too. There had been rope, twine and matches on the shelves, and the kitchen had provided him with bleach and dishwasher salt. Mixed in various combinations there was more than enough for a decent firework display, and with twine soaked in sugar and white spirit he had useable fuses. Nails and screws were a staple shrapnel of the bombmaker, and King had found a good lighter in the chiminea barbeque, along with some burned charcoal which when pounded into a powder with some rust he had scraped from a rusted metal gate, and some borax he had found in the tool shed, made a decent gunpowder.

He had used a handsaw and hatchet to trim branches and fell two small pine trees, and he had hacked off the branches and used the rope and some complicated knots to lift and hold the trimmed trees in place with the addition of wooden pegs he had whittled. All the while, he looked about himself, but the men never showed themselves.

Night fell and King ate what was left of his cheese baguette and drank plenty of water. Upstairs, the light remained on in the master bedroom, but the rest of the house was unlit, King's eyes slowly adjusting to the gloom. He was seated at the kitchen table with the Sig Sauer 9mm pistol in front of him next to the old, worn fishing tackle bag he had found inside the shed. Inside the bag were seven IEDs or Improvised Explosive Devices. They were nasty little pint pots of chemical explosive and gunpowder with screws and nails heavily sealed with tape, and King expected that despite the archaic fuses, would be every bit as lethal as British L109A1 hand grenades.

King checked his watch, then stood up and slung the bag over his shoulder and tucked the pistol into his waistband. He lifted the two petrol cans onto the kitchen table and unscrewed the caps then went back outside, his eyes straining against the gloom for any signs of lights in the forest. Nothing. He walked around the rear aspect of the house and kept in the lee of the building while he studied the land towards the village. The church spire was visible in the moonlight. King made his way into the forest and slipped under the hide he had made earlier. A simple trellis of pine branches lashed together with twine. Behind him, he had made a rudimentary alarm system by taking lengths of hessian gardening twine and stringing them around the trees to create a perimeter to his hide. At the end of the trellis nearest him he had attached a few of the plastic pots with some gravel inside. Enough to hear if the line was stepped on or walked into but not as obvious as tin cans for his enemy to realise that they had walked into a trap.

From his hide, he had a good view of the house and the two most likely sides that his enemy would come from. All he could do now was wait.

Chapter Fifty-One

The Russian border with Estonia

Luger was breathing hard. He had been running for twenty minutes, desperate to get back to the motorcycle, but the chase had taken him off course and now that the automatic gunfire had ceased, he could only now hear the movement of troops behind him and to his right. Which forced him to move to his left, and that was back towards the border and further from the motorbike and further from his plan. Timing was crucial, because the police were already at the vehicle transporter that he had stolen and parked into position and although he had discarded the keys, they would soon move it from the fence once they had enough armoured vehicles in place.

A chorus of barking dogs pierced the night, their voices carrying in the stillness. Sounds often seemed louder or nearer at night than they did in daytime. The ambient background noise of the day was something everyone lived with but barely noticed. He clutched the pistol firmly, but he knew that if it came down to a shootout against trained soldiers with automatic weapons he would be done for. He would always need surprise on his side and to pick up a fallen weapon from the first person he shot. It bothered him that until tonight, he had never killed in cold blood before. He had been forced into a gun battle on his last mission, but it had been a chaotic affair with bullets flying everywhere and if he had not joined the melee then he would have certainly died. Tonight though, had been an order. However, after seeing the roadblock in the darkness he knew that in killing Ivan he had escaped death, or perhaps a fate so much worse than. The Russian intelligence services did not play nice. They beat people to death in their interrogation cells, denied them legal representation and couldn't care less what the world's media said about it. Often inviting the media to film trials in a kangaroo court. And then, when they'd finished with you, they either shot you whilst trying to escape, or you met with an accident. And if the world's media did not agree with the cause, then the Russian government wouldn't care anyway. Jack Luger was under no illusion that Ramsay's text had alerted him, and the single bullet he had fired into the man's skull had saved him.

There were shouts behind him and he realised that the soldiers had come across a patch of mud that he had gone through. He had known at the time that the fresh footprints would give him away, but he hadn't had the time to cover his tracks. He veered to his left and started back through the alleyways. He was aware that he was heading back towards the soldiers and police, but unless they had spread out and broken to their left after seeing the clear set of tracks, then he would pass close to them, and may even miss them. He kept a good grip on the pistol but kept it down by his leg so that his silhouette would not show him holding a gun, and he jogged along the walls, pausing each time before entering the next grid of alleyways. He had barely made it across the third alleyway when a shout went out, followed by a burst of automatic gunfire. Windows smashed and concrete splintered off the unfinished walls and Luger sprinted for his life. The gunfire continued with no regard for the resident's safety, and he felt masonry debris shower over his back. Luger took the right-angle bend so quickly that he slipped and fell, sprawling in the mud. He clawed himself up and continued to run, darting left into the next alleyway, but skidding to a halt as he saw two soldiers running towards him. He turned and ran, gunfire erupting behind him, and as he darted around the corner of the next building he dropped to the ground and rolled onto his stomach, aiming the pistol in front of him. Two seconds later both soldiers ran into his sights. He fired two shots at one, and one shot at the other who was by now nearer to him. The two soldiers fell, the last man he'd shot landing just a metre from him, eyes wide and disbelieving, a gaping bullet hole in his forehead. Luger snatched one of the rifles off the muddy ground and tucked the Makarov into his waistband as he ran, but it fell out and clattered to the ground a few strides later. He cursed but did not stop as he sprinted into another alleyway, trying to keep a tab on how many turns he had made, and how far he had come since the initial contact. He could hear the commotion behind him, heard gunshots in the distance. Scared soldiers or police officers shooting first and asking questions later. Lights were flicking on in the buildings all around him and dogs were barking incessantly. Luger veered to his left as he left the settlement and ran into the trees. He caught glimpses of the road a hundred metres to his right, briefly lit by the lights of traffic, but after a few minutes the vehicles stopped coming and he realised that the police or military must have put up a roadblock already. Time was running out.

Luger smelled the rubbish before he saw it. As he approached, he could see the over-piled bags of rotting waste and the overflowing wheelie bins. The smell was intolerable, and he knew that would have played to his advantage. Nobody would ever choose to go near the bins. The refuse collectors clearly left them alone. He found the motorcycle where he'd left it, beside a low wall with some plastic sheeting that smelled every bit as bad as the rubbish pile covering it. He pulled the sheet away and walked the machine out from the wall and away from the putrid, fetid stench of abandoned waste. The motorcycle was an old Suzuki Bandit 1200 that its previous owner had cherished but customised the machine with questionable taste. The bike was now a 'street fighter' with less dials, tiny lights and indicators, short handlebars mounted low and a cannon for an exhaust pipe. All traces of fairing had been removed and made the already large engine look huge nestled into its tiny frame.

Luger ditched the rifle because it would only get in his way now. The ignition whined briefly, and the engine fired into life. The engine was larger than those found in most small hatchbacks and tuned for acceleration, and when he pressed the gear selector down with the ball of his left foot and slowly released the clutch with his left hand, the machine surged forward on the merest twist of throttle in his right hand. He rode through the woods with his feet near the ground to prevent him from slipping on the mud and eased on some more power and lightly touched the clutch lever to control his speed, then when he eased out of the trees and onto the road, he accelerated and eased the gear selector up through neutral and into second gear. A twist of the throttle and he switched up two more gears and saw a hundred miles per hour on the miniaturised odometer. Ahead of him, a sea of red taillights indicated the start of the roadblock. All for a stolen vehicle transporter that had been abandoned butted right up to the border with Estonia.

Luger overtook the stationary vehicles, his eyes on the two police vehicles blocking the road. He already had the attention of one of the police officers, who held up his left hand, his right on the butt of his holstered pistol. He accelerated towards him, and the officer was swiftly joined by another who was already aiming his pistol at the oncoming motorcycle and rider. Luger hammered on the front brake and downshifted. He dropped his left foot to the ground in a scrambler turn and pulled between two vehicles and onto the grass verge. The heavy motorcycle was difficult to control as the slick road tyres slipped on the mud and wet grass, and he kept the motorcycle in second gear as he headed into the trees. Gunshots rang out behind him, but he was soon out of pistol range and weaving through the cover of the trees. He veered to the right and could finally see the vehicle transporter. Another two police vehicles blocked the road from the south and military armoured transport vehicles were backing towards the transporter with two men preparing a pair of tow ropes. It was now or never. Luger accelerated and went up through the gears. He knew nothing about jumping a motorbike, but he did know that Bud Ekins, the Hollywood stuntman who famously jumped the fence for Steve McQueen in the famous Great Escape scene, took off at thirty miles per hour. Luger was about to jump a twenty-foot-high fence that was ten feet wide. The vehicle transporter was twenty-feet high and five feet from the fence. As he crossed the verge and hit the tarmac at thirty miles per hour, he decided to put on some more speed and hit the ramp of the transporter at forty-five. It seemed hellishly quick. Dangerously Quick. Too quick...

Gunfire erupted, bullets whizzing past Luger's face and some catching the motorcycle's front forks. He felt bullets striking the engine, exhaust, and rear wheel. But he concentrated only on the end of the ramp ahead of him. It was evident that he was travelling far too quickly, and he touched the brakes, but it was too late, he was already airborne and cleared the two fences in an instant, carrying on for a further thirty feet as the machine dropped quickly through the air. Luger felt the giddy sensation of weightlessness in his stomach, the fall paradoxically feeling both rapid and eternal. The ground loomed, ever approaching, and then in an instant both wheels impacted at the same time, the front forks and central rear suspension compressing, and Luger compressing with it. He took the impact, his spine jarring and his elbows hitting his knees. His chest smashed against the fuel tank, but fortunately his face and head did not strike the handlebars. The gunshots stopped altogether – even excited border guards knew not to spray automatic gunfire into another country – and as Luger fell from the bike and the machine slid across the gravel, he knew he'd made it. There were shouts behind him, and he did not want to chance a guard risking a single shot. He struggled to his feet and limped away from the ruined motorcycle, already seeing approaching vehicle lights in the distance as the Estonian border guards motored across the waste ground to see what had got their Russian counterparts so excited.

Die Trying

Luger did not want to hang around to be questioned. The Estonians were a NATO member state, but stranger things had happened than a country wanting to gain favours with a neighbouring dominant country by simply handing a person back, and if the Estonians did not do that, then he would face questioning for hours – days even - with everything far from straightforward. They weren't going to simply deliver him to the British Embassy for tea and biscuits.

The shadows welcomed him to sanctuary, and within a minute of stepping into the suburbs, he could tell he was out of Russia and back in the West, despite Estonia being a former Soviet state. It was evident that time moved differently for countries out of Russia's clutches and despite being a fugitive, Luger felt safer at once. After fifteen minutes of walking the quiet night-time streets, he was confident that he was in the clear. Pulling out his phone, he headed towards the station where he would easily hail a taxi that would take him back to his hotel, a drink, and a good night's sleep.

Chapter Fifty-Two

L acanau, France

They came at dawn. Only there were four of them and not two. Two men from the south and two from the west. King watched them emerge from the forest with confidence. A few minutes earlier, two deer had done the same, only the deer had been difficult to spot and had taken their time. They had used the long shadows and the fringe of the forest for cover as they grazed on wild garlic in the long grass. King had glanced fleetingly away, and when he looked back for them, they had disappeared without trace. The men could have learned much from nature as they stomped across the grass.

King uncoiled the rope and picked up the tension. There was a good deal of stretch in the rope, and it required a lot of strength before it gave completely, meaning that the rope had either snapped, or had successfully released the wedges that he had whittled earlier, that had freed the two trimmed tree trunks and allowed them to fall across the road. The trunks would have fallen between two trees and pinned them tightly a metre off the ground. Nobody was going anywhere on that road without a chainsaw.

It had not occurred to King that the two men would become four. Although he supposed it should always have been a possibility if the contract bounty was indeed large enough. He wasn't going to take the fact as flattery. Not yet at least.

The presence of the other two men was unexpected, though not too problematic. King took out two of his IEDs and the small gas blowtorch he had earlier purchased. It fitted in the palm of his hand, lit at the press of a button and the fiercely hot blue flame could not be blown out. He waited until the men had crossed more than halfway from the woods to the house – even in fight and flight nobody took the longer route – and lit the two fuses with the flame. He had earlier tested a fuse and knew that the length was good for a ten-second burn. He counted off three seconds as he got to his feet, then another two as he picked them up and lobbed the first, switched the second to his right hand and tossed the other towards them. One of the men turned as he either heard something or detected movement and stared at the two, pint pots arcing through the air. They both exploded a second apart, smoked and shrapnel spreading everywhere. One of the men went down and the other three sprinted for the house. Already, another bomb sailed through the air. The felled man was struggling to get up, but the third IED landed just a few feet away from him and exploded. When the smoked cleared he was writhing in agony and screaming like a banshee. The men reached the house, the other injured man struggling to stand now that he had reached relative safety. King aimed and fired two shots from his seventy-metre distance and the injured man went down for good. It was a long pistol shot, but that's what hours at a time and hundreds of thousands of rounds of ammunition over the years did for you. Training was everything. He moved as soon as he had fired, knowing that the muzzle flashes would have been clearly visible in the treeline and one of the men emptied his pistol at the trees, fifteen rounds finding nothing but tree bark and the forest floor. The man reloaded, King noting that he was well-practised. The second man was breaking into the house using a lock-pick. Again, King did not want to make it too easy for them, and the delay at the front door had enabled him to take down two of them already. King fired again just as the two men made it inside. He was already running and got to the house before he heard them shatter the windows with the muzzles of their pistols. He lit the fuse to one of his IEDs and waited before trying the door. It made it to around a foot ajar before bullets struck the wood, but the solid oak door with its thick bracers and hundreds of antique nails was as good as a barricade for King, with only a few bullets making it through and bouncing harmlessly off the wall on the other side. King tossed the IED inside, as close to the table and the two open fuel cans. He ducked his head, already lighting another fuse and tossed it inside a second before the first bomb exploded and destroyed the table. The fuel cans ruptured and were ignited by the second fuse before the device even exploded. King started to pull the door and as the second bomb detonated, the blast slammed the door shut. The room was engulfed in flames, the men screaming desperately at the barred windows and pleading for King to open the door, but he stepped aside, aiming the pistol at the door as the flames increased and the screams subsided. Neither man made it to the door and King tucked the weapon into his waistband as he set out across the grass to clear the roadblock barricade that he had set off on the road.

King heard the bullet impact and the man gasp behind him. As he spun around, he saw the body on the ground just a few metres from him, and the echo of the gunshot filled the valley a full second later. The man had been hit between the shoulder blades and there was blood, organ, and bone matter on the ground next to the Browning 9mm pistol that he would undoubtedly have been aiming at King's back. King caught sight of the tall church tower in the distance, standing proudly above the rest of the village. A guardian angel? Undoubtedly.

King picked up the pistol and checked it before tucking it into his waistband and taking out the Sig Sauer. If there was a fifth man, then there could easily be a sixth. He made his way into the forest and headed for the road; the pistol aimed loosely in front of him so he could bring it easily to bear. A crunch of sticks or dried pinecone snapped like the click of fingers, and he had the weapon ready as the man stepped cautiously into his sights. The man's hands were raised with a revolver in his right hand and his mobile phone in his left.

"Do not shoot, *monsieur*," he said calmly and quietly. He motioned with his left hand, holding out the mobile phone for King to inspect. "The contract... it has been lifted..."

"When?"

"Just now," the man replied. "I switched on my phone to contact the others and call them off. Your traps have blocked in our cars..."

"How many of you are there?"

"Six," the man replied.

"So, it's just you left?"

The man frowned. "Left?" His face dropped. "*Quoi...?*"

King kept his aim steady. "And then there was one..."

"*Oui...*" the man replied hopefully.

King shot the man in the face then stepped forward and picked up his phone. The device was still open, and he scrolled to the messages and read for himself the news he had so desperately wanted to see.

The contract is closed. Do not proceed further.

King heard the vehicle pull to a halt on the gravelled surface and headed towards the sound.

"That was well-timed," he said as Rashid stepped out of the van.

"Always..."

King glanced at the young woman, then said to Rashid, "Who's this?"

"I'm Jo," she said, not waiting to be introduced, and somewhat irked that King should ignore her and direct his question to Rashid. "Jo Blyth."

King nodded. "Good to meet you, Jo." He looked at Rashid and said, "Is she any good?"

"Well, we've been taking out assassins working on your contract," he said. "And I couldn't have done it without her..."

"I'm right here...!" Jo exclaimed, pulling an expression of exasperation.

"That bloke back there makes three out of action, so..." Rashid shrugged and winked at Jo. "She's pretty damned good, I'd say..."

"Thanks," King smiled and held out his hand. "Nobody gets an easy run straight off the bat."

She took his hand and returned a firm shake, "I know

Die Trying

how it works," she replied. "I've worked with silly boys before..."

"I like her," King grinned.

"Still right here..."

"The contract has been lifted," said King.

"When?"

King did not go into detail. The last thing he wanted was either of them questioning whether the man on the lawn had needed to die. He had a gun aimed at King, that should have been enough, but King knew how the mind worked. Especially in the early hours of a sleepless night. "Right now," he replied. "I just captured a guy's phone."

"Where?" Jo asked.

"In the woods," King replied. "Right, let's get out of here..."

"Don't we need to clear the road?" asked Jo. "And get your car?"

King shook his head. "No. The roadblock will slow down the police and fire crews while the fire cleans the scene for me," he said matter-of-factly. "And the car is best left where it is. The owner should get it back soon that way."

"You stole a car?" Jo Blyth asked incredulously.

Rashid put a hand on her shoulder and said, "Jo, you should know that King doesn't do things by the book." He paused. "In fact, none of us do..."

Chapter Fifty-Three

Tallinn, Estonia

Luger had risen early. He was black and blue from the landing. Large bruises to his forearms, thighs, chest, and buttocks had made for a painful, somewhat fitful night's sleep. He had started the morning with a hot shower then had run it ice-cold and had allowed the spray to play on his bruises for as long as he could bear it. Afterwards, he had drunk plenty of water to counter the dehydration that severe bruising caused, and ate scrambled eggs, toast and black coffee ordered from room service. While he scrolled the newsfeed on his phone to catch up after a couple of days, the text from Ramsay made him put down his second cup of coffee and sit up expectantly. The last text from the man had undoubtedly saved his life, so this latest text had his full attention.

Luger frowned as he locked his phone and slipped it

Die Trying

into his pocket, the merest movement causing him pain. As a child he had considered a career as a stuntman but was quite happy to finally put that unrealised dream to bed.

Luger paid the bill at reception and walked to his hire car. The cute and quirky Fiat 500 cut through the traffic with ease. He doubted that he'd ever want to drive one on the open road, but in the city, it made sense. The vehicle was well-equipped with technology, including Apple CarPlay, which connected to his phone and allowed him to read his texts while using Google Maps to cut his way across the city. Ramsay's instructions had been clear and concise. He just hoped that he was in time. He parked his car on the quiet residential street and craned his neck to see the numbers on the houses. Carter stepped out from the building and hovered on the steps while he lit a cigarette. The building housed five comfortable apartments, but being official Embassy accommodation, Luger knew they would be far from luxury. He briefly wondered what the man had done to end up living in a rented flat at fifty with his career going no further than Tallinn, Estonia. It must have been bad. Or he had taken one for the team. Either way, this career-dormant embassy man had attracted unwanted attention once again.

Luger got out of the car and followed the man as he walked along the treelined avenue. It was close to the British embassy and the man took the same walk every morning. In the evening, he went home a different way because he took in several drinks at a local bar to quell the mind-numbing frustration of his work. Luger thought that perhaps this drinking habit had something to do with his career hump, but he was done speculating because he had just spotted how it was going to be done. He cursed himself for dropping the Makarov, but Ramsay had said to be subtle, and street shootings were far from that.

Carter glanced down the road, crossing diagonally as he checked his phone and smoked his cigarette. Luger saw the car pull out, and it made sense really. The white Tesla was full electric and made next to no sound. Luger ran, his body screaming at him to stop, but he wasn't going to do that. He could push through it, had a high pain-threshold. Carter hesitated, sensing something – most likely Luger's rapid movement, the pounding of his feet on the otherwise quiet street – and Luger rugby tackled the man clear of the vehicle with less than a second and a few feet to spare. Carter protested, grunting as he hit the ground and the two men sprawled and rolled into the gutter. Luger got up quickly, the Tesla slowing. He reached inside his jacket pocket, eyes on the driver and the vehicle sped away. His bluff had worked. The driver did not know if he had a gun, and he wasn't hanging around to find out.

"You...?" Carter said, dabbing his bleeding nose with a tissue. "What the bloody hell are you doing?"

"That was a serious attempt on your life," said Luger. He caught hold of the man's sleeve and pulled him with him as he walked.

"That was just a dickhead who misjudged it," Carter said incredulously.

"No, I had a text to say that MI6 would make an attempt on your life immediately and that I should get you to safety."

"MI6?" Carter frowned. "But why?"

"It's a game of chess," Luger replied as they reached the Fiat. "They made a move; Ramsay countered it, and now they have responded. You are now being targeted as a mole.

Die Trying

A double agent. In doing this, they keep the heat off themselves and you die without protesting your innocence."

"But I haven't done anything!" Carter raged.

Luger sped off down the road, the tiny Fiat nipping agilely through the streets. "Bugger," said Luger. "We need your passport."

Carter shrugged, retrieving it from his pocket. "Old habit," he explained. "That came from being posted in Baghdad, Beirut and Damascus." He paused. "Where are we going? I can't just up sticks…"

"There are some very nasty people at the River House who have decided that your life is worth no more than covering their arses, and nothing more. As of now, your career and your life here is over, until matters can be suitably resolved."

Carter nodded, seemingly accepting his fate, and Luger got the impression that the man had little rooted in life and leaving would not be the worse outcome and it was certainly better than being run over on his way to work. "But how did your boss know?" he asked incredulously.

Luger shrugged. "I guess he's just better at chess than they are…"

Chapter Fifty-Four

L**ondon**

"I like the new gaff," King, remarked taking in the office and the stunning view from one side over the River Thames.

Mae handed him his mug of tea. "There you are love. White with one sugar..."

"Excellent," King smiled, taking it from her. King noted that the mug was larger than the coffee cups and teacups on the table. He liked Ramsay's assistant, and he liked the fact that she knew that King did not like fuss. She had made it her business to find out about the team and he noted that Luger had his large, strong black coffee and had placed the plate of biscuits beside Big Dave. Caroline was happy pouring the teas and coffees for the others, and chatted away while she dispensed the sugar and milk accordingly, handing the cups to the rest of them. She had spent time talking to Jo Blyth and making her welcome. Jo was meeting most of them for the first time.

King watched Caroline, realising that something was off. They had reunited last night, and it had been wonderful, the fear of living in the shadows with too many enemies to fight had been lifted, and although he knew that Rashid and Jo had done their part, he still did not know what Caroline had done, and nor did she want to tell him. They had taken a room at a decent hotel and made frantic love, choosing room service over getting changed for dinner, and spent the night in each other's arms, making love more tenderly and sleeping soundly. The hot showers and large breakfasts and a walk along the embankment had felt wonderful, and even climbing the steps to the new building had not filled them with dread. King wondered how long it would last, how long before Caroline felt compelled to wallow in shame or guilt at what she had done. He promised himself never to ask. She would tell him only if she needed to.

"The contract on King's life has been withdrawn. I don't know how you did it," said Ramsay, catching Caroline's eye. "And perhaps I don't want to know..."

Caroline looked at him, her expression suddenly sullen. "I don't think you need to," she said, then engaged with the others, her eyes resting on King "I don't think *anybody* needs to..."

Big Dave shifted awkwardly in his chair. "Any news on those shits across the river?" he asked, changing the subject.

"Evasive, is all I can say. They don't seem too eager to speak to me," Ramsay replied. "But on the face of it they shared some information pertinent to our enquiries but allowed me to send an agent to gather further intelligence knowing that he was likely walking into a trap. They used us in a mole hunt, and we confirmed their suspicions. Jack would have been captured and exposed to all manner of hell on earth." He paused. "I took a chance and gave Jack new orders, and he managed to escape," he said, leaving out the part where Jack Luger put a bullet in another man's skull. There was only so much his team had to know about their teammates. "Once I worked out their plan, I anticipated their next move and Jack saved the life of a Foreign Office employee that Devonshire was going to use to cover their tracks. This man helped Jack into Russia. I used him as a local asset, and in doing so I compromised him. Saving him went without question. I was the one who put him in danger."

"Where is this man now?" asked King.

"We have a few safe houses at our disposal, and he's safely installed in one of them," Ramsay replied. "Jim Kernow is minding him until we can resolve the matter."

"What's the plan for him in the long run?" King persisted. "He can't stay there indefinitely."

"He won't be missed. Divorced his wife fifteen years ago and has no relationship with his daughter. Hasn't seen either of them in years." He paused. "No house, no finance or credit and just a few hundred pounds in savings."

"Sounds dodgy," commented Caroline.

"Drink, affairs and disgrace will do that for a man." Ramsay paused. "But we shouldn't judge. Once we can be sure that MI6 no longer need to cover their backs, then I will try to integrate him back into the real world. He's an experienced hand, there might well be use in him yet." Ramsay paused. "Once MI6, or rather this chap Devonshire, knows that we know, then there would be no stock in having a mid-level *security consultant* killed. In fact, by removing the man, we've probably done Devonshire a tremendous favour."

"And what about this bloke, Devonshire?" asked King.

"What about him?" Ramsay replied.

"He's made a direct attack on us. He was willing for Jack to rot in a police cell, probably condemn him to death." King shrugged. "Does this Devonshire bloke need to have an accident?"

"Seriously?" asked Jo. "This is what goes on here?"

"No, it doesn't," Ramsay said emphatically.

"Well, I'm not sure if going by what I saw in France necessarily backs that up," she replied.

"I'm sure Neil could do with another secretary if that's a better fit for you," King said tersely.

Rashid rolled his eyes. He had worked with her for weeks and had learned how to 'manage' her. Or at least, manage them working together. She was forthright and could be a little undiplomatic. If he could have bet that there would be someone that she would butt heads with, it would be King.

"You're out-dated, King. All that killing, it's largely unnecessary," Jo Blyth told him.

"Largely, but not wholly," King replied coldly.

"Time will tell."

"You didn't seem to have a problem when your boyfriend killed two assassins to save me."

She flushed red and glared at him. "He's *not* my boyfriend!"

"Well, give it time," King smirked.

"Hey!" Rashid protested. "I'm right here..."

King rolled his eyes. "Like you're not trying..."

Jo stared at Rashid. "You've been trying?" Rashid shrugged. "Not very hard, obviously."

"Should I try harder?"

She shrugged and said, "Well, maybe so I'd notice..."

"Sounds promising," Big Dave chided.

Caroline gave the big Fijian a nudge and said, "Stay out of it!"

Ramsay smacked his hand down on the desk. "Goodness me," he said irritably. "It's like being back at school!"

"I went to an all-boys boarding school, so nothing like it for me," Luger said, then sipped his coffee.

"Me neither," King agreed.

"Was that the School of Hard Knocks?" Luger chided.

King laughed. "Yeah, you wouldn't have got in. Not in your short trousers and peaked cap, anyway."

"Well, this is nice. All back together again," said Caroline without any hint of irony.

"That's enough now," Ramsay told them. "Down to business. Here's what we've got..." He flicked the remote and the large screen television displayed three mugshot photographs. One face on, and one in each profile. "Max Lukov, forty-two years of age. Former GRU officer turned Mafia boss. His father, Dimitri Lukov, was a KGB officer, not renowned for his mercy. When the Iron Curtain fell, Lukov senior worked with the newly formed FSB, but he knew enough secrets and had enough influence to forge a criminal empire. Since then, he merged with other syndicates, stabbed others in the back and eventually took a large sector of northern Russia. When he died, his son took over but not without rumours that he had his own father killed. Rumours are rife that he had the man murdered using a female assassin known as The Widow." He switched the image to a rough and dirty-looking man in his fifties, incapable of growing a thick and full beard, but who had given it a try at least. "This is Piotr Krylov, a small-time criminal with aspirations of being a big-time crime baron..."

"Except that he was found dead near St. Peterburg," Jack Luger interjected. "Ivan, the MI6 asset and double agent was taking me to a police officer on his payroll... and I can only assume wasn't to be trusted either... to find out more about the circumstances in which he died." He paused. "MI6, or rather Devonshire and Harriet..." He blushed a little as he mentioned the woman by name. "... said that the modus operandi matched the female assassin that Neil previously mentioned, known as The Widow."

"The guy I went to see on Dartmoor, Tommy Jury," Big Dave frowned. "He was cut up bad, certainly in a way that would match this Widow's MO."

"I agree. And as far as my enquiries have established this Krylov chap was shot in both legs, then tortured. One would imagine, to determine information," said Ramsay. "He was also found with his wrists, femoral arteries and throat slashed. This would point towards Max Lukov having her at his beck and call. Furthermore, it would mean that Lukov wanted answers. Krylov has been traced back to Lukov, and MI6 have transcripts of the GRU admonishing Lukov, right after the bombs went off in port, destroying the drugs. The bombings were never part of the GRU's plans."

"So, Krylov was working for Lukov, and Lukov was reprimanded by the GRU, so he's obviously working for them. Subcontracted by the Russian government," Caroline ventured.

"It would seem so," Ramsay agreed.

"Then by that token, with Krylov being tortured, questioned and murdered, he most likely helped himself to the drugs and replaced them with the explosives," said Caroline. "Not only would the GRU be out of money and drugs, but Lukov would be out of money and influence. Lukov would have to make up any deficit."

"It's speculation, but I would be prepared to run with it," Ramsay replied. "The GRU wanted drugs to come into Europe and Davinder's investigation in Plymouth and Dartmoor found that a local crime boss had been eliminated, one most definitely in The Widow's vein."

"So, it's just about drugs?" Rashid asked. "So, surely we just turn our findings over to the police now?" He shrugged. "We're not vice."

"Normally, yes," Ramsay agreed. "But with the GRU and Max Lukov in cahoots, I can't help feeling that it's something more. With that kind of backing then it's a clandestine attack from the Russian establishment, not terrorists. And certainly not mere drug trafficking."

"It's addiction. Plain and simple," said King. All eyes on him, he took them all on and added, "I know about addiction. My mother was a junkie and overdosed. She was a mess. On the game, couldn't feed her family, stole whenever she could. With huge amounts of free drugs distributed across Europe and the UK, society would become a mess. Health and police resources would be strained, government budgets drained and increasing national debt. The Russians would be free to watch our demise, while all the time strengthening their forces and pushing the boundaries. Just the fear of them growing stronger while we grow weaker would change the world balance, without them even having to invade. What's scarier to a rainbow-wearing, gender confused drug addict and his peers, all with the prospect of national service, than an imposing force of hard-ass Russians who would tear out their livers with a bayonet before breakfast?"

"Eloquently put, I must say," said Ramsay. He stared at

Die Trying

King, then slowly shook his head despairingly. "But on the mark, as usual. It would be like poisoning a forest and watching the trees fall one by one…"

"Could it work?" asked Big Dave. "Logistically, that is?"

Ramsay pondered for a moment then said, "Well, there's certainly nobody policing the Taliban in Afghanistan. Or Iran, for that matter. The production must be prolific now. If the product was distributed quickly and in the right amounts, and in the right strength, then it could prove to be a highly effective means of societal degradation. Their only way to distribute throughout Europe would be to use established networks. The small-time criminal gangs in different regions. That's why they killed Tommy Jury in Plymouth, the body on Dartmoor that I sent Davinder down to look at and liaise with DI Dermott, the investigating officer. Jury obviously didn't like distributing the drugs for a fee, instead of for a hefty share of the profits. Our only saving grace is that many criminal elements will want to con the Russians, too."

"So, where do we start?" asked Jo Blyth.

"I'm splitting the troops," Ramsay said decisively. "According to my sources Max Lukov is currently in Constanta, Romania. Whether he's taking a hands-on approach to the drug smuggling, or whether he's merely putting some distance between himself and the GRU, is not clear. But it *does* make it easier for us to get to him. Now, he'll own the police down there, and he will have plenty of his muscle…"

"So have we," said King.

"Indeed," Ramsay agreed. "General Orlev is the GRU officer who berated Lukov. That's close enough for me. He is a priority target. We also need to find how the drugs are going to come in. They won't use the same method as before, because just about every port authority, coastguard and navy in Europe is on the lookout for huge shipments of heroin." He paused. "Likewise, police and Interpol are shaking down criminals likely to handle the distribution."

"Let's hope that it doesn't put them off," said King.

"But that would be a win, surely?" Jo questioned.

"Sometimes to kill the rat, you need to *see* the rat," King replied. "Just shake down some poison and hope for the best, and you'll never know if the rat is still there or not."

"Don't like rats, eh?" she chided.

"I don't like unfinished business…"

"Nor do I," said Ramsay. "And I don't like coincidence. Lukov being in Romania is significant. I'll bet he's overseeing the operation because farming out the task hasn't worked for him so far, and he won't want the GRU to lose even more faith in him. Now, I'm breaking this down and giving your assignments individually. Mae will make you all tea and coffee in the lounge and I'll call you in." He nodded towards the door, and everyone started to get out of their seats. "King, wait a moment, I'll start with you…"

Chapter Fifty-Five

Constanta, Romania

The country had come a long way in thirty years. The Black Sea had been the Soviet Union's answer to the Mediterranean, but these days the surrounding countries that had emerged since the fall of the Soviet Union had made it their own. Of course, Russia wanted more access to the Black Sea, and that attempt had come from invading Ukraine. The Soviet Union had once lined more than seventy percent of the Black Sea coastline, and now had barely twenty. Ukraine would give them fifty percent, and in Russian logic that would just be better.

Max Lukov watched the sea glistening to his right as his driver made light work of the coast road. The sky was clear and blue, and the sea mirrored the sky. It was days like these that made visitors question the name behind the Black Sea, but when the sky was grey and the wind whipped up the water's surface, it could look ominous, dark, and foreboding. There were many small boats out today towing water skiers, wakeboarders, and parasailers. The craft cut chaotic white streaks in the blue surface and their activity had created foot-high waves that lapped the sandy shoreline where children played with inflatable toys and buckets and spades, and men and women of various sizes and in states of undress caught early summer tans.

The driver took a side road and they wound their way up the hairpin bends into the hills. Lukov rode in the rear of an AMG Mercedes G-Wagon. The rugged-looking off-roader, vaguely reminiscent of a classic Jeep or Land Rover Defender, was a luxuriously made statement vehicle that dominated the road and could tackle any terrain and was indeed faster than many sportscars. Behind him, two BMW X5 SUVs were filled with his best bodyguards and armed to the teeth. Orlev had humiliated him that night on the Baltic Coast, and his only saving grace was that nobody had been left alive to witness it. His recently promoted personal bodyguard rode up front next to the driver. Many of his men were Russian ex-Spetsnaz special forces but using a Global security company he had also employed several Europeans including two ex-French Foreign Legionnaires and a former Greek special forces soldier. He found that travel - even though he was greatly restricted by much of the world's sanctions and travel bans on Russians – was less conspicuous when his entourage was not made up solely of hard-faced Russian men of military age.

The road wound on for ten more miles and after they passed through a small, and typically inland Romanian town with horses pulling carts made from car parts and young men and women herding goats along the side of the road, they entered a vast agricultural plateau and after another ten miles of driving past fields, vineyards and polytunnels, they stopped at an industrial sized farm that operated huge sheds the size of aircraft hangars with various farm machinery moving around a yard the size of a theme park's carpark. The farm was a packing station that shipped produce Europewide to various supermarket chains and there was a constant stream of vehicles coming and going – perfect for their venture once enough palms had been greased and enough threats had been made.

The driver parked the G-Wagon near a block of stacked portacabin offices and the two BMW X5s parked alongside. Lukov got out and was soon flanked by his bodyguards as a man stepped out of the second storey portacabin and walked down the steel staircase to greet them.

"Max, so good to see you…" the man smiled warmly and Lukov embraced him.

"How is it going, Davos?" Lukov looked at him seriously. "We are getting pressured by those pricks in Moscow…"

"This is better than that shit Krylov organised." Davos assured him. "It's fool proof."

"I should have known that Krylov was not up to the task."

"Nonsense, my old friend. He took liberties, you were not to know," Davos said warmly. Sycophancy was always in his best interest when dealing with Max Lukov, and he had seen how it had turned out for the men who thought that they could show the man they were his equal. "Come, see what we have done."

Lukov shook his head. There were vehicles approaching and he looked back at his old lieutenant and said, "We are being joined by General Orlev. He wants to see what his investment is getting him."

Davos bristled. "Then he insults us…"

"The time will come when he realises that." Lukov paused watching the three black Mercedes S-Class saloons pull into the yard. "But by then, my old friend, it will be too late."

Lukov briefly weighed the odds. Orlev's guards would likely be the same men who had slayed his own. They would be confident and slow to react. The vehicles stopped and the men got out. Lukov waited but when the doors were closed and the men stood around looking menacing, Orlev was nowhere to be seen. There were eight men in all. He noted that Sergei Bostock was not among them either. Orlev was showing little respect.

"I am Uri. Orlev sent me in his place," a tall, balding man stepped confidently forwards.

Lukov frowned, indignant that the GRU general should send a lacky in his place, but somewhat relieved after their last meeting in the forest. He had wanted to show the man that he was not afraid, and that bodyguards could be easily bought. "To what end?"

"I am to report my findings," Uri smirked. "If this is to be another failure, he did not want to waste his precious time travelling here."

Lukov glanced at his men. Some were interested in the remark; others were desperately pretending that they had not heard. He looked back at Uri. "Very well, come with me," he said, taking out his mobile phone. "Your men can wait here. As can mine. We don't need our bodyguards, we are men, no?"

Uri shrugged and signalled for his men to hang back. He followed Lukov as the man scrolled on his phone, then placed it back in his pocket. "Krylov was a mistake," he said.

Lukov nodded. "Agreed," he replied. "But your master

has already expressed his thoughts on this, given me a demonstration of his power and influence." He paused as they reached the nearest cavernous building. "So, this is what, then? Your opinion?"

"Yes."

"You think that I need telling what was a mistake, and what is the right way to do things?" He paused, frowning at Uri. "Orlev sent me a lacky, but I have had no previous dealings with you. Your boss was too coward to come here because he knows that he overstepped the mark."

"I will pass on your thoughts to him."

"I hope you do," Lukov replied, opening the pedestrian door next to the double doors large enough to take an airliner. "This is how the heroin is going to be shipped," he said, thinking nothing of the previous exchange. "The canisters are designed to take ten kilos. We will remove the contents, create a false bottom, and replace with five kilos of pure heroin. The remaining cavity will be refilled with the original contents and packed into crates of ten. The first twenty-five metric tonnes of raw product is ready to ship. We will use a variety of methods including air freight, shipping, the train network, and road haulage. There is no smell and no way of detection by x-ray," he said proudly. "The best part is that as a long-standing member of the European Union, Romania finally joined the Schengen area two months ago, meaning that there will be no border enforcement and the product will go through Hungary and into Austria. Romania is now the official gateway to Western Europe."

Uri smiled as he watched the production line flowing and forklift trucks moving crate upon crate to various heavy goods vehicle containers, waiting for lorries to shackle up and take them away. "I would say that this method is a success." He paused. "So far, that is. Just see that the chain has people you can trust, we don't want another episode like in the forest."

Lukov stared at him. "You think I need your fucking approval?"

"Very much so," Uri replied confidently, if not smugly.

Lukov turned on his heel and headed out of the building leaving Uri to trot after him. He continued across the yard, a hundred or more metres ignoring the man beside him as he walked.

"It's just the chain of command," Uri said assuredly. "You must understand that?"

Lukov said nothing as they rounded the stacked porta-cabins then stopped short of the vehicles. Uri continued, then hesitated before he stopped in his tracks. Lukov's bodyguards stood around the bodies of Uri's men. Blood was soaking into the concrete and expansion gaps. Two of Lukov's men held silenced .32 CZ Scorpion machine pistols, and scattered across the ground, sixty brass bullet cases glinted in the sunlight. He grinned as Uri turned and looked at him. "Surprised, Uri? You shouldn't be..."

"You'll never get away with this!"

"I already have," Lukov replied.

"Orlev will have you killed!"

"Maybe. Maybe not." Lukov shrugged. "But I control all the product, and I have Orlev's special project money in an offshore account. If he wants the product distributed, then he needs to stay away and leave me in peace to do what I've been paid to do."

"It'll never happen..."

Lukov shrugged. "Very well. If you think I'm wasting my time, if you think you can't get through to him, then there seems little point in me allowing you to leave. I was hoping you could deliver a message to him from me." He paused, nodding at one of the men holding a machine pistol. "Too bad..."

"Wait!"

Lukov held up a hand as the bodyguard took aim. "You'll deliver a message for me?"

"Yes!" Uri snapped pleadingly. "Of course!"

"You can go back and tell Orlev that he can go fuck himself..." Lukov told him belligerently. Uri stared at him, but he did not protest. "Have you got that?"

"Yes, of course!"

Lukov laughed. "When I was a child, my mother would ask me to do things, and I would often forget. One day, she tied some cotton around my finger and told me that when I looked at my finger, I would remember what she had told me. She was quite right because she tied it too tightly and my finger throbbed all day. But I did not forget!" He paused, staring at the man intently before breaking into a smile. "Yosef! Do you have some cotton on you?"

The man aiming the machine pistol shook his head. "No, boss, I do not!"

"Vladamir?" Lukov asked a large, bulging man with a face that looked like it had once been hit by a train. "Do you have a thread of cotton?"

"No."

Lukov shook his head. "No cotton," he said sullenly. "Perhaps we have something else? Giorgi, do you have a length of string?"

"No, sir."

"Francois?"

"Non, monsieur Lukov."

Lukov snapped his fingers together and four men stepped forwards and held Uri in a vice-like grip. His arms were twisted and two of the men had wrapped their legs over the man's kneecaps so he could not kick out at their boss. Lukov took a flick knife out from his pocket and the blade whipped open at the flick of a button.

"No..." Uri begged. "Please!"

Lukov smiled as he thought of the fear that had rushed through him in those dark woods; the relief when Orlev and his men had spared his life. The humiliation, the anger he had lived with since. Every waking moment, every sleepless night as he tossed and turned in bed and thought of what the GRU general had done. It wasn't like having him here, but as he slowly removed Uri's index finger at the middle joint with the knife, he relished the look on Orlev's face when his message was delivered.

Uri's screams died down and were replaced with sobs and groans. He was pushed harshly behind the wheel of one of the Mercedes, blood covering the interior and his clothing, and the man wasted no time in driving away. Silently, Lukov's men loaded the bodies into the other two Mercedes and the blood was sluiced away with buckets of water and bleach. Two men drove the cars away to be burned on some waste ground off the main road, followed by Lukov and the rest of his men in the SUVs. An old Romanian man with leathery skin and half an inch of unfiltered cigarette poking from the corner of his mouth appeared from behind the portacabins with a hosepipe and nonchalantly sprayed the ground until the blood and frothy bleach had washed away entirely. The old man had seen a great deal in his time but would tell no one. That was why he had become old, and that was why he would grow older still.

Chapter Fifty-Six

"Well, that was unexpected," Rashid said as he watched Max Lukov and his entourage leave through the pair of powerful Zeiss binoculars. He had only just tracked the Mercedes saloon as the unfortunate driver had weaved along the road. The windows of the vehicle had been tinted, but not the windscreen, and the driver had been in visible agony, wrapping a handkerchief around his hand as he struggled to steer. He looked scared, as scared as Rashid had seen anybody, and he had worked in some of the worst places on earth.

"He wouldn't disagree with you," Big Dave replied. Just seven-hundred metres distant, they had found their vantage point when Jack Luger had given them the location of the meeting place. The big Fijian was now uploading the footage he had taken, and the digital photographs taken through a large zoom lens of the man that Lukov had dismembered. The images would go through all databases that the analysts on the floor below Ramsay had legal access to, and some that they officially did not.

Both men looked up as Luger pulled into the clearing

on a motorcycle. He switched off the engine and kicked out the stand, then dismounted carefully and limped across the dusty ground towards them.

"Crikey, it's John Wayne, only more saddle sore..." Big Dave chided.

"Funny..." Luger perched gingerly on a large boulder and winced. "Should have had a car. I've had enough of bikes for a while."

"Cars get detected quickly," Rashid replied. "There's a slab of slate over there that would make a good ramp. Want to show us what you can do?"

"Piss off!"

"Alright, we'll settle for a wheelie," Big Dave chided.

"That would be piss off again..."

Rashid laughed. "Right, let's get sorted. LUP, hard routine and four-hour watches."

"And for someone who wasn't in the super army soldiers?" He smirked. "That's what SAS stands for, right?"

"Everyone knows it's Saturdays and Sundays," Big Dave smirked.

"Nice," Rashid scoffed. "Well, for the former member of the senior service, we make an LUP, that's a lying up place. We eat cold food and shit in a bag, and we take turns on surveillance while the other two rest. Sorry, no valet on this one, Jack."

Luger had picked up Max Lukov in Constanta on his hired motorcycle while Big Dave and Rashid had held back in the hired Jeep. They had tracked Luger using a simple phone tracker app and once it was evident that the agricultural packing station was their destination, he had texted Rashid with the GPS coordinates. Big Dave and Rashid had then found the hill using Google Maps and mounted their watch. Caroline and Jo were waiting closer to the coast, each in a hire car and would alternate the lead to follow Lukov back to his luxury Villa in the hills overlooking the sea. Rashid had let them both know that a person of interest - the unknown man with the severed finger - would require following, and they would sort that out between themselves.

"And the plan?" Luger asked.

"You two are going in to see what's in that building that was worth killing seven men and slicing off a man's finger," said Rashid.

"And what will you be doing?" Jack Luger shrugged. "Sounds like quite a delegation of duties."

Rashid patted the rifle case beside him and said, "I'll be keeping you two safe from seven-hundred metres…"

Chapter Fifty-Seven

London

The third floor of the anonymous looking building with views glimpsing St. James' Park and the River Thames had been designed with sensitive lighting and tinted, light sensitive windows. Heated or air-conditioned to 19c – thought to be the most productive office temperature – gentle classical music played for an hour several times a day. Ramsay enjoyed the distraction when he visited his team of MI5 analysts, who he naturally had more in common with than that of the team. He had worked with, then overseen, many of these people when he himself had worked in the basement office of Thames House, the headquarters of the Security Service. Hand-picked personally for their skills and suitable personality, the five men and seven women that made up his team of analysts and planners – the brain to the team's muscle and physicality – the office worked various

Die Trying

shifts with at least two being on duty throughout the night. The lawyers, financial planners and tech specialists occupying the offices below had no idea that above them the security of the nation rested in the balance, while MI5 and MI6 fought out the semantics of what direction the intelligence service took after MI5's shocking and public security breach.

Charlotte, a middle-aged woman who enjoyed cats and sudoku, and who was refreshingly unaware how attractive she really was, placed a mug of tea and a plate of Jammy Dodgers beside Ramsay as he went over the data. He smiled, remembering how they had both agreed that they were the best biscuits when they worked together years ago in the basement of MI5.

"You remembered," he grinned.

"Always," she smiled.

For a man who could see the angle, see the hidden meaning in so many tiny pieces of data, or slivers of blurred and distorted photographs, he was quite unaware how in love Charlotte had been with him, and still was for that matter. He had met and married his wife, had two wonderful daughters, and still had no idea that the woman who brought him tea with an extra sugar and Jammy Dodgers for eighteen years was his soulmate.

"Uri Milonov, thirty-two, a GRU major who works directly for General Orlev. As special operations, they have a closed remit, unaccountable in other words. As we know such remits have led to the lines becoming blurred... the FSB and the mafia, for instance." Charlotte paused, helping herself to a Jammy Dodger and unapologetically getting crumbs down her front. "Orlev does what he wants," she said, brushing the crumbs off her dress and onto the floor. "But it's more than that. Many people view him as potential competition to other crime syndicates. He has the Kremlin behind him for now, but everything points to him picking up the mantel and running with it."

"Would Lukov know this?"

"Undoubtedly," Charlotte replied. "But he's caught between the two narratives. He has been approached by the GRU in the form of Orlev, and he can't refuse because the GRU put him where he is now. Funding, faith, and favours. But he probably knows that the man is eyeing him as competition. A hostile takeover."

"Just like Max Lukov's father, Dimitri," said Ramsay. "And as Max did, himself. To his own father, no less. These sorts always fall foul to hostile takeovers."

"Indeed." She paused. "You live by the sword; you die by the sword."

"Absolutely. Complete a short bio and send it to Rashid. Let him know who Lukov was dealing with. Get one to King, too."

Charlotte took notes and said, "Where is King?"

"Need to know," he said, hesitating before wheeling himself away from her desk. "Are there any more Jammy Dodgers?"

"Need to know..." she replied glibly and started to type on her keyboard. Ramsay scoffed and she watched him as he wheeled away, a tear in her eye as she thought about what the man had endured. She had daydreamed of being with him for too many years to count. They had shared an interest in puzzles and chess and gothic architecture, and she had longed to walk with him in somewhere like Prague or Bruge and immerse themselves in the city. Sometimes she imagined what it would have been like to share her bed, but her daydreams were nothing more than sharing intimacy and love and closeness. She had never been into the

Die Trying

physical gratification or experimentation. In fact, she considered her attraction to Ramsay as *sapiosexual*, attracted to the man's intelligence over all other attributes. Ramsay's catastrophic injury from an assassin's bullet may have confined the man to a wheelchair, but it made no difference to her, it merely consolidated the strength of his intellect. Charlotte had the bio completed in next to no time, and she sent one each to King and Rashid. Faceless people whom she had never met, and who would likely only achieve their objectives because of men and women like her seated in a comfortable office with Bach, Britten, Strauss, and Gershwin quietly playing in the background for half their working day. The Yin to their Yang, because the objective could only be achieved because of tough and resourceful men and women in the shadows who put their lives on the line, and who took other people's lives when necessary.

Chapter Fifty-Eight

Moscow

He had sought medical attention in Romania, but without the digit there was little that could be done. A thorough clean, some skin overlap, stitches and both steroid and antibiotic shots. He had been prescribed oral antibiotics and painkillers and told not to fly for a few days because of the risk of swelling. He had ignored the medical advice and flown within the hour on an Aeroflot flight direct to Moscow.

Uri wanted nothing more than to see Max Lukov dead, but he knew that he would have to bide his time. The GRU had subcontracted a mission to the former intelligence officer *because* of his mafia connections, not despite them. However, Lukov had seriously disrespected the GRU general, and Uri would lay it on thick enough for Orlev to feel utterly humiliated.

Die Trying

Uri stood up when Orlev entered the room. The table he was seated at alone was fifty-feet long and ten-feet wide. It could seat sixty people in comfort and had done for both strategic meetings and grand dinners alike. The ceilings above the magnificent, polished walnut table were thirty-feet high and decorated with intricate ceiling roses surrounding chandeliers seized from the Romanoff household in the cruel irony that was communism. People were only ever communist when they did not own the things other people did. Equally as intricate cornices framed the ceiling, meeting the oak-lined walls that played host to many works of art that once belonged to the Tsar and Joseph Stalin alike, as well as works by Van Gogh, Picasso and Chagall that had been seized from Hitler's bunker. Orlev was not alone. As usual, his number two and near-constant companion Sergei Bostock walked beside him, if not half a pace behind. Their mirror-polished military boots clipped the parquet flooring, the sound echoing around the room. Orlev frowned when he saw Uri's bandaged right hand with bloodstains seeping through.

"Tell me everything," Orlev said curtly.

"And miss out nothing," Bostock added. "No matter how small the detail."

Uri shrugged. Sergei Bostock was the same rank as himself, and had they not been with the GRU and under Orlev's command both men could be commanding a battalion of men or armour. "Lukov took me to see the product. When we returned, his men had killed the entire protection detail." He paused; the image burned fresh onto his eyes. "Slaughtered..."

"And this?" he asked, pointing at Uri's hand.

"They held me and Lukov cut off my finger," Uri said, swallowing down a sob. He wiped his eyes with the back of his bandaged hand and added, "He said that you should go fuck yourself..."

"What else?"

"Your mother was a whore," he lied. Who else was going to disagree? Uri wanted Lukov dead, and he needed the wrath of Orlev to bubble to the surface in the man usually regarded by his peers as coldness personified. "He said the best of you trickled down your mother's leg..."

"And you did not defend your commanding officer?" Sergei Bostock frowned.

"Of course I did!" Uri protested vehemently. "He said that he could go and fuck himself and his dried-up old mother and he was cutting the GRU out! He has the money, and he has the product and he'll do what he wants with both!" Uri seethed, but he knew that he had gone too far. In wanting Orlev to have Lukov killed, he had jeopardised a legitimate GRU operation. The cat was out of the bag and he would never be able to get it back in. He had allowed his ego to get the better of him and he had just committed an act of treason. And the GRU were quite specific on how they treated traitors.

Orlev shook his head. "I think our partnership with Max Lukov is at an end." He paused, touching Uri on the shoulder. "I am sorry for what happened to you. That was as much an attack on me as it was you, and I know that is no consolation to you at this time."

"What will you do?" Uri asked, looking up at him.

"Lukov will be taken out of the picture, and we will endeavour to retrieve our investment." He paused. "As for the heroin, we seize the factory before they have the chance to ship it." He turned to Sergei Bostock and said, "Sergei, my old friend, I have a task for you..."

The man stiffened to attention, looking straight past the general. "What will you have me do, sir?"

"Your skills are called for once more. I want you to cut out this cancer that infects us. I want Max Lukov killed. Immediately."

"Yes, sir!"

"At ease, major." Orlev waited for the man to relax and said, "Once he is dead his men will be leaderless, and we will take over the plant with a small team of Spetsnaz commandos." He turned to Uri and said, "In your opinion would ten heavily armed men provide enough fire power and intimidation?"

Uri shook as he was about to speak but held up his bandaged hand by way of explanation. "The labour at the plant are farm workers. There's no security because the very fact would look suspicious in what is an agricultural area on an industrial scale." He paused, unable to stop the emotion in his voice. He could almost feel the cold muzzle of the pistol on the nape of his neck – the favoured method of execution within the GRU. "As usual, Lukov is surrounded by bodyguards."

Orlev nodded, glancing at Bostock. Both men remembered the night in the forest, a chess move made by Orlev that had quickly been countered, somewhat recklessly, but countered all the same. This time, they needed every one of Lukov's pieces off the board. "Twenty men," he said decisively. "It will have to go through the directorate, but we will be ready to move in two days." He paused, looking at both men intently. "Two days and we will have control of the operation and Max Lukov will be dead."

Chapter Fifty-Nine

St. Petersburg, Russia

There were few places left within Max Lukov's considerable empire that she had not checked, but the realisation that her son could be moved around, back to places that she had checked and subsequently discounted was overwhelming. *Like pissing in the ocean*, her father would say of impossible tasks. A farmer from Ukraine, he had done little with his life other than work the farm, but he knew what was difficult, and what was impossible. Farming under the Soviet Union had been impossible, and often akin to *pissing in the ocean*, but at least with the Russian Federation it had moved from impossible to difficult. She thought of her father and mother – long-dead now – and what their lives had amounted to. She had vowed when she left home at eighteen never to return. She had travelled the world and met her Greek husband in Dubai in her early twenties working as cabin crew for an international airline. Josef had chatted her up on their flight and they had met for drinks in her hotel. They had slept together that night and been together for the next twelve years until she had learned about his business dealings the hard way. Caught up with Max Lukov in a property fraud scam that had cost Lukov millions of euros, the Russian had exacted his revenge not only by killing Josef, but by taking the couple's son. For a month of torment and agony, she had mourned without a body, always aware that her son may still be alive, but utterly helpless and ignorant. Lukov had shown her proof of life and told her to sleep with a fat, middle-aged German businessman. In the restful state after sex, she had been tasked to steal the man's wallet, pass it to someone posing as room service, and later put the wallet back undetected when room service replenished the champagne. She had done what was demanded of her – by both men – and she had showered for an hour afterwards, never once feeling clean. And she would never again drink champagne. She thought that she would be reunited with her son, and it would be an end to her anguish. But it was only the start. Max Lukov had used her for three years now, and she never got more than a fleeting glimpse of her boy and a few snatched words. He would have changed by now, reached puberty. Could he have been influenced by his captors? Undoubtedly. Would he even know and still love her? Perhaps not. But she would not give up on him, and she would kill Lukov when she found her son. About that, there was no question.

The first time Lukov had asked her to kill a man, it had been his own father. He was an experienced killer, and he would have undoubtedly recognised a fellow spirit. She had been given the poison with which she would incapacitate him, and then instructed on how and where to cut. The man had naturally wanted to have sex with her, and for fear of him becoming suspicious, she had obliged. She had hated herself but was now devoid of feeling anything but the loss of her son. The second time she was to kill a man, it had been by seduction and with a syringe. She was an attractive woman, and her wild, red hair did something to men, released hidden depths of passion. She had seduced him easily, and this time she did not have to sleep with him, simply stabbed him with the syringe and locked herself in the bathroom as he hammered on the door in a rage, his beating becoming weaker by the minute and his shouts turning to rasps and grunts as he died in his underpants on the other side of the door. She would never be sullied again, never use her sex to get to a target.

It had surprised her how easily she lived with the killing. With two men dead – both odious individuals in their own way – the third life she had taken had been with a knife, and it had not been an easy task. It was then that she learned that real life and the movies were far removed from one another, and that when people were stabbed, the variables were vast. The first thrust of the knife went unfelt, and by the time the man had realised, and she stabbed him again, she struck bone, and the knife was seriously bent at the tip, meaning that it was difficult to withdraw. When she finally got it free, the man was fighting back – for his life – and that meant an unparalleled and unimagined degree of desperation. Herself wounded by his blows and cut by her own blade, she had finally slashed the man's throat and he had bled and lost all the fight in him. And he had bled. And bled. Pints of blood, and no sign in stopping. The tiled floor was covered – ten feet in radius and still he had bled. The man's life was draining from him with every drop of precious blood and after a few minutes, he was dead. It was then that she knew if she was going to fulfil Lukov's tasks, get closer to the man who held her son prisoner, then she would have to learn. She researched endlessly, trained daily at the gym and in various martial arts, and learned to shoot. She bought knives and trained on punchbags in her apartment which she would stab and slice and tape back up after use, and she learned how to throw knives and which knives worked best, and from what distance you held the tip of the blade, or the handle, or how to throw a blade straight with no spin. She trained in the art of killing by using her next task as a lesson. She would dissect the experience and see what she could learn from it. All the time, picturing Lukov as her final assassination. All roads led to finding her son, and that ultimately led to Lukov.

She concentrated on the building across the street. A gym was the last place she would expect her son to be held prisoner, but this was one of a handful of Lukov's business interests left to check. The building was vast and boasted fifty exercise bikes alone, let alone the dozens of weight benches and literal tons of free weights. One floor was dedicated to boxing training alone, and another to dance aerobics. A pool, sauna, solarium, and spa appealed to one clientele, while the bodybuilding scene served another, and the reason the place existed. And all because of anabolic steroids and the hundreds of men and women perfecting their bodies with them, and the hundreds of steroid dealers who sold Lukov's wares at other gyms across Russia and Europe. She wondered whether a small room, or storage facility, or even an entire floor for all she knew could be where her son was being held. Regardless, it was another place off her list. All she needed now was to get into the building and check the floors without arousing suspicion.

The text message interrupted her thoughts and she stared at the screen to see the familiar greeting. *Samuel sends his love...* Lukov was the devil, sending her the same greeting each time he wanted her to take a man's life. Her hand started to shake with rage as she read the rest of the message. She would have no time to investigate the building now, for all the good it would do her, but she would come back soon and cross another place off her extensive list.

She re-read the text, trying to ignore the introduction. This would be a difficult job, and she wondered whether the man had taken leave of his senses. The repercussions to Lukov would be severe, but she did not care. The enemy of her enemy was her friend.

Chapter Sixty

Romania

"Well, this is problematic," said Rashid.

"Impossible, more like," Luger observed.

"Difficult," Rashid replied. "But not impossible."

Luger scoffed. "Whatever they're doing down there, they're not closing for the night. There was a shift change and they're working round the clock."

"Like I said, problematic."

"We can't just walk in there. They'll notice us."

"Well, they may notice six-four and eighteen stone of black Fijian, but you're about average height and weight and if you're in the same kit..."

"You're kidding?" Luger stared at Rashid, then said, "You're not kidding."

"I'll be watching and protecting you from here with the

sniper rifle," Rashid assured him. "Mind you, it'll have to be a life-or-death situation for me to shoot a non-combative."

"So, just watching, then." Luger paused. "With me in spirit."

"I'll go down with you," Big Dave told him. "But I'd better hang back. I'm going to be noticed if I go inside."

"Great."

"It looks like the smaller building next to the area of interest is where shift workers clock in and get into their overalls. They all wear gloves and face masks, too. So that should keep you anonymous," Rashid said helpfully.

"Right, thanks."

Rashid checked his watch and shrugged. "You'd better get cracking, then."

Luger tutted and took off his motorcycle jacket. The late spring night air was chilly, but he'd soon warm up. He checked his clothing for anything that rattled, then took off his stainless-steel Omega watch and slipped it into his pocket.

"Turn your phone to vibrate," Rashid said.

"Already done."

"Come on then, sunshine," said Big Dave. "Let's have a wander down there and see what's what."

The two men made their way down the hill using the rocks and bushes as cover. The terrain reminded Luger of Mediterranean Spain or France with sun-baked earth and hardy foliage with the sound of insects and scurrying lizards all around them. The climate clearly grew far hotter in the summer months. With their eyes well accustomed to the darkness they crossed over the road and made their way down beside the stacked portacabin offices and over the ground that had only been sluiced of blood earlier that day.

"I'll wait here," said Big Dave.

Die Trying

"Superb, couldn't be happier," Luger said morosely.

The big Fijian shrugged. "Rashid's right, I'll be out of place in there," he said apologetically, although the grin made it look far from sincere. "You go on, I'll be ok here fending for myself."

"I'm sure you will," Luger replied tersely.

"Don't worry, Rashid has you in his sights."

"But he won't shoot non-combatives…"

"And nor should he."

"At least he's got a good view from up there." Luger wasted no more time and walked confidently and easily across the yard towards the smaller building. There was nothing to be gained by running or stalking his way across the open ground – that would only attract attention.

At the smaller building he checked the windows, then walked between the two buildings to search for a side entrance. There was a door halfway down the wide alleyway – wide enough to accommodate tractors and trailers - and he checked the door but wasn't surprised that it was locked. It seemed foolhardy not to check all the way around the building and he rounded the rear and froze, cigarette butts lighting the night like fireflies. Suddenly, he had flashbacks of that night on the Baltic coast. An outside illuminated and he ducked back into the lee of the building as a worker stepped outside and lit a cigarette as he walked down the stairs. The light was movement sensitive, and after a minute, the group of smokers were plunged into darkness, their cigarette tips visible once more.

Luger made his way back around the front of the building and tried the door. It opened smoothly, indicating that it had a lot of use, and he found some used overalls and masks in a laundry basket. That was good enough for him, and he pulled them on over his clothes and covered his head with the hood. The mask buoyed him with confidence, and he found used gloves and shoe covers in a waste bin and helped himself. The protective clothing covered him from head to toe, and he walked confidently across the wide alleyway and opened the door to the aircraft hangar sized building and stepped inside.

Chapter Sixty-One

Luger placed the fire extinguisher on the table and picked up his beer. The bottle was nicely frosted, and the Romanian beer inside was ambered and hoppy. It wasn't a bad reward for his hike back up the hill with the 10kg fire extinguisher and uncomfortable ride back on the motorcycle, his bruising from the fall from the motorcycle in Estonia still coming out.

"Really?" Caroline asked.

"It's perfect," Luger replied. "They depressurise the fire extinguisher, cut off the bottom and remove the contents. Then they wash it out and insert a metal container filled with heroin resin. After they weld it back together, they refill the cylinder with powder fire retardant and re-pressurise it with CO_2. It's a huge production line and they are packaging them in crates and loading them into shipping containers as we speak."

"Well, I wouldn't have known," said Jo getting out of her chair and putting down her glass of wine. She picked up the fire extinguisher and examined the weld and touch-up of red paint before saying, "No, it's perfect."

"Where are the fire extinguishers from?" asked Caroline. "They must have bought enough to arouse suspicion."

"Worldwide, I suspect. That would be the most subtle way to do it and I did notice different languages on some of the crates of original fire extinguishers," Luger replied. "There were all different sizes with various colours denoting the type of fire retardant, so I presume that the larger ones hold more heroin. It looked like the ones that size..." He pointed at the one in Jo's hands. "... take five-kilos of product. I suppose we'll see when we open it."

"There's nowhere open now to get the tools to open it," said Rashid. "But first thing in the morning we need to get the canister open to verify."

"I have verified," Luger protested. "I took that one out of one of the finished crates. I didn't risk going in there for nothing."

Rashid nodded. "But it won't hurt to check." He paused, checking his watch. "Big Dave is on watch at Lukov's villa. He'll need relieving at around two-am. Volunteers?"

"I'll do it," said Caroline. She could see that with King not present and both Luger and Jo being relatively new to the team Rashid had assumed charge. She had noticed too, that Big Dave, whom she had always considered a safe pair of hands had eased back and allowed Rashid some rein. Rashid had stepped up, and there was nothing to be gained by a power play. Besides, that wasn't the big Fijian's style, nor hers for that matter because they had nothing to prove.

Rashid nodded. "Jo, you can take over at eight." He paused. "I'll fill Ramsay in with what we have and then I'll get the tools we need to open that thing in the morning." Everyone started to disperse. It was late and their hotel rooms beckoned. Rashid nodded to Luger and said, "Jack, can you stay behind? There's something I want to run by you..."

Chapter Sixty-Two

**Moscow,
Twenty-four hours later**

King watched the target as he stepped out of his Mercedes SUV and walked to the restaurant. He had watched the target for twenty-four hours. He no longer needed to see an image of the man because his features were indelibly burned into his memory. He knew the man's mannerisms and he knew his movements. He would have recognised him with a hood covering his features. He knew the man's closest three bodyguards as well. The largest of them walked two metres in front of his principal, the ugliest walked two metres behind and the man's personal bodyguard, a smart-looking man of medium build and intelligent eyes walked to the man's right, keeping around a metre from him with his right hand unhindered so he could draw his weapon.

King could see that the bodyguards were confident. He

could also see that from the bulges under their suit jackets that they were armed with machine pistols. He would have guessed MP5K compacts, but they could be mini-Uzi submachineguns or Mac-10s. It made a difference because the former was an accurate weapon and the other two were 'spray and pray' types. The four men all wore body armour, too. The Russians had devised a light-weight Kevlar system that could stop high-velocity rounds up to 7.62x51mm without the need for steel or ceramic trauma plates, so it would have to be headshots only, and for that he would need to either get close, or he would need a rifle with a good set of optics. He had picked up a Tokarev TT30 pistol in 7.62x25mm and although it was a powerful weapon, it held only eight rounds and he did not fancy getting up close and personal and having to perform a magazine reload in the thick of it. No, with the pistol, he would have to approach from behind. It was placing a lot of trust in a weapon he had not test fired and a misfire or stoppage could be the death of him. He wondered whether there would be a better opportunity in the restaurant. A better angle. Perhaps he could use his knife for the first kill or disarm a bodyguard to give him a tested weapon, with his own street purchase as back up. He'd worked with worse plans.

King crossed over and made a point of not looking at the Russian delegation as he asked the waitress for a table. He sat down at a table for two, choosing the chair with its back to the wall for practical as well as security reasons. He ordered a beer as she left the menu with him, and he looked over at the table for the first time. Orlev was seated at a table for two, with a young woman. She looked too young for him, but her dress and manner told King that she was being paid for the lunch date and quite happy about the arrangement. He wondered whether she would be as happy afterwards in the hotel room and whatever deviance he had planned for her, which the man's wife would most likely soundly object to.

The three bodyguards occupied a table set for four and like most bodyguards had to make do with bread and water while their principal started his three-course meal by sharing a carafe of vodka with shavings of garlic and some cured pork fat known as *slalina*. King ordered a charcuterie board and a basket of bread, and he picked at it as he took out his phone to look like he was simply killing time or catching up on emails.

Starters arrived, were quickly devoured and the dishes cleared away. Orlev was pouring champagne himself, the waiter barely able to keep up, and soon brought a second bottle. King watched as a trolley was brought to the table and the head waiter prepared the flambé table. Diners were always curious when a dish was cooked or carved at the table, and it gave King the opportunity to watch, if not Orlev himself, then at least in the general direction. The dishes arrived by a stream of waiting staff and the head waiter started frying onions and garlic in a little oil and shaking in paprika. Copious amounts of butter followed, and then the shredded fillet steak. The meat had barely kissed the pan when the man gave it a great stir and added the brandy. He pulled the pan away and tipped it towards the naked flame and the brandy ignited and a flame three-feet-high licked the air and diners gasped in surprise and delight. Orlev's date clapped her hands enthusiastically and the head waiter tried not to look too supercilious as he quickly added the mustard, chopped parsley and thick reduced beef stock with panache. Paper-thin slices of button mushrooms were added next, and to keep them perfectly white, cream followed before they could cook too much. The man seasoned with salt and pepper and with well-practised efficiency, waiting staff arrived with bowls of French fries – the traditional accompaniment that has been largely forgotten in favour of vegetables or rice. King watched the performance, a female diner sidling past the head waiter with indifference as he begrudgingly made room for her, then served the classic Beef Stroganoff with a further dusting of paprika.

King had seen enough. The man was already as good as dead. He dropped a handful of rubbles beside his unfinished food and drink and headed out of the restaurant.

After twenty paces at a jog, he slowed down and said, "What was it?" to the woman in front of him.

She turned and stared at him, her eyes darting around checking that he was alone. "What?" she replied indignantly.

King raised his shirt to reveal the pistol, then let it cover it up again. "It was a nice move," he said. "What was it?"

"Powdered death cap mushroom," she replied, still keeping her eyes on the street.

King knew about death cap mushrooms. *Amanita phalloides* – it destroyed the liver and brought death within forty-eight hours, and there was no cure. When knowingly digested, a liver transplant may be possible, but ingested innocently with time lost through testing blood samples and there was nothing that could be done. It was a painful death, too. Meant to be one of the worst ways to go.

King shrugged. "Goes well with the stroganoff, I suppose."

"Homework," she said. "Orlev always orders the beef stroganoff when he eats there."

"You're The Widow," he said.

"Am I meant to be impressed?"

"No."

"And who the hell are you?"

"Nobody," he replied. "If you've heard of me, then I'm not doing my job properly."

"Well, goodbye Mr Nobody," she said and started to walk away.

King followed. "What about the woman?"

She spun around and glared. "Leave me alone!"

"We need to talk."

"I am not bothered by the death of a whore!"

"Not about that," said King. "About Max Lukov."

She stared at him. "Who are you, really?"

"Nobody."

"You are British. You are secret service."

"I have no qualms with you," he told her.

"Eh?"

"*Problem*," he emphasised. "I have no problem with you."

"Good. Then keep walking," she glared. "In the other direction."

"I know Max Lukov has your son," said King. "You were an air hostess. You have no formal training. Why else would the woman whose husband Lukov had killed be working for him?" King looked at her earnestly and could see the woman's expression softening. "I can help find him. We have surveillance taps on Max Lukov and are monitoring all his communications. I can have our analysts run his phone records through some software that will flag up anything about your son. From there, it will snowball until they have a phone number, a GPS location or embedded video file..."

The woman stopped in her tracks, and when she turned around and looked at him, her expression had softened, vulnerability seeping out of what had before been arrogance and indifference. "Really?"

"Really."

"What else do you know?" she asked, glancing at the entrance to the restaurant.

"I know that Lukov allows you to walk around free. That must be humiliating, knowing that the man has control enough over you to hold you as a prisoner without walls."

"You know nothing," she hissed. "What do you know of pain and fear?"

"Everything there is."

"I doubt that," she sneered. "I know things, too. I know that you think Lukov to be more than he is."

"He's head of the mafia family, but he gets his orders from Orlev." King paused. "Who you've just killed, or as good as."

She laughed bitterly. "Orlev is a fool. Max Lukov works for someone else, that person gives Orlev the orders and that covers Lukov. Orlev was the unwitting middleman in a secret organisation."

King frowned. "Have you heard of Iron Fist?" he ventured.

She smiled thinly. "When he was in a drunken, power-hungry state, he let slip that name, yes." She paused. "But I know who really gives him his orders, through that pig Orlev."

"Perhaps we can help each other," King mused. "In fact, I know we can." He glanced behind him and watched as an ambulance stopped outside the restaurant. He looked back at The Widow and said over the wail of a siren, "But not here."

"Where?"

"My hotel room."

"Not a chance!" she scoffed.

"Yours, then."

"No way." She backed away and stood in the lee of the building beside them as she watched the commotion at the restaurant's entrance. Orlev's bodyguards were overseeing the paramedics loading their principal into the ambulance. The poor woman who had been his lunch date was nowhere to be seen as the ambulance pulled away, Orlev's personal bodyguard riding with him in the ambulance, and the other two sprinting back to their car. "Very well, I know a place," she conceded. She reached into her handbag, noticing King's hand gliding to the butt of the pistol, and she smirked as she took out a pen and piece of paper and scribbled an address. She handed it over to King and said, "No tricks. If you try to trick me, I will slice you and watch you bleed to death.

"I believe you," he said sincerely.

"Tonight. Nine pm. You can buy me dinner."

"Just as long as mushrooms are off the menu."

"Naturally."

King smiled, then turned and watched the commotion as a member of the restaurant staff pulled up to the entrance in an old Honda Civic and a chef and two waitresses helped the hooker into the car. She was barely conscious and had vomited down her pretty dress. When King turned around to look at The Widow there was no sign of her, and a shiver ran down his spine as he turned on his heel and walked back towards his hotel.

Chapter Sixty-Three

Westminster, London

It was at times like these that Ramsay felt the vulnerability of his wheelchair. There was plenty of difficulties that he had discovered in a short time and had been oblivious of before. Poor disabled access generally, high pavement kerbs, steep ramps, push-button door openers mounted too high, impatient bus drivers, restaurant toilets with no thought of location – it was a whole new world to navigate. But those were difficulties. This was different. This was people's lack of understanding, but then he supposed it was intentional. The six-foot-plus old Etonian was standing unyieldingly in front of him, looking down on him and dominating the conversation. Not that it was a conversation at this point and hadn't been from the start.

"A little birdie?" Ramsay questioned the man, unable to keep the contempt from his tone.

"Yes, a little birdie."

"And by little birdie, you mean Marcus Devonshire of the Secret Intelligence Service."

"My sources are protected, Neil," he replied. "You should know that by now."

"Devonshire went to Eton as well, didn't he?"

"I'm sure I don't know what you mean."

"At aged thirty-nine, he would have been in your year."

"This is not about Marcus..."

"Home Secretary, this is not the time to play quid-pro-quo with old school friends."

"I will decide what time it is!" The Home Secretary paused. If anything, he had made himself appear even taller as he took a step closer towards Ramsay, forcing him to crane his neck to hold eye contact. "You have stumbled into the drugs game, when you were given this remit to fight terrorism and foreign spies!" He paused, looking down at him somewhat derisively, briefly a sneer, but he checked himself in time. "You have carte blanche, you have deniability, and you write your own cheques. You have clearly wandered into something beyond your remit, and you need to stand down. The Romanian police and Interpol can take over from here."

Ramsay shook his head at the Home Secretary and said, "Sit down, Kenneth..." The Home Secretary frowned, but something in Ramsay's expression told him that he would just be wasting his time. He stepped back and perched on his desk. "No, on the chair, at your desk, please Kenneth. Let's approach this in a civilised manner." He did not give the man time to respond. "These drugs are being smuggled into Europe with the sole intention of creating mass addicts. A Russian operation to weaken our infrastructure and civilisation..."

"For the Russians to attack?" the Home Secretary said incredulously. "They can't even beat the Ukrainians!"

"Then you greatly underestimate Ukraine. The Ukrainian forces have killed more Russian soldiers and destroyed more tanks, artillery, armoured vehicles, and aircraft than Britain possesses, bar our naval vessels. That means that if we were fighting the Ukraine and suffered those same losses, we would have not one piece of equipment in operation, nor one member of personnel left alive. And that's not fighting forces; that's even down to admin and catering staff. *Nothing* left." Ramsay paused. "And Russia keeps sending men and equipment. And will do until they either beat Ukraine or the Russian president dies or is overthrown. Until then, it's a conveyer belt of lives and equipment and bullets. We underestimate Russia at our peril."

"Semantics," the Home Secretary replied. "Whether or not Russia remains a credible threat..."

"Which it does, and always will be," Ramsay interjected.

"Be that as it may, you are wasting your remit on a drug deal." He paused. "Now, the PM is in agreement with me, and my contact in MI6..."

"Marcos Devonshire," Ramsay reminded him. "Your school chum and whatever he is now to you."

"Devonshire thinks that your lot assassinated the deputy director of the GRU."

"Then he'd be wrong." Ramsay paused. "And technically, it isn't an assassination yet. General Orlev is being treated in hospital."

"With no cure and zero chance of making it past the weekend."

"Horrible business," the Home Secretary mused. "Are

you sure that this has nothing to do with your lot?" he goaded him. "Tell me you haven't got a man in Moscow."

Ramsay ignored him. He would never divulge an agent's whereabouts. Besides, King hadn't killed Orlev. He had been beaten to it. "Did Marcos Devonshire that tell you about his mole hunt?" he asked acidly. "And how he risked the life of my agent in doing so?"

"Not my remit, Ramsay. That's the Foreign secretary. You answer to me, and MI6 answer to the Foreign Secretary."

"Who also went to Eton, two years before you both. What was he, head boy? Dorm prefect? Head buggerer of young boys?"

The Home Secretary smiled thinly. "It's a puzzle for you comprehensive school lot, isn't it? The inner workings of public schools, family connections, politics."

"Not a puzzle difficult to solve, Home Secretary." He paused. "I am far from stupid. I know how class, status and politics works. And I remain at my post to keep the injustice and corruption that lies at the heart of that at bay."

"Don't fight me on this, Ramsay. Turn it over to the police and get back to the business of hunting terrorists and foreign spies." He paused. "You know? Some people, many as it happens, said that it was too early for you to return to work, let alone head a department. Are you sure that they were not wrong? Perhaps a break would be in order, or early retirement, maybe?"

"I don't take breaks," Ramsay replied. "And I'm certainly not retiring. Not while the game is in play."

"Game, what game?"

Ramsay wheeled himself to the door and opened it. As he positioned his chair, he looked measuredly at the Home Secretary and said, "It's a game of chess with a politician, cabinet member or member of the civil service making up the pieces. Some are biding their time, others are crashing in boldly and without consideration, and others are on the run. But the pieces are all in play, and I'm coming for them. I'm several steps ahead and exceptionally patient."

"I don't play chess," the Home Secretary scoffed.

"No, you don't, do you..."

Chapter Sixty-Four

M oscow

He was travelling on a Russian passport that he had last used seven years ago. His Russian was passable, but not fluent. Conversational was the true definition, so it was easy to navigate if he simply gave nothing away and asked few questions. King liked it that way, anyway.

The bar she had chosen was a lounge affair that along with the many and varying comfortable chairs and sofas, boasted over five-hundred different vodkas and an array of vodka-based cocktails, which judging by the neatly written blackboards in Cyrillic and English must have been nearly all of them. In King's mind, at least.

King arrived early, as was his habit, and he had already checked the exits and chokepoints before securing a favourable alcove and ordering water with slices of lime and plenty of ice. It looked the part, and he needed a clear head.

Die Trying

He tipped well to balance the low value sale and sat with his back to the wall while keeping an eye on the entrance. Three tables over, a woman with long, straight black hair wearing a cocktail dress walked over and sat opposite him. King was about to say that he wasn't interested in 'business' – as it seemed that on first appearances that Russian women were either old, weathered babushkas or young, attractive prostitutes - when he realised that it was The Widow. A wig and some carefully chosen and applied makeup had changed her appearance considerably, and he felt irked that he had allowed her to get the better of him.

"Did I fool you?" she asked.

"No," he lied.

"You lie terribly," she smirked. "Not good. For a spy."

"Ok, you fooled me," he conceded.

"You said that you could help me. Is that true?" she asked earnestly, before her expression hardened and she stared at him dubiously, accusingly. "Or are you just trying to get me into bed?"

"No," King replied, somewhat surprised at her reasoning. "I can help you, but I'm not trying to sleep with you."

She sat back in her chair, sipping her drink as she regarded him closely. "You are a handsome man. But I am not sure you are kind. Your mouth and expression, maybe. Your eyes? No. They are cold. Perhaps you are kind..." She pointed at his chest. "... in there. A kind heart, but seldom allowed to be."

"All that from looking at my face?'

"You can tell much from someone's face. Their journey is written."

"I don't buy that."

She leaned forwards and said, "You have lost someone, I can see that in your eyes. She was taken too soon..." She tilted her head, scrutinising every part of his face. "Her death was sudden it took all your love away."

King stared at her. It was true, Jane's death had been sudden. But her illness hadn't. That had taken everything from her – her strength, her humour, her sparkle – King had returned to a note and her body. She wanted to go out on her own terms. "Leave it," he said quietly.

"She wasn't the only loss in your life. I think your parents died when you were young, I think you know what poverty is like. It's worn on your face like my father's..."

"I said, leave it!" he snapped.

She sat back in her chair, satisfied with her response. "I think you need a woman who understands you. If you can find my son and help me get him back, I will be that woman," she said matter-of-factly. "You can have me. On your terms, to do anything and everything with. For a night, or for the rest of my life..."

King sipped from his glass wishing it was vodka. He didn't know what to say, but he knew he wouldn't bother mentioning this conversation to Caroline. "I'm going to kill Lukov," he said. "Those are my orders."

"And?"

"If I kill him, then you won't find your son."

"Why do you care?"

"I suppose you were right about me," King shrugged. "My mother died when I was young. I never knew my father, either. My siblings were all younger than me. We ended up in care and lost each other."

"That was just now. You were always going to do this thing, despite what I just said to you."

"Those were my reasons."

"You are soft, for a killer." She paused. "I am surprised you have lived this long."

Die Trying

"Fine," he said. "Then we're done here..." King put down his drink and stood up.

"Wait..." she said, her expression showing vulnerability for the first time. "Can you *really* find my son?"

"It's as good as done," he replied, sitting back down, and picking up his drink. "AI algorithms with keywords, times, dates, and locations. You'd be surprised just how easy it can be."

"And you have done this?" she asked eagerly.

"Not me, but the people I work for."

"And it is done, you know where Samuel is?"

"So, I'm told."

"But you do not know, yourself?"

"No."

"Why?"

"Because you could drug me and extract the information. My boss is rather good at planning the moves on his chessboard. Someone knows where your son is, but it's not me. Yet."

"And you will tell me where Samuel is just because you are a good Samaritan?"

"Oh, fuck no," King replied glibly.

For a moment she looked taken aback, but she recovered well and said, "Then what?" she asked, then nodded. "Because you now want what I said, about being your woman."

"Relax. I don't want you as my whore."

"Then what?"

"Because you can be of use to us," King shrugged. "That's how my department works. You can be useful to us, that's all."

"Go on..." she said dubiously.

"I want you to flush out Lukov for me. But if it's done

right, then we can get your son back."

She seemed to ponder for a moment, then said, "But I know something that you would like to know. Earlier, on the street. I said that I know who Lukov works for. This Iron Fist... I thought it was the egotistical ramblings of a power-hungry drunk. But no, you know of them, and you want to know who tells Lukov who to kill, or how to raise money for their organisation."

"Yes," King shrugged. "We do."

"Then you are not just helping me. You say that you want me to flush out Lukov, and that is true, I have a connection. But this is two favours for one..."

"I can find your son," replied King. "That kind of balances the equation, don't you think?"

"We shall see," she replied somewhat cryptically. "Tell your superiors in London that I can let you know the name of someone significant in this so-called Iron Fist. But I want my son freed and delivered to me before I give the name, and I want a new start. A coastal villa in Spain and a hundred-thousand euros. Tell them that, or it's no deal." She paused, seeming pleased with herself that her stock just went up. "Tell them that I will get to Max Lukov and I will torture him to find out where Samuel is being held, and then I will cut the man's throat before you get what you want from him..."

Chapter Sixty-Five

Romania

"Are you sure this is the best way?" asked Caroline.

"Well, it's *a* way," Jack Luger replied. "Whether it's the best way, I have no idea, but I certainly hope so."

"You *hope* so?" Caroline scoffed. "We certainly need more than just *hope*!"

Luger smiled. "We've had less to go on in the past."

"Well, that says a lot about how we work... you've only been with us for five minutes..." Caroline's grip tightened on the old, worn 9mm Makarov pistol. "There's a lot of them," she said, slipping the weapon into her inside jacket pocket. "I do get rather nervous when there are more people than I have bullets for."

"That's why Rashid is holed-up three-hundred metres away with a G3 rifle," he replied. "I just hope he's as good as everyone says he is."

Caroline laughed. "He's probably better..." She caught hold of the doorhandle and said, "Come on, then. Here goes nothing..."

Luger followed, but Romania was a man's world, and he overtook Caroline and greeted the lead man coolly. "Gregor?"

The man, all six-three, and twenty-stone of him stared back coldly, then stepped aside to reveal a man no taller than five-two and little heavier than seven stone. Luger baulked at the sight of a man with so much influence but turned the scoff into a cough before continuing. "I have heard much about you, Gregor," he said. "This is my associate, Caroline Darby."

Gregor stared for a long time at Caroline, and it was clear that he liked what he saw. He extended his hand and before Caroline knew what was happening, the handshake she offered turned into an elaborate kiss on the back of her hand. She fought herself not to bristle at the sensation of the man's plump lips on her skin and said, "We have been told that you and your men could help us."

"No doubt," Gregor replied. He stood chest-high to the other eight men, but he looked well-protected. Pistol butts protruded over waistbands and several of the men wore long leather coats despite the warm weather, and those leather coats boasted ominous bulges. They would have their work cut out if this went south, even with Rashid covering them with an automatic weapon. "If you need anything along the Black Sea coast, then you come to Gregor..."

"And you can handle the quantities of what we require?" Luger asked.

The Romanian shrugged. "Fuel, sugar, industrial cleaner... no problem." He paused. "But the other thing, that will be more expensive." He rubbed his thumb and forefinger together. "I will need to grease the wheels... pay for signatures to be lost, for eyes to look the other way. It will be expensive, especially in the quantities you require."

"Go on..." Caroline told him, but she remembered to smile. The Romanian gangster had clearly taken a liking to her, and she was not beyond a little harmless flirting to ease things along. "But don't disappoint me too much..."

"A quarter of a million euros," he said without flinching. He was staring at Caroline's breasts, directly at his eye-height.

Luger raised an eyebrow. "How about using a little less money to grease the wheels and a little more stick?"

"Stick?" he asked, turning his gaze away from Caroline's breasts.

"Yes. You know, stick?" Luger punched his fist into his other hand and said, "Stick..."

The little man laughed. "Buying people and beating people costs about the same. But when one is bought, they can always be bought. But beat someone too hard..." he shrugged leaving it to their own imagination to fill the gap, but they both got it.

"Well, far be it from us to tell you how to go about your business," Caroline smiled. "It will be a bank transfer. We'll need BIC and IBANs as well as the account number. Offshore, I presume?"

"Switzerland."

"The gold standard," she replied. "The US government have made the Caribbean untenable the way they have seized funds from the Central and South American cartels. I mean, whose money will they take next?"

"The Swiss sell gold without too many questions, too," Gregor grinned. "However, what you ask for will take time."

"Well, that's okay because you've got until tomorrow," Caroline said offhandedly.

"No...!"

"Yes," she replied firmly. "Now, give me your account details so I can pay upon delivery. Say, this time tomorrow and shall we say, twelve-thousand euros less for every hour you run over?" She paused. "And twelve thousand more for every hour you deliver sooner?"

The little Romanian stared hard at her – her eyes this time - his expression serious and for a moment, quite unnerving, before he broke into a grin and laughed raucously. He looked to his men, who all joined in as if directed upon a stage. "I like you, blondie... I like you very much indeed..."

Chapter Sixty-Six

Romania

They had worked throughout the night and progress had been slow. But that was favourable when dealing with explosives. They had found a derelict farm where they could use a large, abandoned cattle shed, and had started their dangerous task. Big Dave was the expert in this field and had set about boiling the sugar, Borax, hydrogen peroxide and the bleach in large catering saucepans over a large gas jet used for heating tarmac before patching road surfaces. The correct quantities and the specific order in which they were added and mixed, and the required temperature all came from memory, and he had been confident that he could produce a manageable and practical, yet not dangerously volatile compound as a detonator. Gregor has been as good as his word and had got the delivery of chemical fertiliser to them two hours before the deadline and had earned himself another twenty-four-thousand euros. Rashid had set about making gaps in the stacks of 25kg plastic bags in which they would place the highly explosive compound that Big Dave had created. The chemical fertiliser, pound for pound, was a quarter as destructive is military grade plastic explosive such as C4. However, they had 100 times what the military would use to destroy the large agricultural building, but they wanted it completely flattened with no trace of the heroin remaining, and with the heroin inside solid metal fire extinguishers, it would take a lot. Big Dave had also created several fuses that would be inserted into the soft, gelatinous compound that he had made. These would be placed throughout the loading space of the heavy goods vehicle. The fuses had been created by soaking lengths of string in a solution of sugar, Borax, and paraffin. A half-metre length had been tested and proven to take two minutes to burn, and two minutes would be all it would take to wipe out the Iron Fist's campaign.

Rashid got out of the car and walked back to the truck. Big Dave was behind the wheel and had found a trucker's cap from somewhere in the cab.

"You certainly look the part..." said Rashid as he looked up at him through the open window.

"It's the small details that matter," he replied.

Rashid nodded. He checked his phone as the text alert sounded. "That's Neil," he said. "He's made the call to Interpol and the Romanian police."

Ramsay had no choice but to turn their findings over to the Romanian police, but dubious of both their integrity and of Max Lukov's reach, he had brought in Interpol in a measure of operational oversight. Once the world-wide police and law enforcement agencies cooperative were involved, the Romanians would have nowhere left to hide, and a thorough and just investigation could proceed under the watchful eye of Interpol. That was the idea, at least, and Ramsay had just rolled that particular snowball downhill.

"Well, that doesn't give us much time, does it?" Big Dave commented. "And we still have to get those workers out of there. They're not Russian GRU, or Iron Fist, or Lukov family mafia. They're just immigrants and Romanian peasants who are turning a blind eye because they need to put food on the table."

"Jo has got a diversion, or at least a delay for the police, if we cut it too fine."

"Well, let's hope we don't need it," said Big Dave, starting the engine of the eighteen-wheeler. "This thing is a bit different from the lorries I drove in the army. Eighteen forward gears and four reverse." He worked the gearbox and clutch, but still managed to make a terrific grinding noise.

"You're not that good in a car, let alone that thing."

"You wanna drive?"

"No."

"Didn't think so," he chided. "Get down there and raise the alarm. I'm going through those doors while I've got some momentum because if they wise up and try and hold us off, then it will be all for nothing."

Rashid rolled his eyes as he ran back to his car. He knew that the big man could be impetuous sometimes, heavy-handed most of the time and lacking self-preservation almost every time that action was called for. By the time he got the engine started, Big Dave raced past in the lorry and sounded the air horn twice.

"Bloody hell!" Rashid leapt with a start, then accelerated and overtook the lorry and headed down the long road and across the vast concrete yard to the hangar-like packing station. He sounded his vehicle's horn and leapt out. At the entrance, a fire-alarm was mounted to the wall beside the personnel door, and he smashed the glass with his elbow and ran to the neighbouring building and did the same. Workers wandered outside, some panicked and others sauntering and seizing the opportunity for an impromptu cigarette break as they headed to the muster point across the yard. He looked up as the lorry thundered across the concrete yard towards him, and he sprinted to the main building as the last people headed out. Somebody caught his arm to stop him from entering, and he shook them off and darted inside to check that the building was clear. He barely got away from the entrance when the lorry hammered into the great sliding doors and the air filled with cannon fire, or something akin to the sound, and sparks lit up the cavernous space. People were heading back towards them, full of concern, and Rashid drew his pistol and fired several shots into the air, dispersing everyone in various directions. Inside, the engine had been switched off and Big Dave sauntered over.

"Got a light?" he asked quite seriously.

"God have mercy..." Rashid took one of the two lighters they had purchased for the task out of his pocket and handed it to him.

"Can you hear sirens?"

Rashid turned around. He could hear sirens and hoped that Jo had managed to carry out her task. Big Dave was suddenly at his shoulder, and he patted him on the back as he jogged past. Rashid launched into a sprint, quickly overtaking the man-mountain, and firing several shots into the air to get the workers back. He got to the car and started it, but Big Dave had hedged his bets and was running across

Die Trying

the yard ahead of him. Rashid slowed as he passed him, and the Big Fijian clambered in on the move.

"That went well," he said as he closed the door, his knees near his chest in the mid-sized hatchback.

"I haven't heard anything yet," Rashid replied glibly.

"You soon will..." Big Dave was cut off by the almighty explosion, the sound deafening them and the shockwave momentarily lifting the rear of the car off the road before they bounced back down.

Rashid's ears were ringing, and as he checked his mirrors, he could see people unsteadily clambering from the ground, the white dry powder from the fire extinguishers and the residue of unburned heroin snowing down on them. Most of the product was on fire along with the rest of the building, and the flames were growing by the minute, and by the time they had reached the road, the flames were licking a hundred feet into the sky and smoke and burning heroin residue had mushroomed a thousand feet into the air.

Big Dave turned in his seat and watched his handiwork as Rashid took the road towards the town. Ahead of him, blue lights were stuck the other side of a car on its roof. Police officers were attempting to move the vehicle, but it kept spinning around on its roof. Someone was returning with a rope and another officer was backing an SUV into position to pull the crashed vehicle to the side of the road.

"That's Jo's hire car, isn't it?"

Rashid smiled. "It certainly is," he replied, pulling into the side of the road while the police officers attached the rope to Jo's mangled hire car.

"She's not bloody in it, is she?" Big Dave craned his neck to see, but the roof and sun visor were in the way.

"Relax, she sent it off the edge of the cliff," Rashid

replied, pointing at the fifty-foot-high embankment. "She came up with the idea. She's quite resourceful."

"Are you shagging her?"

"No," Rashid scoffed.

"Not yet..." Big Dave grinned.

"It's not like that," Rashid protested. "We worked well together for a few weeks, that's all."

"Cool. You won't mind me having a crack at her, then?"

"Oi!" Rashid said a little too emphatically.

"Well, that answers that, then." Big Dave smirked. "Oh, for Christ's sake!" he exclaimed when the car spun in the road and the rope detached. He got out of the car and strode purposefully to the car, braced himself and hammered his shoulder against the upturned vehicle like he was taking on an *All Black's* rugby scrum on his own. The car shifted a few feet and he hammered against it again and powered through his legs. The car shifted again, then met the inclined gravelled surface of the verge and slid off the road completely.

The police officers got back into their vehicles and sped past them, sirens wailing and lights strobing. Rashid pulled alongside Big Dave and waited while he folded himself back inside. "You're a bloody show off."

"Don't change the subject," Big Dave grinned. "Don't worry, your secret's safe with me." He nodded to the other side of the road where Jo Blyth had just stepped up the embankment and stood waiting for them on the verge. "Or perhaps I could ask her if she feels the same." He waited for her to catch hold of the rear door handle before he added, "Or I could always ask her out?"

"Fuck off!"

"Sorry, what did I miss?" Jo asked as she slid in. "Who's fucking off?"

Die Trying

"Nobody, just some banter," Rashid replied quickly.

"Oh, silly boys with their silly banter," she sighed. "And I gave up the police service for this?"

"There's something I've always wanted to ask a cop," said Big Dave.

"Fire away," she replied.

"How do you handcuff a one-armed man?"

"Good one," she shrugged. "Hey, I've got one. What's black and always in the rear of a police car?"

"Hey, what the hell...!" Big Dave looked over his shoulder at her.

Jo laughed. "The seat!"

"What?"

"What's black and always in the rear of a police car? The seat!" she laughed. "Got any more police jokes because I've probably heard them all..."

Chapter Sixty-Seven

Tbilisi, Georgia

"Remind we why we're doing this again?"

"Because it's the right thing to do," replied Caroline. "And because she would not give the name of Lukov's Iron Fist controller if we didn't."

"I don't mean that," Luger said tersely. "I mean why are *we* doing this, and not a Georgian police SWAT team, or some of our boys from Hereford, for that matter."

"Because of time," she replied. "And because of influence, trust... perhaps just because we do things for ourselves."

"We're not hostage rescue experts," Luger said pointedly.

"Semantics," she replied, checking the pistol in her lap.

They had travelled from Bucharest to Tbilisi, Georgia's capital city, by a flight with Turkish Airlines. Ramsay had arranged for an embassy contact to provide a left-luggage locker which contained two 9mm CZ P-10 pistols and four loaded magazines. There was also a thousand pounds in Georgian Lari and a British passport for Samuel Dimitriou under the surname name Luger. Both Caroline and Luger had the return tickets on their phones in their wallet folder. Caroline had pocketed the passport intended for Samuel, thinking that mothers would be most likely to carry a child's passport, and she thought fondly of the holidays with her parents in Tuscany or the South of France and those wonderful hot summers, or in Meribel and the Three Valleys skiing for Christmas, when her mother would carry all the documents and her father would struggle with too much luggage. The memory, the normality of it seemed a hundred years ago now.

They watched the house across the valley taking turns to use the powerful pair of Swarovski binoculars Caroline had bought at Bucharest airport. The slopes of the hill were lush and green, the rocks white like giant's teeth along the ridge. There were poplar trees around the house, and it reminded her of properties she had seen in Tuscany and Umbria.

"I fucking hate this place," she said quietly.

"What? It's beautiful," Luger frowned at her.

"I hate this country, too." She handed him the binoculars and looked the other way. "I was taken hostage in London and trafficked here." She paused, her hand shaking as she clutched the steering wheel. "They held me and threatened to lose me in the sex trade." She scoffed. "I was around ten years older than the other girls, but they said that they had no shortage of buyers for me..."

"Oh my God..." Luger put down the binoculars and

looked at her curiously. "That's incredible. How did you get free?"

"The woman holding me..."

"Woman? Jesus!" Luger interrupted. "What the hell?"

"Oh, yes," she sneered, the thought that a woman could do such a thing to fellow women was lost on her, but that was the reality of the world we live in. "Evil personified. She used me so that King would do various jobs for her... and we're not talking shopping and gardening or washing the car... she wanted people assassinated." She sniffed and wiped her eyes. "Enough!" she said to herself. "I've wasted enough time on her, and that episode in my life."

"Wow." Luger shook his head. "You think you know people and then they blindside you." He put the binoculars back to his eyes and focused on the house once more. "You never truly know what people have been through, do you?"

Caroline did not respond. She wished that she had not brought up the subject and wondered why she had. King always moved forward, never really dwelled on the past and shrugged off memories of pain and suffering. Whether it was Luger's youth and relative innocence that made her feel able to unburden, or whether she had been compelled to explain herself because she knew that her mood had been off, she did not know. But this was the first time she had mentioned it since she had escaped. King had known what she had gone through, and in his typical manner, he had never mentioned it again, because that was how he dealt with trauma. Lord knows what would happen if he ever unburdened himself with therapy, he would have to move into the therapist's office and live there full time. The thought made her smile.

"How long has this kid been here?" Luger asked, his eyes on the house across the valley.

"Best guess? Three years. Certainly, three years away from his mother, anyway."

"Could the kid have Stockholm Syndrome?"

"Alex said that his mother had fleeting contact with her son. Snatched conversations and FaceTime. It's how Max Lukov asserted power over her." Caroline paused, handing Luger the binoculars. "So, I doubt it. However, hostages can become scared of the unknown, or at least, the world outside their immediate bubble. But I think if Samuel believes that we are taking him directly to his mother, then he should get on board."

"You never suffered from Stockholm Syndrome, then?"

"Hell, no! I killed to get out of there!" She had returned and fought to get the girls out, but that was for another time, if at all. "There's little security up there," she said, mercifully changing the subject. A camera you'd get from a home improvement store, and an iron gate and railings. If we go in fast, we should be able to snatch him and get out of there inside five minutes."

"When?"

Caroline checked her watch and said, "If we go now, then we'll get there in fifteen minutes, watch for ten and do it in five. Another forty minutes and we can make the next flight. We can check in online now."

"It'll be tight," Luger commented flatly. "And if there's one thing that I've learned it's that things seldom go according to plan."

"I know," Caroline smiled. "But that was *hardly* a plan. Maybe it's so simple that it just can't fail?"

Luger laughed and replied, "Fair enough. Let's go and find out."

Caroline drove them through the suburbs and across the river to the other side of the valley. The suburban sprawl gave way to patchy orchards and areas of ground left fallow either through financial difficulty or simply because young people moved away, anywhere, to avoid taking over the small-holdings or farms and being held forever prisoner by manual labour and an uncertain economy. The houses became larger and the plots bigger, and after they drove through woodland for a mile, she pulled up just short of the clearing surrounding the house.

"Over the fence or over the gate?" Luger asked.

Caroline shook her head, swung the car around and selected reverse. "Through, I think..."

"What happened to watching the house for ten minutes?"

"Change of plan..." She floored the accelerator and reversed at speed through the wrought iron gates, smashing them inwards and tearing one from its hinges. Sparks spewed in her mirror as she wound the steering wheel around and slid through a J-turn, the traction control fighting her, but for the gravelled surface of the drive. The manoeuvre had been necessary as driving straight through would easily have resulted in damage to the radiator and airbox. As they reached the steps to the house she slammed on the brakes, and Luger was already out of the car and climbing the steps swiftly. By the time Caroline was at the bottom of the steps, Luger had kicked the front doors quite unsuccessfully, and as she reached the top, she jutted her pistol downwards against the lock – minimising the chances of the bullet going through the door and into the house – and fired twice into the lock.

"Again!" she shouted. "Kick it again!"

Luger did so and the door gave significantly. Another kick and it splintered open, and Caroline took aim through the open doorway.

Die Trying

"Ar isrolo! Ar isrolo!" the old and frightened man screamed, his hands above his head, then looking at them quizzically he said, "Don't shoot!"

"Where is the boy?" Luger shouted.

"Samuel! Where is Samuel?" Caroline bellowed; the gun still aimed at the centre of the man's forehead.

"Don't shoot my husband!" a woman screamed as she bustled in from a side door. She wore an old-fashioned pinny and had clearly been drying her hands on a cloth that she had dropped to the floor. "The boy is safe," she assured them. "Samuel is quite safe..."

Ten minutes later, and they were drinking coffee and eating biscuits at the kitchen table. Samuel was drinking chocolate milk on the old man's lap, and the woman was tearfully, yet somewhat relieved in her mannerisms, packing a bag of food for the boy. They had been looking after him for three years, and at the same time, paying off a debt to Lukov in housing Samuel and living like virtual hermits to avoid suspicion. In the village-like suburb on the edge of Tbilisi, the old man had taken care of the shopping and planted the story that his wife was unwell and could not get out. Soon, people had avoided asking after her for fearing the worse. Better not to ask than be told the inevitable and make for an awkward encounter. The couple had known that the day would come when someone came for the boy that they had grown to love, but had secretly hoped that day would be soon, because of Samuel's near-constant homesickness and pining for his mother.

"He is a very bad man," the old man had said of Lukov. "I took out a small loan when the business was in trouble, the debt was sold to Max Lukov, and the interest..." He shrugged like it had been an impossible amount to repay.

"And then he sends someone to tell us that we must stay here with a child and raise him like our own."

"And we never had children," the old woman said. "Although we always wanted them," she added somewhat wistfully. "But, oh, what will Mr Lukov say when he discovers that Samuel has been taken?" she asked, quite solemnly. "He will take it out on us..."

The old man reached out and held his wife's hand. "It is not right for the boy to stay, my love."

"I don't think you'll be seeing Max Lukov again," Caroline assured her. She checked her watch and said, "I'm sorry, but we have to go."

The old man patted Samuel on his head and said something in Georgian, and the boy got up, turned around and hugged him dearly. He then went to the old woman and hugged her, too. The old woman eventually broke away tearfully and handed him the paper bag full of biscuits.

"You're not getting your deposit back," Luger said, trying to lift the mood as they got into the car.

Caroline did not answer as she sat beside Samuel in the backseat and watched as the boy waved the old couple goodbye. She had never felt the maternal instinct other women talked about, but she could feel something inside stirring. A strong desire to have more, to care for rather than be cared for. It was a strange sensation, and even when they cleared customs and settled into their seats on the plane, she touched her stomach and the feeling had not gone away.

Chapter Sixty-Eight

Batumi, Georgia

Max Lukov had been summoned. He was not a man to be dominated – the killing of Orlev had shown that and thank God he had Sergei Bostock on his payroll to tell him of General Orlev's plan to kill him – but he knew his place within Iron Fist, and it was not yet at the top. He represented the Russian contingent, the other four of the five fingers that made the Iron Fist being Iran, North Korea, China, and Belarus. Orlev had not been a member of Iron Fist, but his direct superior was, and that man was one of two men inside the Russian machine, the other being a top-level FSB assistant director. With a man inside both Russian Federation intelligence and security services, Iron Fist would guarantee Russian involvement in their operations, whether it was by direct action, or through quietly biased influence. Orders came from an Iron Fist sleeper, through Orlev - a Russian official oblivious of the part that they played and thinking it all for Mother Russia - to Lukov, one of the original Iron Fist partisans committed to its agenda.

Lukov did not like the city of Batumi, where harsh and unforgiving Eastern Bloc utilitarianism met faux Mediterranean beach resort. The seafront tried a little too hard to forget communism and austerity when the innards of the beast was built on the severe practicality of poured concrete. Everywhere was a reminder of the past, glossed over with a Ferris wheel and a pretty promenade beside what always seemed to be a dark and choppy sea. But he did like Georgia, and he at least benefited from dual nationality, which with many sanctions imposed upon Russia by many countries made it increasingly difficult for Russian citizens to travel.

He had practised his speech, got ready his excuses. By the time he had finished, he would be granted another mission, a larger budget to attack the West by devious means, and as usual he would cream off some of the capital.

The coast road became less populated, the buildings larger and more lustrous and the scenery became more manicured. He had not driven through these parts in a decade, and it was clear that both money and status had migrated to the area. The austere concrete was behind him now, but instead of the usual buildings of Byzantine revival style, the baroque, neoclassical or Kievan Rus or Muscovite influences that most former Soviet satellite countries adopted for their social elite – such irony during communist times – the houses mimicked Tuscan villas and Cap Ferret gites. Neatly trimmed lawns were punctuated by olive trees and citrus and palms. Lukov sneered at the styling, as out of place as middle-America *McMansions*, or the California

Die Trying

style mid-century modernism designs of wood, glass, and stainless steel in the heart of the English countryside. It was easy to imagine that one day, in generations to come, the Western world would look much the same, with borders and culture no guarantee of a change of view.

Lukov's driver took the right turning and climbed the hill through olive groves and vineyards. The first wine had been made in Georgia eight-thousand years ago and vineyards had remained a constant ever since. Lukov thought the wine to be a little too scented for his palate but was first to accept that growing up in Moscow and St. Petersburg had not equipped him well with the appreciation of wine, and even to this day he found champagne too sweet and would always prefer to drink dark beer and strong vodka.

As they reached the top of the hill the ground levelled out and the villa loomed ahead of them. The driver pulled up at the gate and pressed the intercom. The gates buzzed open slowly and the driver crawled forwards. Beneath the wheels, bright red pavers had been painstakingly laid in a perfect herringbone formation and welcomed them to the door some hundred metres distant. The driver stopped and Lukov told him to wait. The man was his minder as well, but Lukov would not be needing him here. This was home turf and with Orlev dead, he was done looking over his shoulder.

When Max Lukov reached the top step, the door opened, and he was greeted by a tough looking man in his forties with a small scar on his cheek and the most piercing eyes imaginable.

Cold and grey, with a blueish shine as they caught the light. They reminded Lukov of a wolf's eyes and he felt a shiver run down his spine as the man motioned for him to come in.

"Where is Mr Huang?" Lukov asked.

"Zhiyu Huang is a bit tied up, at the moment," King replied. He moved his right hand and showed Lukov the silenced Makarov pistol. "Take a seat…"

Lukov spun around and darted for the door but stopped at the top step when he saw the driver slumped in his seat, and The Widow standing a few paces from the car with an identical pistol and suppressor in her hand. "What the hell?" he exclaimed, eyes glowering at her. "You'll never see your son again, bitch!"

The Widow had just killed the man who she swore she would. The man who took great delight in molesting her whenever he searched her at Lukov's office. She had asked King for the kill, but she did not look in any way satisfied when she looked up at King. She looked purposefully at Lukov and smiled as she walked to the steps. King shook his head at her, caught hold of the Russian by his arm and yanked him back inside. Lukov sprawled in front of a low coffee table and tried to regain composure as he clambered to his feet and slumped in the leather tub chair. His face was flushed red, and he was perspiring heavily. King took out his phone and held it out for The Widow to see when she stepped inside. "He's mine," said King.

"But you said…"

"I've changed the deal," he said coldly. "Your son is safe and well. Here's the proof…" He waited while she took the phone and stared at the picture of her son smiling as he ate an enormous ice cream cone in front of the Academias Hotel in Athens. "There's a room booked, and my colleague is keeping him company until you get there." He paused. "She's actually enjoying taking him to see the sights and spoiling him with sweets and ice creams, so you'd better hurry before all his teeth fall out," he smiled.

"But the deal was for me to kill him, after providing you with information on Zhiyu Huang." She paused. "And then for you to help free my son."

"As I said, the deal has changed. I've arranged for the release of your son, so I've done my part and now you can go." The Widow squared the pistol at Lukov and King raised his own, just a few feet away, at her forehead. "Don't," he said coldly. "Only one person wins this standoff and happily, that's me."

"But..." she stared emptily at the Russian, her heart, and head at odds with one another. She knew that she had lost, but ultimately, she had won. There were two battles that she had been prepared for and conditioned herself to fight, and now there were none.

"This bloke's not worth another thought," he said. "Reset yourself, go to your son and enjoy the rest of your lives together."

The woman looked tearfully at King and mouthed 'thank you' before dropping the weapon onto the chair next to her and peeling off the pair of thin leather gloves as she walked out of the door and into her new life.

Lukov breathed a sigh of relief and King smiled. "Trust me, dickhead, a bullet in the head would have been more favourable than what you're about to go through."

The helicopter rotors thundered overhead, and King saw the shadow of the aircraft pass over the hired Dacia as The Widow drove away. Then, the helicopter was visible, low, and fast over the vineyard as Flymo banked and made another performance of landing behind the house where King and The Widow had hidden the hire car. He smiled, wondering what the man did for kicks when he wasn't flying like a lunatic.

"Whatever they're paying you, I'll double it to let me go," Lukov said confidently.

"I don't get paid much, to be fair."

"Two million, then. In dollars or euros."

"Well, I do need a new boat," King replied. "But the insurance company will pay out soon, so I'm alright."

"Five," Lukov persisted. "Five million to shoot whoever is going to walk through that door and let me go."

King shrugged. "I quite like the bloke about to walk through that door."

"Ten! Ten million!" Lukov begged. "Ten million dollars, and I'll transfer it right now!"

"I can't be bought," King replied.

"Everyone has a price!" Lukov spat at him.

King shrugged. "I *do* have a price," he said coldly. "That price is freedom and democracy. And I will do anything to maintain it."

"Aye, aye, what's going on here then?" Jim Kernow stepped in and looked at the man in the tub chair. "Is this him? Hardly seems worth all the trouble, does he?" He slipped on a pair of blue latex gloves, picked up the silenced Makarov and aimed it at Lukov. "Is it a lift for one or two?"

"Two," King replied.

Kernow fished out a pair of handcuffs from his pocket and tossed them at Lukov. "Nice and tight now, lad."

King stepped out of the room and returned shortly afterwards with a short Chinese man, his face black and blue with bruises, his wrists secured with duct tape. He pushed the man ahead of him and said to Lukov, "Up you get, sunshine."

Flymo had two types of flying. Hell for leather, and parked. He enjoyed scaring the Russian and Chinese terrorists, but fortunately both King and Jim Kernow had known what to expect. The flight took eleven minutes before they touched town at the private airstrip operated by a flying club and air taxi service just outside Batumi. The Cessna Citation was fuelled and ready for take-off, the small business jet capable of making the journey from Batumi to London Biggin Hill in Bromley in a little over five hours.

King and Jim Kernow escorted their prisoners onto the aircraft while Flymo returned the helicopter to the flight school and signed the paperwork. Ramsay had provided enough money and clout for customs checks to be minimal and by minimal, King suspected non-existent as he unloaded the pistol and unscrewed the suppressor before placing in the green FCO diplomatic bag. Kernow did the same and an unassuming young man wearing a cheap suit took the bag in silence and walked down the steps to the waiting Jaguar saloon with tinted windows. Flymo arrived as the car left the apron and he climbed aboard and sat heavily in a single leather chair. Once the two prisoners were seated away from each other and belted into their seats, King sat opposite Flymo and Kernow took a seat on the other side of the aisle. Twenty minutes later, they were cruising at five-hundred-miles-per-hour at an altitude of thirty-two-thousand feet. The lone stewardess had served the three men teas and coffees and had already been briefed not to approach the two men seated away from each other, with handcuffs threaded through their seatbelts.

Chapter Sixty-Nine

The Cape Verde Islands,
Two months later

They had bought the yacht in Saidia, Morroco with their insurance pay out. They had thought, quite correctly, that they would get a lot more bang for their buck outside of Europe. They also benefited from the mild climate and the effect that had on a boat over the inclement elements of Britain, and the craft was in excellent condition, despite being thirty-years old and having circumnavigated the globe on two occasions. Their plan now was to spend until Christmas exploring the eastern part of the Macaronesia ecoregion, the series of islands and archipelagos that stretched from the Cape Verde Islands to the Canaries, the virtually unheard-of Savage Isles and as far as Madeira. They would explore the Azores next summer if they were still inclined. From Madeira, they would sail south and berth in the Mediterranean and take it from there.

Die Trying

At just over a month into their adventure, King felt fit and strong. He swam daily and ate fish and salad for most meals. He had perfected his speargun fishing and Caroline had become a dab hand at spinning with lures. The sun and sea air filled them with vibrancy and purpose, and they could relax in the knowledge that nobody was coming after them. Caroline had not spoken about her time in America, and King hadn't asked. He knew enough about such things to know that if she wanted to talk, then she would. But only in her own time, and maybe not at all.

Caroline sat back in her deckchair, her tanned legs crossed and extended to the wire rail, which she had cushioned with a rolled towel. King was perfecting his dives from the stern, and she had long ago given up scoring him out of ten and turned her attention back to the novel she had already started three times before becoming distracted. Her concentration was weak today, her thoughts coming back to the old couple in Georgia. The fact that they had so dearly wanted children, and had fulfilled it, however briefly, with Samuel. She had never felt a yearning before, but since that moment she had thought of little else. Strong, desperate and with trepidation, yet conversely with glimmers of hope.

King pulled himself out a final time and dabbed himself dry with a towel. "Sorry for being such a child," he smiled. "But it feels good, doesn't it? Being free, not tied to anything..."

"Tied to anything?" she asked. "That bothers you?"

King pulled an expression of distaste. "Can you imagine being tied to anything again?" He paused as he tossed the towel at her. "This is the life. Just the two of us, nobody holding us back, asking anything of us. The world is our oyster..."

"Exactly," Caroline replied, her hand subconsciously

touching her stomach. "Just the two of us, nobody to hold us back…"

"Promise?"

Caroline smiled, but she did not reply as she picked up her book for the fourth time that day and started the first chapter over, the book covering her face, and tears from King.

Chapter Seventy

The Scottish Highlands

Flymo touched down and powered down the engines, keeping his hands and feet on the controls until the rotors slowed to the minimum RPM. He gave the nod to Jim Kernow, who hopped out, keeping his head down and pulled out the folded wheelchair. He opened it and locked it in place and positioned it for Ramsay to slide into once he'd opened the door. Ramsay, who had never been physical, had adapted well and managed to hold himself up as his legs dropped into position and he lowered himself down. Kernow pushed him clear of the rotors, then stepped aside as Ramsay wheeled himself along.

Balfour House was a large manor, or small castle, depending on your architectural inclination and understanding of history. Situated in seven-hundred acres of farmland, it was a small estate by Scottish standards, with most of the land comprising of forest and moorland, with only two-hundred acres of working farmland which had been leased to three neighbouring farms. The property had been many things from private residence for two-hundred years, a hunting lodge, hotel, and country retreat, and for the past ten years had been owned by the UK government and used for secret governmental meetings. Ramsay had requested it as part of his remit, and it now served as a detention facility and training centre. Balfour's first 'guests' had been Max Lukov and Zhiyu Huang, and they had been resident for two months with two of the best 'enhanced interviewers' to have ever worked at MI5. Both women were so expert in their techniques that they regularly attended the SAS selection phase at Hereford, to both advise the directing staff and interrogate prospective recruits. Their favoured techniques with those young, exhausted soldiers hoping to pass selection into the world's most elite fighting unit was to have them stripped naked, let the cold take its effect and ridicule the size of their penises for hours on end. But that was 'soft' tactics – without a pun – and without the constraints of working with the British Army and their soldiers, they could get a whole lot nastier in a remote house on the Scottish moors.

"Thank you for coming, Neil," a sturdy-looking woman of around fifty walked over and wasted no time in escorting them towards the grand front entrance. "We informed your desk as soon as it happened. It's just a matter now of how to go forward."

"Thank you, Matilda. We came as soon as we could. I must say, I'm surprised he cracked without extreme physical torture," Ramsay commented. "But that's the GRU for you. Max Lukov knows most of the techniques."

"I don't advocate torture. They'll tell you anything, even

agree to anything to make the pain stop. I prefer wearing people down until they trip over themselves. Once that finally happens, the lies have gone and only the truth remains." She paused, stopping to look at Ramsay. "Besides, it's not Lukov," she said. "It's Huang. He's singing like a bird. Just couldn't survive any longer on such little sleep. The white noise, the bright lights. The uncertain mealtimes. His body clock is broken. He's had enough."

"What has he said?" Ramsay asked incredulously.

"Well, that's exactly it, Neil." Matilda paused and stopped walking. "It's just so unbelievable. I mean, terrifying, but unbelievable."

"How so?" Ramsay stared at her intensely.

She glanced at Kernow before saying, "Is he cleared at the highest level?"

Ramsay nodded. "You can tell me anything in front of Jim," he replied.

"Alright," she shrugged. "Zhiyu Huang wants to bargain."

"And what has he got to trade?" Jim Kernow asked incredulously.

"The end," she replied somewhat devoid of emotion. Like she had thought of nothing more and now had nothing left inside her. "An E.L.E." She paused, almost finding the acronym too implausible to say. "An Extinction Level Event..."

Author's Note

Hi - thanks for reading and I hope you enjoyed my story. I'm already hard at work on another thriller and can't wait to share it with you. The next in series is All the King's Men and you can get it by clicking the link All the King's Men.

If you have time to rate or review this book, then you would make this author extremely happy!

Did you know that I sometimes give books away, discount them and let my mailing list subscribers know of promotions and new releases? You can sign up and find out more here.

I hope to entertain you again soon.

A P Bateman

facebook.com/authorapbateman

Printed in Great Britain
by Amazon